*Blue Heelers* have made him a household name. The *...* series *Shark Net* and *My Brother Jack* earned him widespread critical acclaim. He has been nominated for numerous stage and screen awards, and has won a Variety Club Drama Award in 1997 and two Logie awards for Most Outstanding Actor in 2000 and 2004.

William grew up in Queensland and has travelled extensively throughout Australia. He now lives in Melbourne with his wife, the film-maker Sarah Watt, and their two children. His first book, *A Man's Got to Have a Hobby*, was an Australian bestseller. *Cricket Kings* is his first novel.

Also by William McInnes
*A Man's Got to Have a Hobby*

# CRICKET KINGS

# William McInnes

| NORTHUMBERLAND COUNTY LIBRARY | |
| --- | --- |
| 30132017972964 | |
| Bertrams | 29/01/2009 |
| F | £12.99 |
| | |

HACHETTE AUSTRALIA

HACHETTE AUSTRALIA

First published in Australia and New Zealand in 2006
by Hodder Australia
(An imprint of Hachette Livre Australia Pty Limited)
Level 17, 207 Kent Street, Sydney NSW 2000
Website: www.hachette.com.au

This edition published in 2007 by Hachette Australia

Copyright © William McInnes 2006

This book is copyright. Apart from any fair dealing for the
purposes of private study, research, criticism or review
permitted under the *Copyright Act 1968*, no part may be
stored or reproduced by any process without prior written
permission. Enquiries should be made to the publisher.

**National Library of Australia**
**Cataloguing-in-Publication data**

McInnes, William, 1963- .
  Cricket kings.

  ISBN 978 0 7336 2193 2 (pbk.).

  1. Cricket players - Fiction.  2. Middle-aged men - Fiction.

  I. Title.

A823.4

Set in Adobe Garamond by Bookhouse, Sydney
Cover design by Christabella Designs
Cover image by William West
Author photo by Rebecca Thornton
Printed in Australia by Griffin Press, Adelaide

Hachette Livre Australia's policy is to use papers that are
natural, renewable and recyclable products and made from
wood grown in sustainable forests. The logging and
manufacturing processes are expected to conform to the
environmental regulations of the country of origin.

*For Clem*

*and for anyone I've ever played cricket with*

# The Question

It won't hurt. It won't, it really won't. That's what he told himself. Blisters the size of Lake Eyre on his heels. He pulled a piece of skin and it flapped back like a broken sail. He heard his daughter scream at the dog from the backyard as he tipped some antiseptic out of a bottle of Dettol. When he was a boy his mother had always told him that the Dettol wouldn't sting as long as he stayed still and didn't wriggle. His mother had never been right. It always stung, but when he yelped she would tell him it was because he wasn't still.

'Don't wriggle and it won't hurt,' she would say.

It won't hurt, it really won't. He poured the Dettol onto a cotton-wool ball and watched as brown liquid dribbled through the sodden lump. He looked at the bottle. There was a sword on the label. A sword. Why? Why was there a sword? I don't want to put this on, he thought. It will hurt.

Had it been worth it? Had it been? He heard his daughter padding up the hall that led to the bathroom followed by the skitting tap of the dog. He rubbed the Dettol over his blister, he tried to remain still.

'Fuck!... Fuck me,' he said.

His daughter stopped outside the door. He heard her voice. 'Daddy said a naughty word.'

'Yes, alright darling,' he said.

'Why did you say a naughty word, Daddy?' she asked through the door.

'Well, Daddy just said a naughty word because...' He saw himself in the mirror. His nose was sunburnt. Bright red... 'Because that's what daddies do sometimes.'

He heard his daughter run off back down the hall laughing.

'Daddy said a naughty word,' she sang to the house.

Had it been worth it? He looked at himself reflected in the mirror. 'You tell me,' he said as quietly as he could. 'And I didn't wriggle.'

He smiled to himself.

'Was it worth it?'

# The Fourths

Chris Andersen's heel had started to hurt on the Friday morning. It had started as soon as he got off the train and walked to his office in the city. He was a big man, Chris Andersen, and as he thumped along the footpath he occasionally felt a twinge at the back of his shoe. The shoe was one of a pair that had been bought for him as a birthday present by his mother. The shoes were huge boats of things that made his feet look twice as big as they were. His mother had bought them overseas, when she had gone trekking in Nepal.

'They're handmade, Christopher, handmade by a Nepalese villager. As soon as I saw them I thought of you.'

Chris Andersen loved his mother and until then had nothing in particular against Nepalese villagers. He thought it was pretty incredible that his mother had gone trekking in Nepal at the age of seventy-two. It was even more incredible that she had brought back these shoes for him. But why did she think of him when she saw them?

Chris didn't want to be too judgemental and perhaps many Nepalese villagers were skilful cobblers. But he knew as he got closer to his office that his mother had not found herself one of those. Whoever made these shoes should probably stick to being a mountain guide. If you want to go up Everest get a Nepalese villager, if you want to buy a pair of shoes go to Mathers.

'You don't like them, do you?' his mother had said as soon as he unwrapped his present.

He looked at the shoes. 'Well, they're great...but you know...'

'It's alright. Some poor little man has made them and I've brought them all the way back but if you don't want them...'

'Mum,' he said.

'Oh no, it's alright. I'll give them to your father,' his mother replied.

Chris Andersen's father shot a look at his son. Earlier, his first words as he entered his son's house were not 'Happy Birthday' but a frantic whisper, 'For Christsake, Chris, whatever your mother gives you, keep it. I don't want the bloody things coming back to me.'

Chris sighed and smiled at his mother. 'No, no, look, Mum, they're great. Very good. Just a bit...unique that's all. But they're great. Very authentic.'

His mother looked at him and nodded. 'Well, I hope you wear them. They look authentic because they *are* authentic. Now, who's for a Fluffy Duck?'

Chris Andersen's father raised his thumb and mouthed silently as his wife prepared a festive drink with advocaat and lemonade, 'Good boy.'

Chris hadn't planned on wearing the shoes. It was Julie, his wife. The night before they had sat around the table eating.

'Please, mate, do you have to speak with your mouth full?' Chris said to his son Lachlan.

'Do you have to call him "mate"?' Julie asked.

'No, I don't have to call him "mate".'

'Good, then don't, Chris, there's enough of that matey, blokey stuff around without you bringing it home.'

'Don't speak with your mouth full, cobber.'

'Chris!'

'Listen, china,' Chris said.

'What?' said Lachlan. 'What do you mean?'

'Your father is being funny in a smart alec-y way, Lachie.'

'Oh,' Lachlan said, not quite understanding.

'Jesus, mate, it's a joke...a joke.'

His son looked at him. Chris Andersen looked at his son.

'Oh, come on, Lachie...' His son turned away.

'Listen, Lachie...' he held out his hand towards his son.

'Sweetheart, don't play with the dog when you're eating,' Julie said to Moira, their daughter.

Chris turned away from his son.

'Yes, Moisy, you really should keep that thing outside.'

'But, Daddy... he has to have a pat. You only yell at him.'

Julie looked at her husband. 'Oh, does Daddy yell at Pixie?'

Moira nodded and Chris Andersen shook his head. 'Only when Pixie deserves it.'

'Chris, don't. Don't yell all the time...'

'Sorry.'

'Your mother rang today.'

'Oh, yeah.'

'She was wondering if you could call a Mrs Martin.'

'Mrs Martin?'

'Yes, that's what she said.'

'Mrs Martin?'

'Is Dad being smart alec-y again?' asked Lachlan.

'*Mate,*' Chris said.

'No, Lachie, he's being thick. Yes, Mrs Martin. Mrs Martin wanted you to ring her up.'

'That Mick's mum... Michael Martin.'

'Tomorrow, could you ring her tomorrow?'

'Listen, Moisy, don't pick up the dog... Moisy!'

'Why do you yell at Pixie, Daddy?'

Chris Andersen looked at his wife. 'Listen, can you tell her to put that dog down?' He looked back at his daughter. 'And I am not yelling at Pixie. I'm yelling at you.'

'Sweetheart, pop Pixie down and go and wash your hands... Your mother also wanted to know if you've worn those shoes.'

'Oh, Christ.'

'Daddy said a naughty word,' sang his daughter as she padded off to the bathroom.

'Swear jar,' said Lachlan.

'Sorry,' Chris Andersen said to his family.

'Why don't you just wear them and then she won't keep asking?'

'Why didn't you tell her I had worn them?'

'But that's lying, Daddy,' his daughter called out over the squeal of water from the bathroom tap.

'She's right. It is lying,' Julie Andersen said and smiled. 'And what about the poor little man who made them?'

'Oh come on... Listen, I am not going to wear them.'

'Why?' Moira said as she sat back up at the table.

'Because they are shocking, evil, woeful looking things... Did you wash your hands, Moisy?'

His daughter rolled her eyes like Maria Callas and offered her hands for inspection.

'What about the little elf that made them?' she asked.

'Little man,' said Lachlan.

'Yes, some little Nepalese man... villager. No elves, sweetheart.' Chris Andersen laughed. 'Snow White and the seven Sherpas.'

'Dwarves,' said Lachlan. 'Snow White and the seven dwarves. Moisy said elves, you said Sherpas. You should have said dwarves after elves or there's really no connection...' Chris Andersen's son looked down at the table. Was he trying to be funny? He looked embarrassed and Chris felt his face begin to burn.

'Yes, alright, mate, haven't you got homework to do?'

Julie was about to say something then changed her mind. He knew it would be about the way he had spoken to his son. It came out sounding more bad-tempered than he had meant. He reached out and patted his son's arm. 'Go on,

Lachie, homework. Elves...dwarves, I really don't keep up...
Elf Dwarf...'

'Elf Dwarf,' his son said and laughed a little. 'Maybe that's
his name.'

'Whose name?'

'The man who made the shoes... Elf Dwarf sounds like
someone's name.'

Chris Andersen smiled, 'Yes, Elf Dwarf the shocking Sherpa
cobbler.'

'Well, why don't you make Elf Dwarf and your mother
happy and wear the shoes... Or throw them out and tell her
you don't like them,' his wife said and smiled.

Chris Andersen liked it when she smiled.

'Are you daring me?' he sounded like he was six.

Julie laughed. 'How old are you?'

Chris Andersen liked it even more when his wife laughed.
He looked at her and his heart was very full. 'I will wear the
shoes of Elf Dwarf tomorrow.'

Julie smiled again. 'You idiot!' She bent down and kissed
his head and then whispered softly, 'Just watch how you speak
to Lachie. Please?'

He smiled back.

There was a yelp from a bedroom.

'Moisy, don't put the dog in your dresses.' Julie headed off
to her daughter's room.

Chris Andersen was left alone for a moment. 'Michael
Martin,' he said to himself. 'Michael Martin...now there was
a player.'

•

Friday morning at an intersection, Chris Andersen looked down at his feet. His feet were in the shoes that his mother had bought from a Nepalese villager.

'Fucking Elf Dwarf,' he muttered. The left shoe was rubbing on his heel. As he looked up Chris could see a couple on the other side of the street laughing, staring in his direction. The lights changed and he walked across. His feet flapped like he had flippers on and he lifted his knees high so as not to trip over his toes. He flapped closer to the laughing couple. They were sniggering now...at his shoes.

'My mother bought them for me,' was all Chris Andersen said as he slapped past.

As he flapped on to his office he thought again of Michael Martin. He had been a terrific player. A cack-hander. A mollydooker. A left-hander.

They were terms that would mean little to most people these days and probably had never meant that much.

They were cricket terms and Chris Andersen, the man in the awful shoes, the big man who walked a little like a hyperactive marionette, loved cricket. Had done since he was a boy. He still played and this day would follow a pattern honed over the seasons.

Today he would ring around and try to gather the semblance of a team to play in the Western Region Fourth Grade Subdistrict Cricket Competition. He had been doing this for years, for Chris Andersen was the captain of the Yarraville West Fourths.

The mighty fourths. Like some sad old battalion they lurched on. They had had their glory days, when people actually used to turn up to training, but these days it was hard even to get eleven to make a team. Answering the phone was too much of a commitment.

Chris had played almost all his cricket at the Yarraville West Club. He belonged to a dynasty. Every club has to have a dynasty and Yarraville West's was the Andersens. The mighty Barry Andersen, father of Chris, Greg and Tony, was a club legend. Barry's name was printed in gold on the walls of the clubroom to prove it. Tony and Greg's names were there as well. Barry was still secretary of the club and Greg and Tony had played their junior cricket with Yarraville West before they'd moved on to a higher calling. Greg had gone on to play for the state and Tony... Tony had played like an angel.

Chris had never played for anybody except Yarraville West. He'd spent a couple of years in the firsts but never really looked like he belonged. Yet he loved cricket.

Well, he must, because nobody would actively go through what he was about to go through that Friday. Soon Chris Andersen would switch his phone on and his day would explode. Besides being a fourth grade cricket captain, Chris Andersen was also an industrial officer with the State Public Workers' Union.

His mother, Barbara, had never really understood why Chris had ended up working at the union. 'You did so well at uni, Christopher... well, you did well enough,' she would say.

Barry would roll his eyes like Maria Callas and wink at his son.

'Mum, I did okay.'

'You got your degree, you worked hard...look at Greg, he worked hard and look at him...his shops.' His mother pointed to a photo of his brother. Actually it was a photo of his brother and his brother's family. They were posed in a smiling lump in front of a rumpled blue drape and grey background.

Chris looked at the photo. It was sandwiched between a collection of wall plates of Old West settings. Indians staring off into sunsets and looking at the stars. A coyote howling at the moon and a man with a buffalo head talking to a cowboy who looked like John Wayne.

The plates came from Barry Andersen, they were gifts for his wife. He saw them on the back of the magazines that she would buy and he read in the toilet.

He had bought the first one for his wife one Christmas. Barbara had seemed to like it and so he had bought more. The Andersens were a family that enjoyed a routine.

Just below the man in the buffalo head and the man who looked like John Wayne was the photo of Greg and his family.

Chris looked at the photo. In a strange sort of a way it didn't look out of place amidst the Western wall plates. It was the way that the faces in the photo looked off to one side of the camera in a glazed, smiling middle-distance vapidness that somehow matched the crinkled faces of the Comanche chiefs.

Chris' brother was a chemist and he had done well. He owned a chain of pharmacies. The crinkled blue and grey background in his family photo was found in the 'Photoland' corner of his pharmacies. Chris had a copy of the photo in the same frame. It was a Christmas present from his brother. Thankfully Chris didn't have any Western wall plates. Yet.

'Do you think he paid for this?' Chris asked.

Barry Andersen unwrapped a packet of ginger nut biscuits. 'Bit of a goose if he did.'

'Greg is a chemist, he worked hard and now he can enjoy his life.' His mother swept a hand towards Greg and his tribe.

'Mum, Greg has no hair.'

His mother laughed as she told him off. 'Christopher, he may be bald but he's happy... You're a lawyer, Christopher –'

'He's actually a solicitor, love,' said Barry.

Barbara looked at her husband. 'Well, thank you, Barry. Is there a difference?'

'Well, slightly, love. In any case, I'm just being specific...'

'You're being a specific plumber then, are you, Barry?'

Barry Andersen was indeed a plumber.

'Yes, love, I suppose I am...and if you are going to be a plumber then you might as well be a specific one.'

'Alright, Barry.'

'Cheers, love.' Barry Andersen dipped a ginger nut biscuit into a cup of tea.

'Well, yes, Mum. I am a solicitor and I'm still doing legal work –'

'For the union, Chris...the unions.'

'Yeah, is that so bad?'

'Well, I don't think so, mate,' said Barry.

'Thanks, Dad.'

'I don't mind...if you like it, if you're happy. It's important to be happy, Christopher.' His mother looked at him. 'It's so important to be happy...' She had that look in her eyes.

Chris moved over to his mother, touched her gently on her shoulder and then took her hand. 'I am happy, Mum, don't worry... I am happy.'

'Alright, then,' she said.

Chris looked over at his father, who held up one big thumb from a balled fist. 'Good boy,' he silently said just before he dunked another ginger nut into his tea.

Chris turned to look at his brother and his family and raised his arm in the practised cowboy way. 'How!'

Both his parents laughed.

His mother asked him often if he were happy. He could see the look on her face, that shadow of wariness, a hint of slight panic before she asked. Maybe panic was too strong a word. Concern. There, that was it, that look of concern.

She should ask me if I am happy now, thought Chris Andersen as he tripped over a gutter, his Nepalese flippers catching on the rim of the cement. Not enough to send him sprawling, just enough to make him jerk awkwardly. Just enough for a man drinking coffee in a cafe to snort out a mouthful.

Chris looked at the man and the man laughed even more. The man laughed and coffee from his cup spilt and fell into his lap. The man leapt up.

Chris Andersen pointed at the man. 'Who says there is no justice?'

Chris felt a little better and walked through the doorway of the building that housed his office and switched on his phone. Within seconds he heard beeps. Messages.

Already.

Fridays for Chris Andersen were review panel days. On these days members of the union would make their way into the city with their complaints, their concerns, or their defences, and address a panel. It was a big union that basically covered any service the state provided. Every Friday Chris would sit with a variety of members and listen. The days were uneventful but the process was time-consuming, although panel day did give him the opportunity to go through the candidates for the cricket team on the sly.

On this Friday, Chris had a full roster of union members to deal with. A rabbit-shooter from Shepparton, Kelvin Ryan; a prison security officer, Ian Sykes; a couple of timber workers, Toni Divaniski and Ryan Pope; a groundsman, Brian Love; and a meteorologist, Meryl Top. As he limped into the meeting room Chris checked his messages. There were two from his mother and one from Julie. His mother had called first to remind him to ring Mrs Martin. Julie's message told him his mother had rung her to remind her to remind him to call Mrs Martin. Julie had told Barbara Andersen that Chris was wearing the Sherpa shoes. The next message from his mother told him that Julie had told her that he, Christopher, was wearing the shoes from the Nepalese villager and that she was pleased. 'I'm happy, Christopher, those are unique shoes.'

He looked down at his feet. He shook his head.

Chris sat down and decided to kick off the Sherpa shoe that was hurting the most, and wriggle his feet free. No one could see his feet anyway as they filed in. As he bent down his phone beeped again, a text message. 'LIVEY IN. PLUS THE FIVE

USUALS ADD TWO JUNIORS. RING ROUND FOR ROB
AND REST. CLUB SEC… PS LUV DAD.'

Chris nodded to himself. 'Oh, very nice.' Livey Jones and
the five regulars in the team made six and these two probable
juniors meant that he had eight as a starting number for
Saturday's team. If he could get Rob Orchard then he'd add
an extra man. 'Yes, very nice.' Maybe he wouldn't have to ask
Lachlan to play after all.

Even though he thought it bad form not to play a full team
when you had the opportunity, he had to admit the last couple
of times he had recruited Lachlan hadn't gone well. Maybe
he shouldn't ask his son to make up numbers. He didn't know
if Lachlan would be disappointed or relieved.

Perhaps if he explained to Lachlan, then it might not be
so hard. Maybe it would be good if his boy didn't play. Chris
had always loved to play cricket with the seniors when he was
Lachlan's age, but then that was him and Lachlan is Lachlan.

He thought for a moment about ringing Mrs Martin and
checked his watch. Still a couple of minutes. He flicked his
shoe off then dialled the number. His foot sprang free like
some harnessed animal and it began to bound about with relief.
He could hear the phone ringing and rubbed his foot. He
flicked up the inside of the shoe and felt rough edges all around.

'Bloody thing is as rough as guts.' The phone continued
to ring. He brought the shoe up on his desk and peered into
it. There was a rough metal label stuck to the tongue of the
shoe. He looked at it. The phone continued to ring. He read
the label. 'Made in Yugoslavia.' As he digested this the phone
stopped ringing. A nice voice spoke.

'Hello, Carol Martin.'

'Yugo-fucking-slavia!' Chris said in disbelief.

'Hello...excuse me, who is this?'

Chris Andersen tried to put the handbrake on but it didn't respond in time. As he spoke a big stomach on a little body entered the room. It was Kelvin Ryan. Kelvin the rabbit-shooter. He wore an aqua-striped shirt and brown pants. His legs and arms looked thin and fine, but his stomach looked like he had borrowed it from somebody for a joke.

He made his way to where Chris sat and Chris Andersen stared for a moment, transfixed by the vision.

'Who is this, please?' Carol Martin said.

The aqua-shirted one spoke. 'G'day...you'd be Chris Andersen, Kelvin, mate. Kelvin Ryan.'

Chris nodded and spoke in a rush into the phone, 'Sorry, I'm terribly sorry, Mrs Martin...'

The problem was that Kelvin the rabbit-shooter decided to speak too.

'What's that?' Kelvin's beady eyes were set on the big shoe sitting on the desk. 'What is that fucking thing?'

'Mrs Martin, this is Chris Andersen. I'm so sorry about that.'

'Is that a shoe? Christ, that *is* a shoe. That is a whopper, mate...'

'Oh, hello, Chris.' Mrs Martin sounded relieved.

'Yes...hello. Look, I was talking about these shoes that my mother brought back from when she was in Nepal. She said that she had bought them from a Nepalese man in a village who had made them...'

'What's wrong with Australian shoes?' grumbled Kelvin. 'Jesus, mate. You're a bloody union man and you're buying bloody crap from overseas.'

'Yes,' said Mrs Martin, sounding not so relieved.

'Yes,' echoed Chris to Mrs Martin. 'Listen, Kelvin, can you just wait a moment?'

'Oh, don't mind me,' said Kelvin as he poked at the shoe with a little jab of his finger.

'Yes,' repeated Chris.

'Yes?' said Mrs Martin.

There was a silence.

'Bloody foreign crap,' said Kelvin.

'Yes, well, they weren't made in Nepal...in the village...'

'Oh, yes,' Mrs Martin said. She was an incredibly polite woman. Kelvin peered at the label.

'These things were made in Yugoslavia, mate... Yugoslavia. Jesus they don't even have bloody Yugoslavia anymore...'

'Kelvin, mate, can you be quiet a minute?'

'You been sold a pup, mate,' Kelvin smirked, completely ignoring the fact that Chris had asked him to be quiet.

'Well, Chris, that's nice...uh Michael, I don't know if you know... Michael is back...'

'Oh, he's back then...great. Back from overseas?'

'Maybe he's bought some shoes too,' mumbled Kelvin.

'Yes,' said Mrs Martin. 'Yes and I was wondering if you wouldn't mind giving him a ring perhaps...' She let the words hang in the air.

'Yes,' said Chris. Kelvin just stared at him.

'He's at a bit of a loose end so...you being an old friend...'

'Oh, I'd love to, Mrs Martin. Do you have his number there?'

'Yes, I'll just fetch it...it's his work number. He's just filling in at a clinic, um.'

Chris was gripped by a thought, but even so he could hear a hesitancy in Mrs Martin's voice.

'Do you think he might be up for a game of cricket, Mrs Martin...does he still play?'

There was a silence.

'Oh, yes, I'm sure he'd love to play, Chris...Um, would you mind not telling him I thought it might be an idea if you rang him?'

'Of course, Mrs Martin.'

'Yes...he's...he's been at a bit of a loose end since he's landed.'

Chris copied down the number and said goodbye to Mrs Martin. He felt a tap on his elbow. It was Kelvin.

'You going to keep that thing up here?' he gestured to the shoe.

Chris smiled and flicked his Sherpa shoe back under the desk.

'Now, listen, Kelvin, you'll be right here. It just sounds bad, but remember this is not a hearing, this is a review panel. You'll be right.'

Kelvin humphed a little. 'Yes, mate, I know...told me all this on the phone. What are you?'

Chris Andersen looked at Kelvin. Kelvin looked back.

'What are you in cricket?...You play cricket, don't you? Batsman or bowler?'

Chris put his head down and went through some papers.

'Yes, sorry. I'm a bowler, Kelvin. A bowler.'

Kelvin sniffed. 'Bowler!' He made a little noise. 'It's a batsman's game, mate, they get all the glory... A batsman's game.'

Chris looked over at him sideways and nodded slightly. 'Anyway, just don't say too much...the facts will sort themselves out. We'll be right.'

The door opened and the department reps came in and sat at a desk that was slightly raised.

Chris Andersen sniffed and shook his head and looked up to check the department reps. Even if these review panels weren't arbitration, the department always tried to make them more austere and serious for the members that sat before them. The first rep was a man he knew. A nice fellow with an awful beard. It was awful because he wore no moustache. Why anybody would bother to grow a beard and not wear a moustache was beyond him. It was like wearing a shirt without any undies or pants.

But still, even without a moustache, he was a nice man. It was the second and then the third reps that made Chris pause. The second was a man with a coffee stain down the front of his shirt. The man from the cafe who had laughed at Chris' shoes. The man whom Chris had laughed at when the coffee had spilt into his lap. They looked at each other.

'Nice shoes?' said the man.

'Not really,' said Chris. 'Nice coffee?'

The man smiled. 'Not really.'

He seemed okay after all. It was the third rep that Chris Andersen couldn't help staring at. Her hair was swept back in a tight bun. She wore a smart suit. He wasn't sure...until she spoke.

'This review panel is of course not a panel of arbitration or of hearing. It is, as its name suggests, a panel of review between the union and employer, the Department of Works... We review cases of concern, complaint and cause. The first item is a complaint received from citizens of Shepparton concerning a contract employee... Mr Kelvin Ryan.'

It *was* her. It had to be. For a moment Chris Andersen thought she may have been a relative. But then she looked straight at him. For a long moment.

She doesn't recognise me, he thought. Was that a bad thing? He didn't really know.

For some reason he dredged his mind and uttered very slowly and quite clearly, 'Hands off Malvinas!'

'I beg your pardon?' she said.

They all looked at Chris Andersen. She didn't remember him.

'Sorry, it's nothing, just something I remembered. Means nothing.'

'Well then, let's begin,' said the man with the coffee stain.

Kelvin was employed on a seasonal basis by the state to shoot rabbits and occasional foxes. The problem was that on one morning two months ago he had shot just about everything except rabbits and the occasional fox. And he had made another mistake when he'd told everyone at the Criterion Hotel one Friday night all about it.

Kelvin had shot a couple of stop signs, a letterbox or two, and a guide dog. Kelvin wouldn't have really had a problem if he hadn't told everyone he'd shot a guide dog.

The woman in the smart suit looked at Kelvin. 'You shot a guide dog?'

'Yeah, most definitely, but you know it already had a hole in its head . . . for the money to go through.'

Chris Andersen gave Kelvin a hard look in an attempt to try to shut him up.

The man with the coffee stain pounced. 'So you admit to these actions?'

Kelvin nodded. 'My word.'

'You shot a guide dog?'

'Yes.'

Chris Andersen tried to clarify the matter. 'We're all aware, I hope, that the guide dog was a plastic one . . .' He looked at the reps. 'A charity collection bin as it is termed by the association, and that it was decommissioned and purchased by Mr Ryan at a selected charity distributor for second-hand goods –'

'The second-hand dealer on Mulberry Street . . . got the receipt,' Kelvin added.

'And the road signs?' the man with the coffee stain asked.

'The road signs were purchased at the same outlet,' Chris replied.

'And I got me receipts,' Kelvin added.

'And there are receipts supporting the purchase,' Chris reiterated.

The man with the coffee stain blinked. 'Mr Ryan is a pest exterminator?'

'A rabbit-shooter and union member . . . he uses these objects as targets on his property so he may . . .' Chris sought a word. 'Follow his calling to its highest possible rate of success.'

The reps looked at each other and then at Chris. His foot hurt and the whole process seemed to make time disappear in the room. The tension evaporated.

'Well, really there's nothing to pursue then,' said the nice man with the beard.

'No, there doesn't really appear to be much point continuing.' The woman in the smart suit was annoyed. She looked at Chris. 'I assume you are going to recommend that your member seeks reimbursement from the department for costs associated in attending the review.'

Chris didn't say anything. He knew that it was the girl from that afternoon all those years ago. And that she didn't have a clue who he was.

'Got me receipts here,' Kelvin replied, holding them out further than his stomach.

'Well ... very well, I'm sure Mr Andersen can take care of those matters for you. Good day.'

Kelvin nodded and left a happy man.

The other reviews went by slowly and uneventfully. In a break the nice man with the awful beard looked at Chris. 'You playing tomorrow, Chris?'

'Yes, I am.'

After a brief but heavy silence, the nice man said 'Chris plays cricket,' by way of explanation. 'For Yarraville West, isn't it?'

'That's right.'

'I don't get cricket. I have a husband who does, but I'm sorry, I don't get it,' said the woman Chris knew from years ago.

'You don't get it?' asked Chris Andersen.

The woman looked at him. 'No, I don't. I don't. But then I don't get unions really. Why bother?'

It was the way she held her head that annoyed Chris. She had held her head that way all those years ago.

'Well,' said Chris Andersen. 'We're a bit like Collingwood. We've got a lot more supporters than we've got members, and the members we've got aren't going anywhere.'

Nobody said anything for a few long seconds. Chris rose and walked over to a door that led to a small foyer. As he walked he looked at the woman. No. She wasn't interested. She had no idea who he was. Well, that was that. She seemed to be engrossed in flipping through the papers of the next subject before the review panel. Chris thought he could squeeze in a phone call to check on Rob Orchard. If Rob was free he could sort out his availability. That would be good. As he went to the door, he heard her voice.

'You have only one shoe on.' She looked at him. And as she did she tilted her head to one side. She hadn't changed.

'Yes,' Chris Andersen said, looking at her.

He pushed through the door and reached for his phone.

Rob Orchard had been at work for almost four hours. And now he was resting his newspaper on the wheel. He flipped a page and as he did so he saw a woman peering at him through the glass of the door. He didn't look at her. If he made too much eye contact then he would have to engage in conversation and that would be no good because then he couldn't read his paper. That was why he had shut the door of the bus that he was driving. Had been driving, for four hours.

He just wanted to have a quick peep at the paper in his break. It was a simple pleasure, at shift break he would get the paper from his leather bag and prop it on the steering wheel of the bus and flip through to the form guide or the horoscopes.

Just a simple pleasure that he didn't want interrupted. Simple things were important.

Rob knew that sometimes a simple thing can make your day. You have to remember that because in some places the simple thing is hard to find. They are usually there, but they can be hard to find. Such a place is the bus to work. The early bus that had been filled and emptied of human beings at least five times so far that morning.

It wasn't really that long ago that Rob had woken in his flat by the gardens in Yarraville and got ready to go to the depot and open his bus. As he walked to the depot he could hear the magpies call, hear the seagulls from the Maribyrnong River sing to the rising sun, hear the long mournful horns from the freighter ships roll across the stillness like great early morning yawns. He could smell the dew. The trees were gracious, green and elegant. The air clear. But that was then.

In the bus the commuters had been sandwiched together. Tightly. Strangers pressed against each other, not knowing each other yet hearing each other's breaths, smelling each other. But then he had smelled someone's sausage roll. And it was a beauty. It was the sausage roll from hell. In a contained space a smell like that can break a man. Especially when you can hear the mouth of the owner of that sausage roll wrapping itself around the pastry and chewing. Masticating. Mulching.

Whoever it was must have been in a seat right behind his screen. He could see a lazy looking man in a suit rustling a brown paper bag. He guessed it was him. The smell of that sausage roll overwhelmed everything else. Deodorant. Perfumes. Aftershave. Hairspray. Cologne. Farts. Maybe even a hint of pee from last night's late shift. These are some of the smells that float through a bus, but on this morning the aroma that blanketed everything was that sausage roll.

Sometimes a few people would ask for a ticket and distract him from the smell.

'Zone one, all day,' they would say.

'Six-twenty,' he would say.

Sometimes there would be a person with a big note. 'I'm sorry, this is all I've got...can you change this?' A fifty dollar note would be waved in front of his face.

'Well, no, as a matter of fact I don't have change and you can fuck off and walk, you fat git.' He turned the page of the paper and the woman looked like she was going to tap on the glass of the door. He never actually said that to the big bill wavers. Even though he wanted to. He would stare and tell them to take a seat. Amazingly, there was none this morning. Now was that the simple thing to make his day? He hoped not.

He held the newspaper in his hand and before he turned the page he thought that perhaps the magpie he'd heard singing in the early morning might have been the simple thing.

As he drove his bus mobile phones trilled. Almost as if mocking the sounds he'd heard while walking to work. Some rings have snatches of music. Well, digitalised snatches of tunes. He would hear this muddled symphony of tunes exploding. As he drove he heard a freakish mixture of Beethoven's Fifth Symphony, Deep Purple's 'Black Night' and Abba's 'Mamma Mia' meshed together. Music for commuters. He liked to hear the little snippets and try to pick the tunes.

That early morning bus. People, sorry, commuters also read, of course. One man tried to read the *Age*. It must have been a dare. Why would anybody want to try to read a broadsheet on a packed morning bus? Rob looked at this man. What was he doing? It was as if he were trying to fold a bed sheet in a telephone box. He has no hope. Most of the other readers had chosen the safer tabloid.

This is how we start the day, my fellow travellers and me, Rob Orchard thought and flicked to the form guide. He turned to Flemington just as his mobile sang to him. Puccini, 'One Fine Day'. He laughed a little as he thought of those ring tones he had heard as he drove. He didn't ever say he was better than his passengers. He watched them in the mirror and it is odd what you see reflected there. Yet he knew he was one of them. His phone fitted with the rest. He picked it up and saw the caller's number. He nodded and pressed the receive button. Then held the phone a distance from his ear.

'Hello Christopher Andersen,' he said.

'Robert, how are you!' blazed Chris Andersen. Rob held the phone further away from his ear.

'How are you?'

'Just after some timetable information,' screamed Chris.

'Oh, up yours, funny man.' He smiled when he heard Chris Andersen laugh.

'What do you want, Chris? I'm on a break.'

'I want some new shoes, mate.'

'What?'

'Don't worry. Are you right for tomorrow?'

'Yes, Christo. I'm right.'

'Now, you know we're at home,' Chris said.

He brightened. 'No, Christo, I didn't know that.'

'Yeah, playing Trinity.'

'Good...that means we do lunch.'

'Yes, mate, we do...and that means you get fine leg.'

'Good,' said Rob Orchard.

'Right then,' boomed Chris. 'Keep yourself nice.'

Rob laughed. 'Up yours, funny man.'

He switched his phone off and sat for a moment. He smiled. He folded away the paper. We're playing at home. Good, he thought.

He opened the door and smiled at the woman.

'Are you right there? Do you need a hand?' he asked pleasantly.

'Oh,' said the woman, 'do you go down to Gardenvale?'

'No, that's the seventy-five. It goes from the corner of Queen Street. Pop in and I'll take you up.'

'Oh, thank you,' said the woman. 'I didn't know whether to ask. You looked like you were on a break.'

'I am on a break, but it's fine... Come on I'll pop you up.'

The woman smiled. 'Nice to see someone in a good mood,' she said.

Yes, thought Rob. I've found my simple thing for the day. We're playing at home. 'I'm playing cricket tomorrow,' he said lightly.

He wondered what she'd be playing.

Ian Sykes was a security officer who was worried about his chicken sandwiches being irradiated by the X-ray machines at the prison he worked at in the northern suburbs. 'I know security is important and I'm all for it, but irradiation can cause certain side-effects in certain foods...but I don't want manual inspection of my lunch either – there are hygiene issues,' he boomed to the panel.

Ian Sykes went on and on to let everyone know that he had purchased the chicken at his own cost and had carefully prepared it in such a way that he maintained his health and therefore his working life. He was proud that he would be operating at a more efficient level because he was a healthier worker.

'That is a good bit of chook, that,' he thundered as he proffered a Gladwrapped chicken sandwich as evidence.

Chris Andersen held his forehead in his hand. Ian Sykes had been banging on about chook sandwiches for over an hour and a half. He was glad when an unhappy Sykes was told emphatically that his chook sandwich had to be X-rayed or manually examined (with gloves). Chris couldn't find it in himself to raise much of an argument.

Ian was followed by Toni and Ryan, two immense timber workers who wore sunglasses and Southern Cross flags on their jackets and looked like they were out of a ZZ Top music video. They were concerned about overloading of overtime and transport weights.

The day dragged on and Chris concentrated on the groundsman's water usage rates and the meteorologist who had car parking problems at the Botanical Gardens. He sat and listened and was there for the members.

They dealt with little things that didn't seem to matter to anybody in the room, except the union member, really. Little things that made up people's lives. Little things that passed the time.

It was late in the afternoon when Chris Andersen managed to find some time to use his phone. He dialled Michael Martin's number and a receptionist answered.

'... mead Medical Clinic... hello...'

'I need to speak to Michael Martin, Dr Michael Martin.'

'He's with a patient at the moment.'

'It's very important, just a quick word.'

'I'll see if he can talk, hold please.'


Michael Martin sat back and looked straight into a penis and two shaved testicles. He then looked up at the face of the man who owned that penis and testicles.

It wasn't the first set of penis and testicles he had seen and most likely it wouldn't be the last.

'Now Mr... Mr Smythe...'

'Call me Doug, please.'

Michael Martin nodded, his eyes half-closed, he could have gone to sleep but he knew that in those few long moments before sleep, he would feel the heat, hear the noise and see those eyes and so he thought what Mr Smythe had to offer was easier to cope with. He spoke slowly, 'I'm not quite sure, Mr Smythe... sorry, Doug... why you are showing me your equipment. It doesn't seem to add any weight to your expressed need for an enlargement.'

'Well, no, look I'll be completely open with you.'

It was hard for him to be anything else.

'Completely open... this is a lifestyle issue.'

Michael gestured for him to raise his trousers but Doug didn't seem to care so Michael leant back further and put his arms behind his head.

'Lifestyle. I know that what I've got is quite adequate... but I want an enlargement. I want it. I want to renovate, I want to be what I want... and I want this.' Doug pointed at his appendage. And while he did the phone rang. Michael answered.

'Michael Martin.'

'Mate... Michael... how are you?'

Michael turned to see Doug Smythe's lifestyle project.

'Hello,' Michael said slowly.

'It's Chris, Chris Andersen. How are you? You in the middle of anything?'

Michael sat still and somehow his thoughts, his racing thoughts disappeared and he saw...

'Hello, Christo.'

He pictured a laughing man leaning on a bat. The afternoon light dying in the sky and shrouding him in a golden veil that shone. He felt like laughing until he remembered.

'Hello, Mike… Listen, I don't mean to be abrupt here but I'm a bit pumped for time. I've got some mad fucking meteorologist who wants to talk about car parks, primary school tours and black holes…'

Michael smiled, this was typical Chris Andersen. 'Yes, Christo.'

'Anyway, I just want to know if you want a game of cricket. Tomorrow. Bull Reserve. Yarraville West Fourths. Not much of an invite, but there you are.'

'Uhh…'

'Come on, Michael. It would be great to see you. What do you say?'

'Well, yes, why not? No that… it'd be good. What time?'

'Bit before twelve. How you been?'

Doug Smythe coughed.

'Look, sorry, Chris. I am in the middle of something… but that will be good. Can you bring some kit for me?'

'Yep, got the club bag there,' said Chris. 'But you might want to bring your own box.'

Michael remembered Mr Smythe. 'Right, a protector. Very vital. Okay, Chris.'

'Ta ta, brother,' boomed Chris Andersen.

Michael rubbed his eyes. The Andersens. They always had loud voices… except for Tony. He shook his head and brought his attention back to Doug.

'Now, you understand that these procedures are not guaranteed of success. I know I'm only a referring doctor, but you must know that this is your decision.'

Doug Smythe, a man who looked very ordinary, breathed heavily. 'I know that. I know. I'm really not here for a lecture. I am here for a referral.'

Michael looked at him. What was the point of arguing? He knew someone would give in – it might as well be him. If he got rid of Mr Doug Smythe and his wherewithal then he would have time to go to the dispensary.

He reached for his keypad to write the referral but paused as he saw the man pulling up his trousers.

'You want to put this consultation on Medicare?' Doug Smythe asked.

He watched as Doug Smythe buckled his belt with a flourish. 'Listen, I pay my taxes.'

Michael Martin nodded. 'I'm sure you do.'

He turned back to the computer but his thoughts were on a game of cricket.


It was on his way home that Chris Andersen remembered. He could have kicked himself for forgetting. He would be waiting for the call. He would have kicked himself...but his foot was too sore to do anything much.

'Christ, how am I going to front tomorrow?' he muttered to himself as he stood on the train platform and reached for his phone. He scrolled through his contacts and found the name he was looking for. Brian Keith.


Brian Keith's mother stood at the window in her front room and looked out at Brian. He was a tall boy. Not a boy. He was twenty-five. He stood there in the early evening light peering into the sky. She watched as he occasionally brushed away the white moths that flew under the bright streetlamp above him.

Mrs Keith held in her hands an awkwardly shaped vegetable strainer that Brian had made for her at the workshop. It was a birthday present.

When he stood still he seemed...she felt ashamed for a moment but she was tired. He seemed normal.

He waved at a moth again. She opened the window.

'Brian, if you want to see it, don't stand under the light.'

He turned and looked at her. Stared in question.

'Don't stand under that light,' she said slowly and with great love, 'if you want to see the first star of the night don't stand under the light.'

He laughed and said, 'Righto, Mum.'

Mrs Keith looked at her watch. Just as she was about to think he wouldn't ring, the phone rang.

She breathed a small easy sigh and picked it up.

'Hello, Mrs Keith!' My God that man has a loud voice, she thought. But she was always relieved to hear it.

'Yes, Christopher,' she said.

'Is Brian there? Can you pass on a message?'

It was a routine. 'Yes, Christopher.'

'Can you ask him if he can play for the fourths tomorrow. We need him.'

She held the phone away from her and called to her son.

'Brian, Christopher Andersen wants to know if you can play cricket tomorrow. They need you!'

Brian turned to his mother and yelled from the semi-darkness, 'I'm ready, Mum. Tell Christo I'm ready.'

Mrs Keith spoke to the phone. 'He says he's ready.'

Chris Andersen listened to the woman's voice as he watched the lights of the approaching train. 'Tell him he is a good man. Mrs Keith...'

'Yes,' she answered.

'Has he found that star yet?' asked Chris.

She smiled to herself. 'Brian, have you found the star?'

'No...not yet, Mum,' her son answered in his light voice.

Over the noise of the station Chris Andersen heard Brian. 'Tell him to keep looking, it'll be there.'

Mrs Keith smiled. 'I will. And thank you.'

Her last words were lost in the roar of the train.

Chris Andersen snapped his phone shut and limped into a carriage. Done. He had a team. He looked down at his feet. 'Bloody shoes.'

He was playing cricket tomorrow. And he wondered, as he looked through the windows of the train out at all the backyards of people he didn't know, he wondered why she didn't remember him.

# Cec Bull's Memorial

The Cec Bull Oval lay under a fine layer of dew. The sort of jewelled dew that would catch rays of light and reflect them for those who were there early enough to see. Little prismed rainbows that shone like diamonds and then slowly disappeared, as the sun grew warmer and the day wore on.

Ted Bright had seen those rainbows on many mornings, for it was now, before the park was claimed by the weekend, that he liked to walk the oval. Sometimes he had the park to himself, sometimes he had to share. This morning he and Newk waddled around alone. Although someone had gone before.

The footprints of an early morning jogger had worn a thumping path into the grass. Ted looked at the prints as they curled along the boundary of the field and went round and round.

'I wonder if he stopped to look at the little rainbows, Newky?' Ted Bright said to his dog.

A great bull-necked Labrador turned his big head and looked at his owner. Newk was a very old and very fat Labrador. His sandy coat fizzed with grey and white. His brown eyes were tinged with misty blue in the middle. A tongue lolled out from his mouth, a mouth that seemed set in a perpetual grin. Newk was the kind of dog who made you smile.

Newk heaved a bit towards Ted Bright and then stood still, waiting for his owner to make some movement. But the old man just stood on the boundary line staring down at the frosted footprints in the grass.

'I don't think he would have stopped, Newky. Why should he? Had better things to do. He had to run around in circles.' Ted Bright laughed a little to himself and then pushed off, clicking to his dog. Newk pushed up against him and Ted scratched and rubbed the back of his big head.

'Come on walk, you fat old bugger.'

Ted Bright had gone for strolls and walks on this oval for years. For nearly all of his eighty years he had walked with one dog or another. By himself or with somebody else. He used to walk around it as a young boy and he used to run around it as a young man playing football and sometimes cricket. Years ago he would come and sit under the tall gum trees that stood on the rise near Essex Street. He would sit there with his wife, Marg. They would sometimes bring a picnic.

Once they had made a picnic. A special one. Well, the picnic was normal; a flask of tea, salad sandwiches, a couple of pieces of fruitcake.

Ted had hurried home from his work at the Kitchen Maid stove factory up by the Defence Munitions Plant on the banks of the Maribyrnong River. It was the day that man landed on the moon. Lots of the workers had had a peek at the television in the accounts office, when the fellow actually plopped onto the moon. After that the day was spent putting together the basic wiring on your stand-alone stove and oven.

About four-thirty they were all given an early mark so they could go and watch the re-runs on the tele at home. Ted and Marg had sat together and watched.

'It's history, Margie,' said Ted.

'It is, it is... but they just don't seem to be doing that much, do they?'

'What?'

'Well, what a way to go... to just fuddle about.'

'I suppose.' Ted had to admit, now that he thought about it, his Marg had a point. 'Yes, they do stand around a bit... but they're up there.'

They stared at their PYE television and the grey rolling pictures from the moon.

'It is remarkable, though... just a bit funny. Like going all the way to Coles just to fiddle with your change and come home.'

'Well, yes... but they're up there.'

'Ted, let's have a picnic down in the park and watch the moon.'

Ted had nodded and washed and changed. And the flask and tartan blanket that were usually taken to the footy were carried to the rise on Bull Oval. There on the tartan, Ted and his Margie had eaten their sandwiches and sipped their tea and stared at the moon.

It was alive and distant in the night sky. They stared at the disc of silver, the sky's twenty cent piece.

'They're up there, up there,' said Margie.

Up there on the sky's twenty cent piece.

It seemed so great a thought, such a huge leap, that Ted Bright and his wife held hands as they looked up.

'What a thing to leave your mark where nobody has ever gone,' said Margie.

That was the point when awe should have struck them dumb, but that was also the point when Ted bit onto a piece of fruitcake and one of his back teeth parted company from its base. It mixed in with the cake in his mouth and he made a sort of a sound. A sound that, at first, made Marg think Ted was ruminating on the size of it all and was expressing his awe.

She looked at him and held his hand even tighter. 'It's history, Teddy.'

'It's my bloody tooth,' howled Ted. 'Bloody almonds!'

The gum trees had gone but he knew where they'd been. He rolled his tongue across a chip on one of his back teeth. He had never really got around to having it seen to. He thought of the moon and of fruitcake and of his Margie.

Ted had sat here with her, in this park, before she was his wife. A playground squatted in the far corner where once a vast old cotton tree had stood. And there under the spreading branches, early one evening, he had kissed her for the first time. Marg Heywood, her name had been then. Marg.

He spoke more to Newk now, he thought, since Marg had died. Sixty years they were married. Sixty years. She had died two years ago. There in bed together one morning she had turned to him and said simply in a weary sort of voice, 'Teddy... Teddy, I feel tired.'

She had died. He had sat with her for an hour, holding her hand and staring at her. Their big fat old dog had come in and looked at him with his friendly eyes. And sat with his head on the bed.

Well, if you could share that moment with a dog then it was only right that you could share a few words now and then as well, thought Ted Bright.

He missed his Marg and he supposed that really, although he still liked what he did, nothing these days really kept him going. He was running down, filling in time without her. Not a bad sort of life but, really, when the highlight of your day was watching a fat old Lab poo on the dewy jewels in the park then...well. Never mind.

'Come on, Newk, let's not fuddle about.' The old man and his old dog rambled off on a tour of the oval.

He saw the footprints of the jogger. They trailed past the playground. They had never had children, Marg and Ted Bright. Just their lot in life. His tongue ran across his tooth. He looked at the footprints.

'What a thing to leave your mark where nobody has ever gone,' he said slowly.

Newk wandered off and stopped by the wire ropes in the middle of the ground where the wicket lay. By the way the dog moved Ted knew what was coming.

'No, Newky! No! I've got no more bleeding plastic bags. Come on, come here.'

The old dog barked a bit.

'Newky... Newk.'

The dog bent his creaky hind legs and let a series of steamers fall on the wicket.

Ted Bright looked at the dog and Newk smiled back, looking very pleased with himself.

'Oh well, better an empty house than a bad tenant.' He clicked at the dog and he moved towards the car park where plastic dog bags were held in a metal dispenser.

Ted Bright and Newk were stopped by a voice.

'Don't worry, mate. Don't worry about the bag. I'll sort it out.' A brisk little man in khaki marched out. 'I've got to roll it. I'll fix it up if you like.'

John Grassi walked past the old man and his dog. Ted nodded. John Grassi took out the wires and poles.

'Are you sure?' Ted Bright said. 'I've run out of bags.'

'No, you'll be right. No bags needed. I'll just roll the shit into the wicket – it'll blend nicely with the rest of the turf.'

Ted Bright half-smiled and even Newk turned his big wobbly head to one side.

John Grassi, the groundsman from the council, took the last pole and tossed it away from the square. He sighed impatiently. 'It's only the fourths, mate. Only the fourths today. They won't know the difference.'

Ted nodded. 'Oh... right then. I thought we might come round in the afternoon for another look-see... but if it's only the fourths...' he trailed off.

'Oh well, you never know your luck.'

'Yes... yes...' Ted Bright said that because he couldn't think of anything else to say and he suspected that the little fellow in the dungarees couldn't give a fig about what he said. He seemed to be in a hurry.

'Righto then,' said the old man and he clicked at his dog and together they went walking around the oval.

John Grassi was in a hurry. He'd come down the night before to water the ground, but because the fourths were playing he didn't have to do any rolling last night. It was a dead track anyway and really it had been years since a top side had played here. The oval was too irregular a shape to have top grade cricket played there, so he did just what he had to do and no more. The dog shit didn't really matter.

This park had seen worse than dog shit in its time. When the junkies used to drift through this suburb they would leave all sorts of crap and gear. Needles, sometimes capped, sometimes not. Even in the playground they would find them, in amongst the swings and the timber cubbyhouse. And that old wooden boat.

There was a wooden boat that had a little platform you could stand on like a deck, so you could look out over the park as if it were the waves of a sea.

In the cubbyhouse one year they had found more than needles.

They had found a body. John Grassi had heard about it when one of the garbos had radioed in after collecting the rubbish bins. John had to go and chalk up the markings for a football match, so he was on his way there anyway. He arrived about the same time as the ambulance.

She was curled up in the cubby. A young woman. Hair dyed bright blonde with the dark roots showing. He could see that quite clearly, he stood that close. She was curled up as if she were asleep. Hunched over, her head turned to one side and her mouth slightly opened. She didn't look any older than eighteen. She looked young. Maybe even younger than she looked. Between her boots were some things that must have belonged to her. A tin of tobacco, a needle and a clear little plastic bag sat in a little mess by her boots. She had a small bag in the shape of a dog. A carry bag. One of the paramedics picked it up and placed it outside the door. He put all the articles back in it.

They looked big, the paramedics, in their grey overalls, as they squatted inside the cubby with the girl. One checked her pulse and then turned to get some equipment. She must have been alive. As he stood the paramedic bumped his head on the top of the cubby.

'Shit…shit,' he muttered as he gave it a quick rub and grabbed a bag.

John Grassi could see that the cubbyhouse had a title plate above the doorway. 'Our Home.' He had never seen it before.

Her skin was so pale.

'Must have snuck in here to get warm last night,' the paramedic who hadn't banged his head said.

They took her out and put a mask on her. Maybe she was alive? They put her on a stretcher and put her fluffy dog bag in a plastic bag and tossed it in the back.

'Bloody junkies,' said John Grassi to hide the fact he felt like crying.

A paramedic nodded at him and rubbed his head as he got in the ambulance. The other paramedic laughed at his mate.

'Need a Panadol?' he giggled.

Junkies. They were a hassle, alright. Still, they had moved on and it was good the suburb was changing. New families, houses being done up and you could see that change here in the park, thought John Grassi as he got out the big heavy roller. New barbecues and the playground had been done up. New cubbyhouse and that new big boat. Nice swings.

No junkies.

But sometimes he would think of that girl and wonder if she was alright. When he marked the centre square and the boundary with the white chalk he would think of her. Her skin was pale. So white. She was so young.

John Grassi pushed the heavy roller and Newk's shit pounded into the turf, mingled in with the pitch. They were only the fourths. They wouldn't notice the difference.

The Cec Bull Oval had changed, John Grassi was right. It had changed a lot. It wasn't really even an oval, more of a peanut shape really. That meant that one side of the ground was shorter than the other, and seeing as how the surface was a little bit rough, the oddness of the ground was accentuated. Oh, it had a lovely grassy surface and had an in-ground sprinkler system to maintain the lush cover. But this summer had been very hot and very dry and even the sprinklers couldn't stop little mangy patches appearing here and there.

The unevenness of the ground gave a hint that the oval hadn't always been a reserve, it hadn't always been the Bull Oval.

Its official title was The Cecil Bull Oval and Reserve. Cecil Bull. Cecil Bull, or as everybody who knew him called him, Cec. Cec Bull had earned the right to give his name to the oval, for he'd spent a vast amount of time running over its surface in various guises. Ted Bright had told John Grassi all about Cec Bull – or as much as one man could.

Cecil Arthur Bull was born and bred in Yarraville West and was one of twelve children. He grew up the son of a meatworker and being the eldest he followed his father's bloody footsteps into the slaughterhouse.

Cecil worked there all his life, save for the four years he spent in the forces of his majesty's Australian Army during the Great War. He left Yarraville as a young man and came home much older a few years later as a sergeant with ribbons on his chest.

People who knew him well didn't really see that much of a change in him. He was loud and liked a drink and played his football and his cricket with a studied violence that was always on the right side of good taste and propriety. He married a girl from Footscray who he had known before he left and she didn't see any change either.

But it was there. It was in the way he drank a little bit more than people realised and it was there in the way he would stand amongst the waste and blood of the animals in the slaughterhouse.

He would stare at the guts and intestines as they tumbled out. Turn and listen and stare at the animals as they smelled their fate and the blood of their fellow kind.

'They can smell it,' he would say. 'They're sucking it in, breathing it deep into their guts...'

And if anybody asked him what he meant, he would turn to them and stare with his dark eyes.

'Death, boyo, and it's a bugger of a thing to take into ya belly.'

Sometimes when the intestines lay squirming on the cement floor, before the boys would come and shovel and sweep them away to the offal trays, Cec would look down and stare. Stare as if he were looking to see where the death had been sucked into, into the corded intestines and the heavy livers and kidneys and gut.

He stared in a way that would let anyone who really saw him know that he had sucked death into his belly. Not just once, as the animals that stood crammed and stockaded in the holding yards had, but many times. Many times locked together with other men. Men he hardly knew, but men he smelled and could feel and hear as they moved and breathed beside him.

He stopped for only a moment and he never really spoke to anyone, not even to the girl he married or to the children they had or to people who knew him well and called him Cec, for if he did, if he had – then they would see, they would notice he had changed.

The closest he ever came to revealing the change was one afternoon when he worked the floor with a young fellow who played in the first eleven at the club. It was a favour for the boy's father, a mate of Cec's from the RSL. A holiday job. The young fellow was studying to be a doctor, so Cec hadn't worried about how the boy would take the butchering. They would do butchering enough, he thought.

45

He'd had a couple of beers at lunch had Cec Bull and so he didn't see that the young fellow was only just hanging on to his stomach.

Cec had probably had a few more than a few beers and when he spilled the stomach of a warm beast upon the cement he had stood too close and the guts had spilled and piled up onto his legs and his apron.

Cec looked down and the memory assaulted him. He remembered running. Running and noise and explosions. Running and turning blind then jumping, falling into a hole, onto a man. Into a man. A French soldier. His stomach slit open. The Froggie could have been alive, Cec didn't know, but Cec could feel him – he was warm. He smelled him, he stank.

Cec breathed hard and looked down at the animal's guts. He moaned a little. He bent down and picked up a handful of the entrails and held them close. 'They don't smell...don't smell like that Frenchie's...he stunk, boyo, stunk like ... high as a Frog!'

The young fella from the firsts looked at him and for one moment thought that perhaps Cec Bull was going to bury himself in the guts of the animal.

Cec Bull realised that he had been seen.

He laughed and said, 'A Frenchie in the war, his guts all over me...he stunk, boyo... As high as a Frog...and they wave flags and play tunes and raise their glasses and that's it, boyo, that's it.'

The young fella looked Cec Bull square in the eyes and said, 'As high as a Frog?' Then he spewed and Cec Bull swore an oath.

'Holy fuck, you dill, you've ruined the guts. Boys, bring the hoses, this silly sod's upended his load.'

Even though he roared and made fun of the young fella, Cec Bull knew he had been seen. That young fella had looked into him and Cec felt a lot less sure of where he stood when the young bloke was about. About the club.

The young fella never mentioned that day to Cec, even though they would nod at each other in the nets and at the ground. And years later, when the young fella had become a doctor and sometimes dropped in to watch a match with his father and Cec would saunter over and laugh about the time the 'Young Doc upended his load over a cow's guts', they would never mention what they had shared. That was fair enough by Cec.

He was a sporting man, Cec Bull, and he bought a house near the park, just so he could be near the oval.

He was more of a football player than a cricketer, as evidenced in his portrait hanging on the walls of Yarraville West Workers and Services Club. Around the bars and through the pokies were dotted photos of stalwarts and club legends. A couple of cricketers had gone on to represent Australia in Tests, so they had pride of place over the entrance to the dining area. Greg Andersen had played two one-day matches for his country in cricket's dark days in the mid-eighties, but national selection is national selection and his portrait was rightfully hung, placed over the entrance to the alfresco area.

So important was Cec Bull to the history of the club that he was given the honour of having two photo portraits on the wall, one in footy garb and the other in his cricket whites.

Both images were starkly illustrative of the man Cec Bull had been – a meatworker, a slaughterman at the abattoirs over in Kensington – and even though he was pictured playing footy or cricket, Cec Bull still looked like a slaughterman. Other legends, with a pleasant fixed smile and wearing a club blazer, held a football or proffered a bat. But not Cec.

No folded arms popped under the biceps to make the muscles look bigger for Cec. His football photo had him tackling the head of an opponent. Cec's big chin and nose seemed to almost touch, and with his mouth agape in a toothless smiley snarl he looked like a malevolent Mr Punch trying to rip the tongue from the poor unfortunate he was manhandling.

His cricket shot was more poetically graphic. Cec sat behind the stumps smiling, robed in the big wicket-keeper's gloves and heavy pads, his enormous frame hunched in a keeper's crouch. He looked for all the world like a gargoyle removed from a gothic cathedral and plopped down behind the wickets.

These two photos were placed over the toilets. Cec the footballer-cum-slaughterman indicating the gentlemen's and Cec the gargoyle-cum-wickety the ladies'. It was an appropriate honour because it was due to Cec Bull's bodily functions that the scrubby park by Essex Street was given toilets, amenities and clubrooms and ultimately his name.

When Cec Bull's playing days were over he settled into a steady roll through life. He continued slaughtering cattle, sheep and pigs and he continued to enjoy a drink or one or two or fifty. He also became the oval's caretaker-cumgroundsman for a while because he lived in a house that spilled onto the reserve.

Cec and his wife had bought the place with a bit of help from his wife's father. They were a growing family and the house was a big one, with nice fruit trees. So for a small fee he was given the role of groundsman because he was handy. It didn't last long because he was caught drinking in the groundsman's shed. He only got caught doing that because he relieved himself through the scoreboard window while the church group were playing a game of social cricket.

A Reverend Donald Mope was bowling pretty ordinary off-spin to a mirthless and heavy-hitting left-handed Baptist when his attention was captured by the squeals and shocked screams coming from the scoreboard area.

Reverend Mope turned just in time to see Cec Bull in action, showering all and sundry with the outcome of a good day's drinking. All the while as he let go, Cec Bull serenaded his audience with a booming, cascading off-key baritone version of 'Yes, We Have No Bananas'.

Reverend Mope gave the ball to the umpire and strutted over to where Cec sang.

Cec later told the council that the reverend only made a 'to-do 'cause that bloody hairy bloke from the Baptists was giving him a right caning...he was bowling pies was Mopey'.

Reverend Mope stood as close as safety permitted under the scoreboard and in a surprisingly high voice for a tall man cried out to the crooning Bull, 'For heaven's sake, stop that.'

Cec Bull stopped. Stopped singing. It was a church match after all. After a few seconds silence, save for drips and flourishes on the tin roof from Cec's appendage – which it must be said sounded oddly like a loquacious conductor tapping his baton before an orchestra – 'Yes, We Have No Bananas' gave way to a mule-like version of 'Jerusalem'.

Cec sounded like a ship lost in the fog on a dangerous sea. Reverend Mope exploded.

'Bull, stop piddling at once...stop piddling.'

A little boy close to the outraged reverend giggled and ducked a backhander from Reverend Mope. He would have caught another but he was too quick and scuttled away and laughed even louder.

'I'll have words with your mother, Edward Bright!' trilled Reverend Mope.

Little Edward Bright showed no signs of caring and laughed even more at Mr Bull's willy.

A young woman with a white parasol stood and looked at the hairy sac and sausage that peered out from the small black window in the scoreboard. She said not a word nor showed any emotion.

Cec Bull pulled himself in and did himself up and put his great ugly head through the window. He stared down at the crowd below. He could see Reverend Mope and a woman with a white umbrella. He smiled. The young woman saw the sac and sausage replaced by the gargoyle and let out a shriek that echoed around the park. It slowly dawned upon Cec what had happened.

A collection of pursed-lipped Methodists looked up at him and he looked down at them. Cec Bull foghorned to the assembled faithful.

'Sorry, Mopey, sorry old son... Must have got a bit mixed up. Thought I was using the pisshole out the back.'

'Mister Bull! There are children here and ladies.'

'Oh, pull your head in you twerp.'

'The council will hear of this!'

'Good for you, Mopey... and Mopey...' Bull paused mid-roar. 'You're a shithouse bowler.'

The council did indeed hear of it and Cec Bull was there the night a quietly angry Reverend Mope addressed a closed sitting. Of course Cec would be there, he was an alderman. As the rest of the council were returned men with whom Cec would drink at the RSL, and even have the odd bottle in the groundsman's hut at the oval, the upshot was a grateful council thanking the Reverend Mope for bringing to its attention the lack of facilities at the ground.

More money was to be directed towards rectifying the lack of proper conveniences and so when the appointed committee sat and directed the development of the ground, somebody decided that the park should have a name. What name better than Cecil Arthur Bull to be laid down upon that peanut-shaped piece of land.

There were a few minor issues to be dealt with as far as the churches' cricket competition was concerned, but a nice ground is a nice ground and after all Mr Bull was a decorated returned man.

At the dedication ceremony on a Saturday in early summer the mayor paid tribute to a fine son of the western suburbs, a keen citizen, Mr Cecil Bull.

'We have fashioned from bush and scrub, from rock and stone, a place where young men can come and compete in the pursuit of healthy competition. To dedicate themselves to the service of their suburb. Ladies and gentlemen, I dedicate this reserve – the Cecil Bull Oval and Reserve.'

There was a smattering of applause and a band played and Cec Bull belched quietly to himself. They played a game of cricket. Then everyone went home.

Later that night, Cec Bull walked from his house and onto the oval. His oval. He had a bottle with him and he went and stood in the centre of the paddock and took a huge swig.

Cec smiled and raised the bottle to himself. He could see the lights of the houses that were being built around the park. Now that money was being spent on the amenities, people thought it was a place where they'd like to live. He looked back at his own home. The fruit trees were growing. It looked like a house an alderman should own. Hadn't done too bad, Cec, old son. Down at the corner of the ground two new houses were being built, one of them a brick home. A brick home. Cec Bull nodded his head.

'This place is coming ahead,' he said to the empty field.

The stars were out over his oval. He pawed at the earth with his foot. He remembered as a boy this oval being a bluestone quarry. Many of the lanes around the back of the houses were cobbled with stones that had lain beneath the grass of the oval, 'My oval,' thought Cec.

He took another swig.

The quarry had been winding down when Cec Bull had been a little boy, but he remembered it. The dry acrid smell and the grey men covered in dust, the thin skinny horses with their big tongues rolling as the rocks were pulled clear on the big wooden drays.

As a little boy, Cec remembered playing one evening with his three younger brothers, seeing who could throw stones nearest a dead dog on the floor of a small pit. Whether it had been dumped down there or had crawled by itself he didn't know. He didn't care. It wasn't unusual to have stuff dumped at the quarry. The quarry was closing and the holes were to be filled, so people would throw lots of stuff down there.

They were throwing their rocks and laughing and pushing when Cec saw him. A black. An Abo, standing off to the right of them. He was an old man, a man who was dressed in clothes that hung indifferently to him. He held a bottle that he sometimes drank from. In between mouthfuls he sang to himself.

The Bull boys all stopped and looked.

'He's singing in Abo.'

The boys mimicked him and laughed. The black man turned to them and yelled. None of them could understand what he said. His left arm flicking up as if to tell them to go away.

'He's as drunk as a fiddler's,' said young Cec Bull as he held a rock in his hand. He didn't know why he threw it, he was just a boy and boys love throwing rocks. Soon they all threw their rocks. No longer at the body of the dog but at the old black man.

They laughed as he jerked and tripped as their stones crashed near and clipped him. He yelled and they laughed.

They would often go to the quarry and look for him. Sometimes they found him. They were just boys having fun. He was just a black man.

One afternoon Cec Bull saw him. Lying down. In his clothes that didn't really seem to belong. Lying down at the bottom of the pit, where people would throw things they didn't need anymore. Instead of a dog or an old bike or a broken basin there lay a body. A black body. Cec Bull and his little brother looked down. They threw a couple of rocks and the man didn't move. Cec's little brother peed down into the pit. He didn't hit the man but they thought it funny. After a while they got bored and anyway it was time for tea.

Cec Bull's little brother told their mother about the body of the black man in the pit.

'Oh well, good riddance to bad rubbish,' their mother had said.

Bad rubbish.

People kept on throwing their rubbish into that disused quarry and soon the pit wasn't as deep as it once was. The council brought sand and soil in from the Maribyrnong River flats and the ground evened out in a rough sort of a manner.

By the time Cec Bull went off to the Great War, they played games of cricket and footy on that patch of grass.

Cec Bull thought of that old Aborigine. He took another swig.

'Hey, boyo,' he said. 'Hey, you old darkie, hey you down there! Underneath my oval.'

He did a silly little blackfella song and took a swig.

Cec Bull laughed and his big head lolled back and his eyes filled with the stars. He would have only taken a second to fall, but to him it seemed like an age as he tumbled back. He tumbled back onto the grass of his oval and as he tumbled he was filled with a shooting pain that flashed and stopped and his mind cleared and then he saw a girl with a white parasol, her mouth open in a shriek; an old black man singing; and heard the chatter of gunfire; of roaring noise; of the warmth of the mud. But it wasn't mud. Cec Bull moaned a little. It wasn't mud. It was the stomach of the French soldier.

'Oh,' sighed Cec Bull. 'As high as a Frog.'

Then Cec Bull died.

They found him the next morning. Spreadeagled and dressed in his suit, lying out in the centre of the oval. His big ugly head drawn back in that leer.

'Oh, well,' said a copper, who had been woken early on a Sunday morning by a group of parishioners, who then headed off to the Methodist church to spread the news of the body on the oval.

'Oh, well,' he said as he looked down at Alderman Bull and his bottle nearby. 'At least he died happy.'

Where Cec Bull had died, John Grassi's roller squashed and compacted down the turf.

Ted Bright was just finishing his lap of the oval. He turned back to see the groundsman rolling the pitch. 'Oh, well, maybe we won't come back and watch the cricket this arvo, Newky.'

He scratched his old dog.

Ted Bright looked at the leaves of the big fruit tree that hung so close to the fence of the park. He looked around and reached up. A rich fat fig fell into his hands. He walked along and held it to his mouth. It smelled sweet.

'Ooo, Newky, this is a beauty, can't wait till home.' He peeled back the soft skin and leant against the park sign.

The park sign was sponsored by the council and a real estate company. Bull's Realty. And above the council's name and the Bull Realty logo was the title of the park, The Cecil Bull Oval and Reserve... but above that was the word Yirrindi Wilam. The word given by the traditional owners of this land to describe the area. It was Aboriginal for 'A Place of Song'.

The fig was tasty, and Ted Bright looked at Newk.

'Well, maybe, Newky. Maybe we will pop down and watch the fourths later on. If the cricket's no good, there's always the figs.' He laughed and his fat dog barked. 'It looks like it's going to be a cracker of day, but a hot one, Newky.' He whistled softly to himself and Newky followed, wheezing in time.

Behind them the sun was out and warming and the footprints of that early morning jogger were already disappearing. The oval waited. Waited for the fourths.

# Let's Get Physical

The woman in the leotard must have been at least sixty. Chris Andersen was walking on a treadmill in the gym at the Yarraville West swim centre. The treadmill was placed on an upper level, in front of a glass wall, which enabled Chris to look down on the aquatic area below. That is where the woman in the leotard stood, when she wasn't jumping up and down and doing strange leg-lifting movements. She was a water aerobics instructor and she barked at people bobbing in the pool, and the bobbing people would try to mimic what this leotarded screamer was doing, and they would get it wrong and the woman in the leotard would scream louder.

She had been here on Saturday mornings for years. For as long as Chris could remember, he and his wife had been bringing their children to swimming lessons on a Saturday morning. The whole time they were there the woman would scream and play the music that people bobbed to.

From behind the glass wall Chris could see them all. Lachlan lounging on the long wooden bench, changed and dressed. Waiting and reading. He was always reading. Moira in the learner's pool with a clutch of others, the water teeming with thrashing little bodies, their arms and legs churning the water. Teeming with little bodies the way the creeks teem with tadpoles after the rains.

He could see Julie stroking up the pool doing laps. In the lap lane, safe from the bobbing people. Her strong sure stroke and her shoulders, gliding through the water. He could see his family amongst the throng and he felt a surge of emotion, a burst of happiness. Many men have felt such a surge in their lives. Some would have written great music, done great things, climbed mountains. Some would have tried to involuntarily skip and jump and throw in a yell for good measure – like Chris Andersen did. But men who would do great things and perhaps write marvellous music weren't on a treadmill.

And they didn't have a bad foot.

The woman in the leotard brought her own music. He heard that Kenny Rogers song. The one about the gambler.

Chris Andersen stumbled a little on the treadmill. He clutched at the handrail like an old man. His knees were bad; he used to love jogging around Bull Oval or down along the river but those days were long gone. Now it was six k's on the cushioned treadmills with various fitness programs. Even with cushioning his heel hurt.

Chris looked around at the other podgy bodies wobbling along a computerised version of a Marine boot march. The wobbly bodies did okay, maybe the Marines weren't so tough after all.

Some of the other treadmills had television monitors in front of them, welded into the wall above the big panes of glass. You could tune your Walkman in to a channel and march away while watching the box.

Everybody seemed to be watching a music clip show. Chris Andersen looked up sometimes to see groups of black American singers in baggy tracksuits with baseball hats and lots of jewels surrounded by half-naked women gyrating their hips at breakneck speed.

'Gonna put gonna put, gonna put a cap in your ass.'

That was what the muscly black man with a backwards baseball cap sang. Chris didn't want to make any judgement on what he was seeing. He didn't really understand the context of the song. He remembered watching television late one night when Kerry O'Brien used to host *Lateline* and Kerry, with his green pen and red hair and broken face, was talking about what the 'music of the streets of Black America meant'.

According to Kerry's guest it was all about sex. Kerry's guest was a sweaty-faced fat man. A sweaty-faced *white* fat man.

Chris Andersen told himself that the music and images were probably as mystifying to him as the music and images he'd liked when he was Lachlan's age had been to his father, Barry.

Even so, the music all looked and sounded manufactured. Not that the stuff he used to watch with his brothers wasn't manufactured, but it wasn't as slick. That's the word, slick.

He remembered sitting in front of the television watching Donnie Sutherland on *Sounds Unlimited* on a Saturday and

*Countdown* on a Sunday. He remembered the time Greg cried because their father had made fun of a band that Greg had liked. Hush. And their song about a girl called Boney Moroney.

'Christ, you're a bloody dill, Greg. Look at 'em.' Barry stood in front of the television.

Greg looked up at his father. 'They've got a couple of Chinese boys playing, look.'

Two guitarists in the band were Chinese. Chris Andersen remembered thinking, What's so unusual about that? They all looked a bit skinny and hairy and thin. The lead singer had a dog collar around his neck. It was all very homemade. Even Chris knew that Hush were pretty daggy.

'We've missed out on the cricket because of this show, you know,' said Barry Andersen. He laughed. 'Come on, what you reckon?'

'They're alright,' Greg had said but he was going red. Chris had giggled.

'Is that it, just alright? We're missing the cricket and it's just alright?'

Greg went completely red. Chris snorted.

'You'd think it'd want to be a bit better than just alright,' Barry grumbled.

Just when Chris thought Greg was really going to sook up, Tony Andersen had laughed. He was reading on the brown couch.

'I don't mind them, Dad.'

Their father looked at Tony. Tony smiled. 'They're alright in a funny sort of way – they're just having a go.' He smiled at his father.

Barry Andersen looked at his son Tony and nodded his head. Then he smiled, too. 'Fair enough then, but it looks pretty ordinary to me. Come on Boney Moroney.' He gently nudged Greg with a thonged toe. Then he touched his son's head. 'They're just having a go.'

Greg stopped tearing up. Chris Andersen had looked over to his brother Tony reading on the couch. Tony smiled and winked at him.

Chris shook his head and stared at the writhing bodies on the screen. Now some skinny white woman was gyrating in a strange tight suit with platform heels.

From down below he could hear the sixty-year-old leotarded water aerobics instructor screaming at the bobbing heads.

'No no! Listen to the music. Look at the action, roll your thighs… ROLLLLLLL!'

She started shouting along to the lyrics of 'The Gambler'.

She must have been the only aerobics instructor who taught to Kenny Rogers.

The woman started doing some odd leg lift, as if she were trying to hoick a leg over a fence. The heads bobbed in the water. It was like a bizarre video clip. In fact, Chris Andersen flashed back to a *Countdown* afternoon and remembered some weird Olivia Newton-John music clip, well, they had been called video clips back in the eighties. Olivia had worn a leotard and although she wasn't sixty, Chris Andersen remembered the way Olivia's leotard had sort of hung and bunched and clung in a weird way. She wore those odd stockings and a big towelling ring around her head. This is how the leotarded aerobics instructor praying-mantised her way through her poolside session.

In fact, the woman looked like she was going off to an Olivia Newton-John convention. The name of the song came to him – 'Let's Get Physical'. Olivia and lots of fat men in gym shorts.

I bet Greg liked that song too, he thought. He made a mental note to ask Greg, the next time his brother was holding forth about the dangers of unions to small businesses like his own.

The skinny gyrating woman on the TV screen gave way to sulky looking men with wispy beards, heavy pouts and guitars that looked ten times too big.

Chris Andersen stepped off the treadmill and walked down the stairs. The place was full of the most amazing bodies. Not because they were sculptured and god-like but because they were so real. So varied.

Every race seemed to be gathered under the roof. Vietnamese and Chinese and Anglos thrown together like some packet cake mix. The only thing in common being their exotic and magical sense of aquatic attire. The western suburbs dress sense was purely functional, basically anything that covered the genitals was deemed suitable. Undies, striped pyjama shorts and bathers that looked like they had been borrowed off old wrestlers, like Mario Milano and Killer Karl Cox.

There were shaven-headed Middle European men with heavily tattooed arms, there were old men and women whose folded stomachs spilled slowly downwards towards the water as they dripped into the pool. Africans, impossibly tall and long, their trailing limbs flowing through the air as they walked and laughed. Some wore sombre colours, business shirts and dark trousers. Some women wore flowing robes and burkas.

Chris Andersen walked and wondered why it was only sometimes that he would notice the different people. Yes, they were just people, but sometimes he would see their different colours, hear their different languages and feel the different cultures, all heaving and breathing beneath the peeling roof of the swim centre. It made him feel wise somehow.

It was on the occasional Saturday that he noticed it and he couldn't really say why. Chris walked past a Vietnamese man with bathers pulled high who hawked deep in his throat but didn't spit. He watched as the man walked into the toilets and Chris heard him hawk again. The music of the aerobics instructor drowned him out as the leotarded Olivia bounced up and down to an old sixties tune called 'Needles and Pins'.

'And stretch...riiightttttt out...until you feel those needles and pinnnnnnnnnnnssssaaaah!' she bellowed.

Chris walked to the end of the pool and waited for Julie to finish her last lap. As he did he looked over to his son. Lachlan was still reading his book. It wasn't that he was reading, it was the way he held his head to one side on an angle. He looked so much like his uncle.

Chris felt a splash and he looked down at his wife. She was smiling and her hair spilled out of her cap as she peeled it back.

'How's your foot, Chris?'

He looked into her face and her eyes; they were ringed with the marks of her goggles. They looked soft and brown against the blue of the pool's water. He loved her very much.

'It's still there...it'll be right.' He wondered why he didn't tell her he loved her.

She laughed again. 'Oh, well, at least I can tell your mum you've worn them.' She raised herself out of the pool and stood. He handed her the towel.

'I think I'll take Lachie to play today.'

Julie stopped drying herself and looked at him and then over to her son.

'Have you asked him or are you just going to make him?' She wasn't smiling anymore.

He told himself he should have told his wife he loved her when he felt like saying it.

'Chris?' his wife said.

He looked at her and knew he shouldn't tell her now.

'Look, I'll go ask him. If he doesn't want to play, that's alright.'

'You say that and then you crack the shits if he doesn't do what you want...'

'Oh, come on.'

'You do, Chris. I don't want you yelling at him.'

'I yell at everyone.'

Julie looked at him with a gaze that stopped him dead.

'Look, Julie, I just thought it would be good for him... and me, to see Michael. Michael Martin.'

'He's playing, is he?'

'Yep. Talked to him yesterday and you know it's the last game for the season...and I'd like to...spend it with Lachie.'

'Well, ask him. Say that to him. Don't trot over there and tell him he's going to have to make up the numbers. Don't conscript him, Chris, ask him.'

He looked away and saw the hawking man wander past the screaming Olivia and then saw Lachie looking over at him.

He nodded to his wife. He couldn't help himself.

'You know my dad would always drag me along.'

'Chris.' She looked angry now. 'You are not your dad and Lachie is not you. If you want to spend time with him, ask him. Have you ever asked him if he likes cricket? Talk to him.'

Chris nodded, he felt hot. 'Yes, I will. I will.'

He looked over at his son. Lachlan turned his head back to his book.

Julie wrapped the towel around her waist and went to collect their daughter, Moira, who was climbing out of the tadpole pool.

'Ask him. If he wants to go alright. But don't order him.'

'*Okay!*' The leotarded Olivia punched her arms out in front of her. As Chris Andersen walked around behind her towards Lachlan 'Macho Man' blared from the speakers. The heads bobbed up and down like hyperactive corks.

Chris climbed the wooden benches and sat next to Lachlan. His son didn't look up.

'Good book?' he asked.

'Okay,' said his son into the book.

'What is it? What are you reading?' He went to take the book but managed to draw back his hand.

'*To Kill a Mockingbird*,' his son said into the book.

'Oh, yeah...oh yeah. I remember reading that...at school. Would have been your age.'

Lachlan put the book down and looked at his father. His light eyes were steady. The look surprised Chris, it was a look that Lachlan gave every now and then and when he did it always took Chris by surprise. It was a searching look.

'Is that why you became a lawyer? Like Atticus Finch?'

Chris stared back at his son. I should probably say yes, he thought. I should probably say yes. *To Kill a Mockingbird*. He searched his mind briefly. He couldn't remember a thing about it. The girl with the weird name...and...the weird bloke next door and no...nothing else. He looked at his son. What did he want?

'No. No, not really. Had to read it for school.' His son blinked and looked back to the book. He remembered not finishing it. The movie was on one Saturday night and so he watched that instead. Maybe he shouldn't tell that to his son.

'I became a solicitor...because... I could...'

His son looked back up at him with a blank expression and nodded.

An old man moaned from the pool in front of them. His bathers were baggy, like the skin of an elephant. 'Macho Man' kept thumping from the speakers. The heads kept bobbing.

Chris Andersen looked at his son. 'Macho Man'. He sang along with the song for a moment. He remembered seeing that music video on the same show as he'd seen Olivia Newton-John getting physical. The old man's bathers reminded him a bit of Olivia's leotard.

He glanced at his son and realised that he knew the words to 'Macho Man' but had no idea what *To Kill a Mockingbird* was about. He felt slightly embarrassed.

Chris clapped his hands and his voice came out louder than he meant. His son snapped his head back up to look at his father.

'Now listen, Lachie, come and play cricket...' He winced. 'Would you like to play cricket for the fourths today?'

Lachlan looked down again, but this time to the ground, not the book.

'Look, I won't yell... Well, I probably will, but I'll try not to... It's the last game of the season and we'll probably get hammered...and we can spend a bit of time together...' He was running out of time. Julie and Moira would be coming out from the change rooms at any minute. The old man kept moaning and was shaking his hands, water flying from them, some of it landed on Chris' legs.

Chris flinched a little and went on. 'Look, I won't not say you'd be making up the numbers – you would. You'd be doing me a favour. If you don't want to, then that's fine.' He paused a while and then cranked up again, clapping his hands. 'You know there's a fella playing today that I'd like you to meet. Michael Martin. He's an old friend.'

'A friend?' asked Lachlan.

'Yeah, he used to play cricket with us...with me and your uncles. Me and Greg and...' He stopped.

'And Uncle Tony?' His son gave him that look again.

Chris Andersen turned back and focused on the bobbing heads. He nodded as they bobbed, 'Yes...yes...'

He saw his wife and his daughter walk from the change rooms and head towards the exit. Julie waved for them to follow.

Chris shook his head as 'Macho Man' finished.

'Yeah,' screamed leotarded Olivia. 'Give yourselves a big clap!'

Chris turned to his son. 'Look, don't worry about it. Don't worry. Come on.'

He walked off towards the exit and a pair of laughing young women who had originally come from some part of Africa walked past. They looked like they wouldn't be out of place on a catwalk at a fashion show. They wouldn't be out of place in one of those music clips. Their hair teased, their lips pink with colouring.

Chris Andersen looked back, not at the girls but at his son and he saw him bow his head again and blush. Another woman originally from another part of Africa and draped in flowing robes looked away. One of the Wobblies from the treadmill Marine boot camp looked at the two young women with empty eyes.

At the exit Julie stood with Moira. His daughter had hold of Julie's hands and was leaning out at an angle. They were both laughing, but Julie had her eyes fixed on her husband.

'Well?' she said.

Chris Andersen flicked his hand. His wife looked at him and pulled her daughter up.

'What's that supposed to mean?'

'What?'

'That thing you just did with your hand?' She did the thing with her hand.

Chris Andersen did another thing with his other hand. 'Oh, well, you know.'

He looked over his wife's head at a television that was playing more music shows. More rich Afro-Americans from some well-lit street scene were thrusting away on the set.

'Lachie, are you okay?' Julie called to her son.

Chris heard her tone and winced.

He saw his son nod his head.

'I'm good, I'm good, Mum.' Lachlan looked up to his father and back to his mother. 'I'm playing for the fourths this arvo.'

Julie looked at her son. 'Good, is that good?'

'Yeah, it is. It is good.' Lachlan smiled and then looked at his father. Lachlan wondered if his father would be pleased.

Chris Andersen looked at his son. He wondered if his son was going to play because he really wanted to. He thought of Tony smiling on the couch. Whatever happened to Hush?

They all moved off together and walked out to the car park and into the hot morning.


'Could you just drop us off at the rooms down the oval? We should probably go there and set up,' Chris Andersen said to Julie almost as soon as they drove out of the car park.

'Won't I need my kit, Dad?' Lachlan asked.

'He's right, Chris,' said Julie.

'I've got his kit,' Chris replied. Julie looked at her husband. 'I packed it . . . this morning, before we came . . .' He trailed off.

'Just in case?' said Julie.

'Yeah, just in case,' said Chris giving her a lukewarm grin. Julie looked at him. For a normal man he was odd sometimes.

They drove through the streets and stopped at a crossing as a gaggle of young men in baggy tracksuits and back-to-front baseball caps strolled across the intersection. Chris felt a little odd. He looked at Lachlan in the rear-view mirror. His son was looking out the window.

'You right, Lachie? You right to go straight to the oval?'

Lachlan Andersen listened to his father and nodded. He looked at the young men in their baggy clothes and then as the family car sped up, he saw an Aboriginal man down a lane standing, staring up at the sky.

Lachie thought about the book he was reading. He thought of how many different colours and people he had seen this morning. Perhaps it was easier for Atticus Finch to be brave because the people in the book were all so similar. Black or white.

There were so many different people where he lived. He looked back at his father. Atticus Finch. Chris Andersen. Both were lawyers. Maybe it was easier for Atticus Finch.

As they turned into a side street, Lachlan could see piles of rubbish on the footpaths. Hard rubbish collection day was on Monday and the piles were getting bigger. People were using the weekend to turf belongings they no longer needed.

Lachlan had another thought as he saw an old man and woman carrying out a small table to their rubbish pile. He wondered why the Aboriginal man was wearing clothes that were old and baggy when the big, tall, black men he'd seen today on TV wore clothes that were new and baggy.

He sighed a little and rubbed his eyes. He could smell the chlorine from the pool. He pinched one of the lollies Moira was arranging on her hand and she roared. He bent his head back into his book.

Michael Martin sat on the low step of the clubrooms at Bull Oval. He closed his eyes even though he had sunglasses on. It was hot and already he knew it was going to get hotter. He had a headache. Not a bad one, but one that might get worse. He'd slept well enough with the help of the bottles of pills he'd taken from the dispensary. He patted his shirt pocket and felt the other bottle of Valium. Just in case. It was hot. He blinked and reached for the water he'd bought from the shop down by the old pub on the corner.

He hadn't been there for years. The last time he'd walked into the shop he had bought a Coke and a Mars bar. That would have been years ago. Then it had been owned by a fat man who always wore singlets and called people Chief.

'Thanks, Chief, thank you very much,' he would rasp as he took the money from his customers.

As soon as he walked into the shop he knew everything would be different. The smell tipped him off. He knew a Vietnamese family ran it. It smelled of incense and rice, of cooking oil and coriander. A pungent smell. The father came to serve him holding a tiny baby. She was almost newborn. Dark tufts of her hair fluffed up. The man was more interested in whispering to his child than engaging in conversation with his customer.

Michael Martin stared at them both. There was a confidence and almost a laziness in the way the man held the baby. Michael could tell he had other children.

Michael asked for water and the smells took him away from the shop in Yarraville West and opened the door to times in clinics in lands far away. He had seen parents with children carried like this. They had come to see him, sought him out to offer their children to him for immunisations, for healing. Back then there was an assurance in his manner, a belief in the injections and treatments.

Michael Martin stopped himself; he had to find something else to concentrate on. The man with the baby named a price and Michael handed over some money.

'Hot day today, matey,' said the shop owner. His accent took Michael by surprise. It sounded so Australian. A Vietnamese-flavoured Australian accent. This man would be my age, Michael thought. As old as me.

'Staying in today? Best idea I think,' he said as he cuddled his daughter. 'We'll stay in today.'

Today...Michael remembered it was a home game, so that meant the home team had to bring the lunch. The lunch at subdistrict cricket was a most important event.

He scanned the shop. There was no bread left. And then, just for old time's sake, he knew what he would take.

'I'll have some of those packets of little Mars bars and a couple of big bottles of Coke. Thanks,' he said.

'Okay,' replied the shopkeeper.

Michael Martin laughed and muttered quietly to himself, 'Thanks, Chief, thank you very much.' Keeping faith with the past.

The shopkeeper fetched the Mars bars and Cokes. He placed them in a bag, all the while cradling his child.

'There you go,' said the shopkeeper. He said it to Michael but he was really speaking to his child.

Michael wondered what had happened to the fat man and his singlets. Dead and gone most likely. Dead and gone. Time passes for everyone. He closed his eyes and felt for the bottle of pills in his pocket. He would need them today.

Michael Martin left the shop and stepped into his car. He drove down to the oval and pulled into the newly bitumenised car park.

He sat for a few moments. He was early.

'Shit,' he muttered. 'Shit, shit, shit.' He listened to his radio and then turned that off. He looked at the plastic bags holding the Mars bars. They might melt. He scanned the oval. Nobody else was there. 'Shit,' he said again.

Michael put the plastic bag under the seat, stepped out of the car and onto the oval. He walked slowly over to the clubrooms.

He couldn't quite believe he was early. He was seldom early, and if he was it was never by design. He flicked up his one piece of cricket equipment, a box. He had stopped on his way and picked it up from a sports store in a shopping centre that had an old Vampire jet fighter mounted on a stand outside its car park.

While he'd been in the sports shop he'd seen a poster on the wall. It was a glowering giant of a man with a crew cut. 'Just Do It' was written across the bottom of the poster. He had seen the poster before, on the wall of a hospital he had worked in.

'Christ,' he said to himself. How early was he? He sat on the steps and tried not to think of anything much. Too many doors could open and he couldn't be sure where they would lead.

He looked up at the sky and across the oval. A woman stood at a window of the house at deep mid-wicket. She looked like she was staring out across the oval. Maybe she is looking at me, thought Michael Martin.

But she turned and headed back into the room, away from the window. Michael lost his distraction. That house. It had always had an Alsatian that barked if the ball went anywhere near.

Michael remembered the time a big fat tail-ender had got onto one and sent it flying over the fence at mid-wicket into the yard of that house. He had jumped on top of the fence and the dog had gone off, as dogs like that do. He remembered Chris Andersen laughing a lot. Then a young girl had come down the stairs and called to the dog, it had a funny name, but he couldn't remember it. A strange name.

The girl had called the dog and it had stopped barking and gone to her. She took the ball from the mouth of the dog, walked over and gave it to Michael. She hadn't said anything to him as she gave him the ball. Michael remembered her wearing a T-shirt with a face on it.

Perhaps the woman in the window was that girl all grown-up, thought Michael. He looked over at the window but she had gone.

No, no distraction there. He stopped trying to remember. Remembering could take you to places you don't want to go. He tried to think about as little as possible. He tried to empty his mind. He tried to, but one thing remained, the dog. What had been the name of the dog?

That is how he came to be sitting on the low step of the clubrooms staring out across the ground, staring at the grass and trying to think of nothing but instead thinking about that dog. It was good to try to think about that dog. Flicking his protector up with one hand and catching it with the other, closing his eyes tight every now and then, even though he wore sunglasses.

Michael Martin had drifted off to somewhere else. He had no idea how long the yelling had gone on before he heard his name. He looked up and somebody was yelling. He could see a big man in white and a tall boy in white. The big man was waving his arms and yelling. No, he was exploding.

'Marto! Michael!' the big man boomed.

Michael Martin smiled to himself. Chris Andersen. He waved back with his box. The tall boy carried a heavy bag. The club kit. This must be Chris Andersen's son. Michael knew it had to be because Barry Andersen had always made one of his sons carry the heavy club kit bag.

Michael stood as the pair got closer, and as he did he had a feeling, a feeling that surprised him, a feeling that today might be a good day.

Chris Andersen had stopped yelling and nodded to Michael Martin. He put down the two drink coolers he carried and slung down his own kit bag.

He held out his hand and grabbed Michael Martin's. Michael's still had his box in it. Chris Andersen shook Michael's hand and his box vigorously.

Chris looked down at the plastic protector he was shaking. 'Michael, you haven't come empty-handed. Good to see.'

'Well, you never know when they might come in handy.'

'That's your kit, is it?'

'I travel light, Christo!'

'I hope it's clean.'

'Straight off the shelf, hasn't been broken in.'

'Well, then, it's a pleasure to shake your box. Lachlan, come over here and shake this man's box.'

Lachlan stumbled a little as he shuddered the big kit bag onto the concrete of the low step and looked at his father.

'It's all right, Lachie, trust him, he's a doctor.'

Michael Martin smiled easily. 'Hello, Lachie.'

Lachlan nodded.

Michael looked at the boy. He was an Andersen alright. 'I saw you walking over with that bag.' He nodded his head in the direction of the big shapeless kit. 'Your father and his brothers used to have to carry that bag.'

'Yes, mate, nothing like tradition.'

Chris Andersen was jangling some keys.

'We'll get this thing open. The boys will start rolling up soon.'

He opened the door to the clubrooms and hauled the coolers in.

'Lachlan, give a hand will you. Give me a hand with these tables.'

Michael smiled. Chris Andersen sounded just like his father.

'Don't worry, Lachie, I'll give your dad a hand.'

He disappeared into the clubrooms and helped Chris drag a trestle table out.

The clubrooms were really just a set of toilets, a bar and two change areas. There was a big fridge squatting in a corner where the water coolers were plonked.

Chris turned to Michael. 'Did you bring any stuff for lunch?'

'Coke and Mars bars.'

Chris laughed. 'Mate, you haven't changed, the old Coke and Mars bars.'

'Thanks, Chief...'

'Thanks very much!' both men laughed.

Chris Andersen took one end of the table and Michael the other.

'That fat bloke with the singlets...He's turned into a Vietnamese man with a little baby.'

'Well, there you go.'

Outside, Lachlan watched the two men as they carried the table and set it up just by the doorway. They disappeared back into the rooms and Lachlan supposed they were fetching the foldout chairs. While they were gone, just as his father said, the boys started to roll up.

Lachlan looked at the car park. A few minutes ago it had been bare, save for a small black Saab that he thought must belong to Michael Martin. He thought he looked like he would own a car like that. Now the Saab had been joined by a growing collection of cars, some that Lachlan knew.

Lachlan noticed that although the cars of the opposing team would differ from week to week, they would always be the same type. Big station wagons and four-wheel drives that shone and never looked like they left the bitumen. He could almost tell what the men would look like as they stepped out from their vehicles. They would either be a bit tight in their movements and carry a bit of weight, or they would be younger and walk slowly but without a limp. So many smoked.

He would watch them gather together, looking slightly anxious and watchful. They would look just like the team he would be playing in or more correctly would be making up the numbers in.

Sometimes he would see a few boys his age. They would come in late in the order, do most of the fielding and be yelled at a lot by older men, who he supposed were their fathers. He knew all about that.

Lachlan leant down on the table and looked at how the opposing team had started to gather. None of them had reached for their kit, but they looked this way and that as they got out of their cars. He was always surprised at how nervous and tentative grown men could look if they were alone.

Even Michael Martin had looked a little hapless when they saw him from the car as his mother had dropped them off.

'There's Michael, there's Michael Martin,' his father had boomed.

'Alright, Chris, you don't have to yell,' said his mother.

'I didn't yell,' his father yelled. He wound down the window. 'But I will now if you like? Michael! *Michael*!'

His mother laughed and shook her head. 'Your father's a dag, you know that don't you, Lachie?' He could see her eyes in the rear-view mirror.

Lachlan had nodded back.

'And you still want to play cricket with him?' Now his mum turned to look him in the face with her soft eyes.

Lachlan had nodded and smiled.

She had smiled back.

His father kept on yelling.

The man he yelled at had looked a little lost, thought Lachlan.

His father had turned back into the car.

'Jules, can you maybe bring down that stuff I put in the fridge for lunch about two-thirty...please?'

His mother had nodded. 'Chris, come here will you.'

His father had leant back into the car and his mother had given him a kiss, murmured something and then said, 'Have a good game.'

His father had laughed.

And then they had walked down onto the oval with his father yelling as they walked. The lost man had looked up and it was Michael Martin. He seemed nice... But a bit... Lachlan didn't know...a bit something.

The opposing team had all parked in a clump so they could be together.

A mid-seventies Mercedes hiccupped into the car park and weaved its way this way and that. It narrowly missed a fat, bald man and then a municipal bin. The fat, bald man yelled and the window of the old golden Merc was wound down. An emaciated head with a great turban of greying hair poked out.

Music blared from the car. 'Ra Ra Rasputin'. Lachlan had no idea who sang the song but it sounded like the old stuff that his father would sometimes play in his shed and then laugh himself stupid about with his mother.

The music stopped the fat little bald man dead for a minute and then the owner of the car with the turbaned, emaciated head yelled out, 'Sorry, matey. Sorry you old lover of the Russian Queen.' It was Livey Jones. Beside him sat Rob Orchard.

Lachlan could see that Rob Orchard was laughing.

The big old car rolled to a halt and both men got out. Livey wasn't very tall so when he stood up from the driver's seat of his car he really wasn't that much taller than when he was driving.

He wore a translucent hair cap; he had forgotten to take it off, like he often did. He must have come straight from work at the butcher's market and picked up Rob Orchard on the way.

Livey was a butcher and he seemed to Lachlan a strange, loud little man, who would snort and hawk a lot, and always smelled of disinfectant and meat.

The first time Lachlan could remember meeting him was when he had gone shopping with his mum and dad one Friday afternoon. He must have only just started school as he could still fit in the shopping trolley.

He liked to go shopping with his parents and as his father pushed the trolley he would sometimes reach his hand out and touch his mum's swollen stomach. He was sure the baby was going to be a girl and he wanted her to be called Esmeralda.

He touched his mother's stomach and he smiled at her face. She smiled back and the trolley stopped.

'Here we go! Here we go,' said a voice.

Lachlan turned to see a grey moustache below two beady watery eyes and above them a white paper hat. The hat looked like the old bath caps his mum sometimes gave him to play with. What was alarming was the grey stuff that was all piled up underneath the translucent cap. It ballooned up and about and some even poked out at the sides. It looked like his brain had exploded.

'Hello, Livey,' his mum had said to the man. His mum had said hello so this man must have been okay.

'This the young fellow?' said Livey.

'This is him,' replied his father.

Lachlan thought he should smile. So he did. He couldn't detect any change in the apparition before him. He couldn't tell if the grey moustache smiled or not. Although the eyes did squint a bit.

'Just a big barbie pack, thanks, Livey,' said his father.

'Oh yes, the famous barbie pack,' Livey answered and then disappeared.

Lachlan had looked down at some white, greyish things below the shiny glass.

He bent down and pointed. 'What's them, Mummy?'

He felt her hand gently fall down the back of his head and neck.

'What's that, Lachie,' his mum said softly.

'What's that, Mummy?'

He heard his father murmur and shudder a little. 'Oh... brains.'

His mum had shushed his dad but before she could answer Livey returned. He saw what Lachlan had pointed to.

'Oh that's where they went!' Livey looked a little panicked. Then, relieved, he flicked a few fingers that had little flecks of meat on them. 'Me brains! Me brains! Thank God I found me brains. These buggers are trying to sell them on me.'

Lachlan stared. Livey laughed, a snorty honk.

His father had said brains. He looked at the grey stuff beneath the paper shower cap. Brains. Lachlan felt a bit odd. That feeling he sometimes still got in his stomach, a churning.

His mum laughed a little and then stroked the back of his neck again.

But Livey hadn't finished. He produced the barbie pack and an enormous tray of meat, with bits of green stuff filling it out.

'You like the sausies? Do you like the sausies, Lachie?' said Livey.

His mum answered for him. 'He loves his sausages, don't you, Lachie?'

He nodded slowly. He still felt odd.

'Well, everyone loves me sausies, matey,' Livey said. 'And why wouldn't they? Special ingredients, special ingredients. But the problem is, matey, we're running out of special ingredients!'

Livey wriggled his hands in front of Lachlan's face. Two top joints of his fingers were missing and little beads of meat and breadcrumbs flew about Lachlan's face.

He stared for a minute longer and the two fingers without their top joints wiggled in front of him.

'And I want me fingers back!'

Lachlan screamed for nearly an hour and never looked at a sausage the same way again. Livey hadn't really changed in Lachlan's eyes, and now as he strutted towards the doorway, he waved his stumps at Lachlan.

'Lachlan, mate, how are you.' It was a statement rather than a question that demanded any answer.

Lachlan smiled wanly and nodded.

As Livey walked past into the rooms Lachlan could see that he had his butcher's shirt still on as well as his cap and a white cotton apron with a smiling pig and sheep and cow all winking out from the legend 'Buy 'n Bulk 'n' Save Butchers'.

Rob Orchard was not far behind. He carried a tray of sandwiches.

'Hello, Lachie, how are you?' This one was a question.

'Good, thank you...and how are you?' replied Lachie.

'Oh, I've barely survived that trip with Livey...'

From inside the rooms Lachlan heard Livey fart a welcome. Chris Andersen roared.

'He's been letting rip ever since he picked me up. I'm a bit worried about the safety of these sangers,' said Rob.

'I'm just building up for a big arvo, boys,' snorted Livey from the doorway.

'Jesus, Bony M and farts from the arse of Livey Jones,' said Chris Andersen.

'Mate, I was keeping time with the old ra-ra-rasputeeeen!' said Livey.

'Well, you're keen then, Rob, you're keen,' Chris said.

Rob Orchard laughed.

'And Livey...'

'Yes, my Captain,' Livey said and snorted.

'Are you going to take that thing off your head?'

There was a moment's silence.

'Why didn't you fucking tell me, Rob?'

•

Lachlan saw an older man heave himself out of a small white car. He knew the man wouldn't talk to anybody for a while. He would wander out to the pitch and poke around out there, before going back to his car. Then he'd look at his watch and listen to the soft music on his radio. He might even have a drop of tea or whatever it was he kept in his Tartan thermos. Lachlan's nanna had one like that. Perhaps it was only older people who owned a Thermos like that. Thermos. It sounded like a country. Thermos.

The man who was the ruler of Thermos was Ron Sparrow, and as well as being the ruler of Thermos he was also the umpire. He was also the reverend from the church down in Cross Street. Sometimes Lachlan would see him in his little white car on the streets and Ron Sparrow would toot at Lachlan and smile his nice smile.

Lachlan would wave back. He was always surprised when Mr Sparrow waved.

He heard his father's phone ring. It was in the bag somewhere. 'Lachie. Lachie, get my phone will you...' His father's voice came out from the dark of the clubrooms. Almost as an afterthought he heard, 'Please, mate.'

He smiled and rummaged through the bag.

It stopped just as he thought he had it. He pushed aside a second pair of whites he knew were for Michael Martin and stared into the bag, seeing not much. Two Gray-Nicolls batting gloves and inners for the gloves, and a box that had a skull and crossbones drawn on it in Texta. He looked back to where his father's voice had rumbled in the dark. He remembered his mother's kind brown eyes.

'You do know your father is a dag, don't you?'

Lachlan laughed. He made a note to remember the skull and crossbones. He heard the beeping of his father's message tone. The phone was under his father's pads, and he reached down past the pads and grabbed where he thought the phone would be. He pulled back and in his hand he saw a glove. An old Slazenger batting glove with a phone popping out the bottom of it.

Lachie held up the glove and took out the phone. As he did, he saw a name written in pen on the finger of the glove. He held both the phone and the glove in his hand.

The name written along the finger of the glove was Tony Andersen.

Without thinking, Lachlan took the phone from the glove and then put the glove into his own kit. He blushed and called out immediately to his father.

'Dad...Dad, message for you.'

He walked to the doorway and held the phone out and his father's big hand grabbed the phone from him.

His father stared at the phone. Pressed a few buttons. Pursed his lips and blew out a breath. 'Why doesn't that surprise me?' Chris Andersen said.

'What's that, Christo?' Rob Orchard appeared at his side.

'Oh, it's bloody Neil Greene. Can't make it. He's caught up with a client.'

'Oh hello, what...else is new. Neil the great pretender,' snorted Livey. He farted.

'Do you have to keep doing that here? You know it's not going to be funny in a minute.'

'It's not going to be pretty that's for sure, but farts are always funny, Christo.'

'Perhaps he just knew you were going to be on fire, Livey.'

Livey snorted.

'Does that leave us down?' asked Rob Orchard.

'Well, yes, by two. It's good Lachie's put his hand up.' Chris Andersen looked down to his son. 'Thanks, Lachie, for this. Thanks.'

The boy smiled a bit and fidgeted in his bag. He was quiet. Chris looked at him for a moment until a car horn tooted.

They looked to see another four-wheel drive.

'Here's Matthew.'

'The rocket himself.'

Matt Halley waved to them and jumped down from his car. He was a stocky man who wasn't that small, but his lack of height was accentuated by the way he held his pants high. He walked very quickly.

'Why does he wear his pants up around his ears? He's got no idea,' said Livey.

'When you say that, can you put your meat helmet back on? It gives you more authority and covers up that ragged grey mane of a mullet,' said Chris Andersen.

Rob Orchard laughed.

Two young men, more teenagers, sauntered behind Matt Halley.

Matt marched up to the clubrooms.

'Fellas, these blokes are from our mighty under-17s. They've volunteered to give up their Saturday afternoon to help uphold the honour of the fourths,' Matthew said.

'They are fine men, Matthew, and we welcome you to our happy band.' Chris Andersen saluted them but the two under-17s just stared back. Right, thought Chris. Not much humour there.

'Neil couldn't make it, so we're two down.'

'He's as weak as water,' Matt said.

'Does he pay his club fees?' snorted Livey.

'He does, he's completely financial,' said Chris.

'Well, he's still a tool,' said Livey.

Livey Jones farted.

'Oh come on, please,' Matthew Halley said.

'Why do you always sound like a teacher?' said Livey.

'Well, that's probably because I *am* a teacher, and from where I'm standing it's better than sounding like a butcher.'

'We might be three down, has anyone seen Brian Keith?'

The men all looked at each other.

'He's usually the first here, isn't he?'

'Usually, but he hasn't turned up yet. Marto was the first.'

Livey turned to Chris.

'Is Marto here?'

'Yeah, yeah, he's just gone to the toilet, I think...look, I think I might have a chat with the other skipper and see if we can bat first. That way some of us can keep a look out for Brian and maybe do a bit of a ring round to get some other fellas down here.'

Rob Orchard laughed. 'Come on, you're talking about Trinity, Christo.'

'Well, maybe I'll appeal to their softer side.'

Chris Andersen started to wander off towards the clump of Trinity players when he heard Lachlan's voice.

'There he is, Dad, by the playground.'

Chris looked past the Trinity team and saw the gangly frame of Brian Keith. Brian walked with a sideways stagger. If it had been anybody else Chris would have thought Brian was looking over his shoulder, but it was Brian being Brian. Still, he had never known him to be this late for the start of a game.

As he got nearer to the Trinity team Brian's stagger got worse. Maybe he was trying to look over at something. Chris craned his neck to see what it might be. He could see the playground and past that a pile of rubbish set on the pavement and then a bus stop. There was a woman at the bus stop. He looked back at Brian and saw him almost trip and then fall into one of the Trinity players. There was the sound of a dull bong.

'You fucking right?' Chris Andersen heard a pissed-off voice and broke into a run.

Brian had tripped and brushed against the end of a large green wagon.

A tall powerfully built man was standing over him. 'You fucking fool. What's your problem?'

'Brian! Are you right there?' Chris Andersen's voice cut through the wall of fat, white-shirted backs. Some turned towards him.

'I'm okay. I tripped. I'm sorry. I tripped.'

'You're a fucking dick. You hit my car,' the tall man said.

'Hey, listen, it was an accident, mate, and it's not a car it's a bloody truck. Go easy, mate.' Chris Andersen stood in front of the tall man and picked up Brian's bag. Brian reached for it. 'I'll be right, Brian.'

'My bag.'

'I'll be right. I've got your bag.'

'Yeah, Cairnsy, it is a truck, it's supposed to be able to take a bit of punishment.' It was the bald, fat man who had yelled at Livey.

'No damage done, is there?' asked Chris.

The tall man looked at him. 'Not yet, mate.'

Chris Andersen rolled his eyes. He knew this man. He was a grade bowler from the higher Trinity teams.

'You carry his bag? You wipe his arse as well?' the tall man said.

There were a few titters.

'Hey, Cairnsy, come on,' the bald man was trying to keep things sweet.

Chris Andersen sighed. He remembered this tall man. He knew his reputation and knew he shouldn't say anything. But he couldn't stop himself. 'Mate...mate...'

The tall man looked at Chris Andersen.

'What?'

'Mate, just don't... just don't. It was an accident. So just don't.'

The bald man stepped in between the two of them.

'Come on, Cairnsy. Come on. You've got all afternoon to sort it out. Come on. Sorry, Christo, she's sweet. I'll see you for the toss in a sec?'

Chris Andersen walked away with Brian. Behind him he heard a few titters. 'Don't!' somebody said in a silly voice.

'You okay, Brian?'

'Uh, yes...yes... Can I carry my bag, Christo?'

'I'll carry your bag, mate, don't worry. Why were you late? You get lost?'

Brian knew that Chris Andersen would think that he had got lost. He knew that. It was nice but it wasn't right.

'No...no. I just got worried for her.'

'Your mum? Is your mum okay?' Chris Andersen held his hand on Brian's elbow.

'No, Mum is fine. She is fine.' Chris Andersen did go on a bit but it was nice. 'I was worried about her and the bus.'

Chris Andersen looked at Brian. 'Well, you're here now, mate. And I'll ring your mum if you like.'

Brian shook his head. 'No, no...' How could he make him understand? He looked back at the playground and beyond.

'Don't worry about that mob, mate. They're okay. Don't worry about them.'

Brian shrugged. He wasn't thinking about the Trinity team. He gave up trying to tell Christo. Maybe he would tell Lachlan.

'Is Lachie playing?'

'Yes, he is.'

Good, thought Brian.

Chris Andersen thought that today might not be a great day for Lachie to play after all. A fucking A-grade bowler in the fourths. A grade bowler.

•

Michael Martin stepped out from the shower area. He had taken his time deciding whether he would take another couple of the pills in his pocket. He had taken his time and thought about the bloody dog's name. He had thought and taken his time and suddenly it was time to get ready to play.

He hadn't taken any pills. He stepped out into the light of the day and smiled. He saw Christo frowning and walking with a tall, thin young man. The young man was looking over his shoulder.

Michael looked to where the young man might be looking. He saw a woman sitting at a bus stop. She wore a burka and a long flowing robe. He stared at her for a minute. Then, for no reason, he turned to the window of the house that used to have the dog. There, standing in the window and looking out was the woman he had seen for a moment when he had first arrived at the ground. She was looking out over the ground. He looked back to the bus stop. Both women were looking over the ground.

He shielded his eyes and felt a little punch. He turned to see Livey Jones.

Michael Martin laughed loudly. 'Jesus... Livey the walking corpse.'

Livey snorted and pointed out to the middle. 'Christo's gone out for the toss.'

Chris Andersen walked out across the oval and the day's heat already stung his skin. The paddock was baked hard by the long hot summer and his heel throbbed as it jarred against the earth. The old umpy was waiting to toss the coin. The fat bald man whose name was Dougie Wright was there as well. He was chewing gum and rubbing his hands together.

As Chris Andersen reached the middle, Ron Sparrow smiled. 'Hello, Christopher, how are you?'

Chris nodded. Ron Sparrow was the only person aside from Julie and his mother who called him Christopher.

'Good, Ron. Yourself?'

'Pretty fair for an old friar. Now, you know Dougie, of course.'

Chris nodded. Dougie was okay even though he did play for Trinity.

'You've got a grade bowler playing, Dougie?'

'Too right,' Dougie said, smiling beneath his blue Trinity cap and chewing energetically.

'In the fourths?'

'Come on, Christo, you know the go. If we play him in the home and away he's eligible for the finals for us. You know the deal.'

Chris Andersen looked at Ron Sparrow and then Dougie. 'Just keep him on a leash, then. We've got a couple of juniors playing.'

'Mate, you put the pads on, you play the game,' Dougie said, not seeming so okay

Chris Andersen looked at him.

'Do me best, Christo, but you know…' Dougie shrugged his shoulders.

'You've got a full team, Christopher?'

Here we go, thought Chris Andersen. 'As a matter of fact we are down a couple but we might be able to grab a full list if we were to bat first.'

'Let's toss the coin and see then,' said Dougie.

The coin was tossed and Chris called.

Heads.

It was tails.

Chris Andersen looked at the Trinity captain.

Ron Sparrow looked at the Trinity captain.

'We'll bat,' Dougie said and smiled. He shook Chris Andersen's hand, said 'Good game, mate,' and waddled off.

Chris watched him go and then turned to see Ron Sparrow smiling at him gently. 'Never mind, Christopher. It's a nice day for cricket.'

Chris Andersen nodded and smiled tightly back.

He turned and yelled as only he could, 'We're fielding. Yarra Fourths! Out here. We're fielding.'

His voice echoed across the oval.

The woman at the window stood up and leant forward. The woman at the bus stop bowed her head.

The game was on.

# Game On

The Yarraville West Fourth Eleven, shy two of their number, began to form a clump around their captain, Chris Andersen. He clapped and yelled, 'Come on, come on in here.'

Chris kept on clapping long after the clump had been formed.

Lachlan knew his father was clapping to fill in time so he could come up with something to say.

Michael wondered why Chris Andersen continued to clap and looked to see if the woman at the window was still there. She was. Chris kept clapping.

Matt Halley pulled his pants a bit higher.

Brian Keith looked over towards the bus stop.

Livey Jones struggled into the keeper's pads and gloves. They seemed to hang on him so he looked like a toddler wearing his father's clothes.

Chris Andersen kept on clapping.

Livey tugged the keeper's gloves on with his teeth and Chris stopped clapping.

The two teenagers from the under-17s looked relieved.

'Right... right. In here.'

'We are here,' Rob Orchard said and rolled his eyes.

'Right,' said Chris Andersen, ignoring Rob. He paused.

Don't start clapping again, thought Lachlan. He felt himself going red.

Chris Andersen went to clap, stopped himself and threw both his hands up. 'Right, we're bowling. They could have done the right thing and asked us to bat but they didn't. It's not the end of the world. It says a lot about the way they play the game... in short, they are a pack of turds... well, you know they're not really. Steve Waugh would never have given the other team a break. I suppose I would have done the same... and you know...'

Eight blank faces looked back at him.

'We'll just play cricket. We'll just have a go, and that's all we can ask of ourselves. Now, they'll probably cane us. And that's life... but you know anything can happen on a cricket field...'

Livey farted.

Chris pointed at Livey. 'Yes, you see anything can happen.'

Chris waved a hand around the clump.

'We've got a few young blokes playing today. Thanks for coming along. Shame we couldn't get a full complement, but there you go. It's not the end of the world.'

Chris Andersen kept wondering what on earth he was supposed to say. 'Look, you two,' he pointed to the two juniors who had arrived with Matt Halley. 'Say hello to the rest of the crew... Now, who are you?'

The two boys looked at each other and then back at Chris Andersen.

Chris Andersen looked at them.

'Who are you? What do they call you?' Chris Andersen yelled.

Lachlan went red again.

Rob Orchard giggled. Chris sounded like a bad actor speaking to someone who didn't speak English.

He took a breath. 'Yes?... Yes?' he said as calmly as he could.

'Tim,' said one.

'Tim,' said the other.

Chris Andersen nodded. 'Tim... Tim...' He clapped. 'Good... Good, there you go. Good symmetry. Very good. Tim and Tim. Right, okay. Feel at home and have a go. What do you do?'

'Bat a bit and bowl a bit,' said Tim.

'Bowl a bit and bat a bit,' said the other Tim.

Chris Andersen nodded.

'Right,' he said. 'Well, Tim Two, you said you could bowl a bit and bat so you can open the bowling with me and Tim One, you go first change along with Rob here.'

Chris took another deep breath. 'Right, okay... what's the word, Matt Halley? Do you have the word.'

The two Tims looked at each other.

'I do,' Matt said as he tugged at his pants.

'What have you got?'

Rob Orchard noticed the look on the two Tims' faces.

'Christo,' he said, nodding at the two open-mouthed under-17s.

'Oh right…yes, sorry. Fourths tradition…first appeal is done in another language…so no "How is he?" Alright? No appealing for the batsman's wicket in English. Do you understand?'

The two Tims looked at each other and nodded.

'Look, it's like a tradition – you know how in the first session of a Test match the Australian team, when they're in the field, always wear their Baggy Greens?' asked Chris Andersen.

The two Tims nodded.

'Well, not appealing in English for the first wicket is our tradition… A celebration of our multicultural nation.' Chris Andersen laughed and the two Tims looked at each other and nodded for the third time.

'Look, it's just a bit of fun,' Chris added.

It was indeed a fourths tradition and it dated back four years to when an enthusiastic butcher who had worked with Livey came down to make up the numbers. His name was Zlatko and he had an almost obscene amount of energy and not much interest in cricket. And even less interest in the English language.

The team was taking a beating and so Chris had thrown him in to have a bowl.

Zlatko had run back a mile and steamed in as if he were running the hundred metres. He leapt high in the air at the bowling crease and then let the ball drop slowly from his hand. The ball hit the bat and the batsman padded the ball along the wicket.

Zlatko spun onto the umpire and let rip with a blood-curdling shriek.

The umpire jumped back and Zlatko yelled again and the umpire's finger went up.

'Holy Christ...sorry about that,' the umpire muttered to the departing batter. The umpire's arms shook for two overs.

Chris Andersen had never forgotten the one game Zlatko played and the impact of that foreign language. So he had come up with the idea of always appealing in a foreign language.

It had never really worked. The success of Zlatko's Croatian yell had more to do with the fact that the umpy, who was never seen again after that match, was an overworked air-traffic controller on stress leave.

But the tradition stuck and Matthew Halley would spend a bit of time in the school library searching for a suitable phrase to use on Saturday afternoon. Chris Andersen explained the reasoning to the two Tims.

'Takes the umpy by surprise sometimes, and you never know your luck. So that's what we're about...'

'*Hvor er Han,*' Matt Halley said. 'With the accent on the *Vor*!'

'Right,' said Chris. 'Now speak us through it, Matthew.'

The two Tims looked at each other again. It was like being at a Star Wars convention.

Matt Halley slowly pronounced the words, '*hVOR er HAN...*
*hVOR er HAN...hVOR er HANNNN,*' he whispered energetically. 'Really let rip on the *han*.'

'Nordic is it, Matt?' Chris Andersen asked.

'Norwegian...*hVOR er HANNNNN*... Norway, fascinating country when you look at it. Only about six million of them but they have one of the healthiest economies in Europe. They don't want membership in the EEC – now that's confidence. And did you know –'

He was stopped by a noise.

'That German one's better,' snorted Livey. 'Why can't we use the German one? It's got a bit of balls about it.'

'Listen, Matt has gone off and done the work so the least we can do is back him up a bit. Now come on, all together.' Chris Andersen quietly clapped his hands and all the Yarraville West Fourths muttered and whispered in an attempt at solidarity.

'*hVOR er HAN…hVor er HANN…hVOR er HANNN… hVOR er HANN,*' nine voices whispered.

'Sounds like "forehand",' said Livey.

Michael Martin started to laugh.

'Well, it fucking does,' Livey said. 'The German one we used has got more grunt to it.'

Chris Andersen clapped his hands again. 'Come on, come on, Norwegian, Norwegian…now we set?'

Livey farted.

'Jesus,' said Chris.

Michael Martin thought Livey looked rather like a cross between a burnt-out old rocker from the seventies and a rather emaciated Muppet. Definitely not like Jesus.

'Right then,' thundered Chris Andersen. 'Let's go and remember, think Norwegian for the first shout.'

Ron Sparrow stood at the clubroom end and watched as the two openers for Trinity came out, Dougie waddling and a younger man sauntering. They could have fielded, thought Ron Sparrow. Trinity could have fielded, it was a bit weak. Not a great sign for a man of faith, Trinity being a bit weak. Never mind. It was a nice hot day for cricket. Still, he thought, they could have fielded.

He looked around as he heard Christopher Andersen behind him.

'Here we are, Ron.'

The big man offered him his blue Yarraville West cap. 'Right arm over.'

Ron Sparrow nodded and took the cap.

Chris Andersen walked down alongside the pitch. He looked around and shrugged. 'Oh, bugger it.' He looked around and placed his field. He gave himself two slips, because it was always good for a bowler's self-esteem and self-worth to see a bit of a cordon... Chris Andersen believed in supporting the bowlers, especially when he was bowling.

A mid-off and a mid-on. He put Rob down at fine leg, of course, Tim One in the covers and Tim Two out at mid-wicket.

Chris flexed a bit and rolled his arm over. The two openers took their places. Dougie was about to face him and was taking guard. The Trinity captain held up two fingers to indicate he was after middle. The middle stump. Ron Sparrow gave it to him and Dougie scratched away with the toe of his boot.

Chris Andersen took eight paces back and looked around the ground. Oh, bugger it, he thought, taking in his field, it'll have to do. It's not the end of the world. He flicked the ball up and there were a few cries of encouragement.

Pitch it just short of a length, just on off-stump, nice and straight. He trundled in, a nice, slow approach and dropped it just short of a length, nice and straight on the off-stump, and Dougie put his fat little leg down the pitch and smote the ball.

Ron Sparrow thought it was almost biblical how hard Dougie hit the ball. It sped away and crossed the boundary line before anybody could really look like chasing it.

Cheers came airily across from the Trinity bench.

'Get him next time, Christo,' snorted Livey.

The ball made its way sadly back to Chris Andersen's hands and he looked at it. 'It's not going to be the last time you'll be punished today, my little round friend,' mumbled the Yarraville West captain.

He took his eight paces back and trundled in again. The ball moved off the pitch and this time Dougie didn't move his front leg. It hit him, just above the roll but it hit him in front and Dougie was short.

The whole team went up and then the whole team held their breath. No one could remember the words.

Chris Andersen turned and filled his lungs with air but all he could remember was 'How is he?' The timeless plea of a hopeful bowler. He searched his mind for the bloody Norwegian phrase...

'*EVA FOR ON*,' he bellowed.

Michael Martin just laughed.

Tim One and Tim Two leapt in the air like Brett Lee and Warney combined. All they needed were the blond highlights in their hair.

Brian yodelled like some drunken Swiss cheesemaker. But Livey outdid himself. 'Fuck! What is ... Forehead ... Fore arm fore arm fucking fore arm.'

Matthew Halley skipped across from backward point. '*hVOR er HAN*! *HVOR er HANNN*!'

Lachlan bent his head and his shoulders shook. He did all but laugh.

Ron Sparrow looked at Chris Andersen.

'Is that an appeal? Are you appealing, Christopher?' he asked uncertainly.

Chris Andersen nodded enthusiastically.

Livey Jones yelled again, 'Forehead.'

'Well, not out, not out,' Ron Sparrow said.

'Oh, Ron, why not?' said Chris Andersen.

'Well, it was close ... Close ... not out though,' Ron Sparrow said.

'I told you the German had more grunt,' shouted Livey.

Ron Sparrow squinted back down the pitch. I would have given him, I think. Perhaps I should have ... you can never tell with leg before. They didn't have to yell like that though.

Chris Andersen walked back and he ran in and bowled the ball in roughly the right spot. And Dougie and his younger partner would invariably belt the ball to almost every part of the ground. They did that for another five overs. It didn't really get any better. The portly Dougie had a good eye and, of course, a bit of luck. One of the Tims dropped him but it was a difficult catch low to his right and then in the next and last over of Chris Andersen's spell, the other Tim fumbled a high catch out at mid-wicket.

Chris Andersen grimaced a bit and then clapped his hands. 'Bad luck, Tim Two, bad luck...good for the symmetry though...good effort.'

The fact that Tim Two could bowl was good. And bad. The Yarraville West Fourths dropped Dougie's opening partner three times, all from Tim Two's tidy medium-pacers.

Matthew Halley acrobatically missed a thick edge, got up and profusely apologised then pulled his pants a little higher. He obviously hoped it might help, thought Chris.

The second dropped catch was an edge that kissed the glazed side of the bat, spat into Livey's gloves and then dribbled out onto the grass in front of the wicket-keeper.

The next spilt catch was courtesy of the captain.

A ball came high and Chris Andersen flung his big arm up and the ball clipped the top of his fingers.

He had wrung his hands for a few balls and had thought of giving himself a rest. His heel was sore and now his fingers felt as if they had been hit by a teacher's cane.

He looked down at Rob Orchard.

No, he thought. Let Rob have a few extra overs down there.

He grabbed the ball again and walked slowly back. He smiled out at the young Tim Two, who had dropped the catch.

'You'll be right, Tim...you'll be right.' The boy smiled back.

The game had taken on a certain quality. A drifting quality that only happens when the result is beyond doubt. Chris Andersen knew that Trinity would score a mountain of runs and just as surely he knew that Yarraville West would stutter along and fall in a heap.

But he also knew that this was when cricket took that path that few other games could take. The meditative, almost dream-like mode that would take a mind anywhere and perhaps nowhere. All that was needed was a prompt, a nudge down the path of thought and reflection.

Chris Andersen's came on the next ball.

The ball pitched in line. Well it looked that way to Chris. In line enough to go up for an appeal. It came out a little stronger than he thought. Nobody else backed him at first. Perhaps they didn't think it was out, or perhaps they were still searching for the Norwegian phrase. Livey had obviously given up trying and went with the German. '*Wie er ist!*'

It was a bit desultory. So Chris Andersen made up for it with an enthusiastic shriek. He didn't bother with the translation.

'How is he?'

'He's not going anywhere,' said Ron Sparrow.

Chris Andersen looked at the umpy.

'Hit outside...just...but it hit him outside.'

'Bloody close.'

The old umpy smiled.

'Closeish...ten millimetres outside.'

'Ten millimetres,' Chris repeated.

'Good areas, Christo, good areas. Get him next time,' Matt Halley hooted from third slip.

Chris Andersen turned back towards his mark...ten millimetres. His mind went somewhere else. He could see...

Him standing in the new room in Chris and Julie Andersen's house.

People liked the new room that Chris Andersen had put on the house. They told him so. 'Very good. Very nice, mate.' Then they would look down and they would stare a bit and they would purse their lips, look up and then look around. Couldn't help themselves. He could see them biting their lips. They all wanted to know why Chris Andersen had put the strip of paisley carpet on the spotted gum floorboards. Ten millimetres, that's why. Even when Chris Andersen says, 'Ten millimetres,' Chris sees Him, the damn building inspector.

Chris Andersen watched as he nodded in the direction of his yellow tape measure.

'Ten millimetres,' he repeated and then snapped the recoil on his tape.

Chris Andersen, a man who had just renovated his house, stared at the man who wasn't going to give him a certificate for the work done.

They stared at each other because of ten millimetres. An interior step was too deep by ten millimetres. Never mind that the same building inspector had passed the step the last time the house was renovated four years ago. What at the time had seemed like a good idea had come to this. Two grown men staring at each other saying nothing.

It had been just a small renovation this time. Nothing too big, just an extra room and a verandah. Why not? The rest of Australia was doing it.

Almost every player on this ground, save for the youngsters, were doing it, thought Chris Andersen as he wandered back to his mark.

People at barbecues talk about their tradesmen or architects or their designers the way people used to talk about their hobbies or their pet. Three years ago they would have talked about their financial planners in a similar way. Whatever happened to footy or cricket? Whatever happened to hobbies or pets?

It was at such a barbecue in the backyard of a house that had just been renovated that Chris Andersen had stood by a water feature with a friend called Neil. Neil Greene, who always promised to play but turned up once in a blue moon for the game.

Neil happened to be an architect and had known Chris for years. Neil had been a friend of Julie's before Chris even knew him. Neil had known Julie at uni. Known Julie enough to have gone out with her for a year.

A year.

Chris Andersen rubbed the ball against his groin and flicked his eyes down at the cracking surface of the ball.

Chris liked Neil. And the history that Neil and Julie shared never entered his mind. Well, rarely.

What had she seen in Neil?

Chris Andersen began his approach. As he ran he thought of Neil. Neil was friendly and very relaxed, which is much easier when you have had a ridiculously large amount of success in your life. Your business life. Chris liked to remind himself.

Chris let the ball go and it was slightly overpitched. Not much, but enough for the Trinity batsman to swing his bat full and long and hammer the ball through the covers and out towards the boundary.

Brian wound himself up to chase the ball. His arms and legs nearly working in unison. As he watched Brian move, Chris Andersen realised that Brian moved like a fast ungainly crayfish, with arms and legs going in all directions. As Brian ran a big white stretch limousine glided on the road behind him. A white ribbon fluttered from its bonnet. It was a wedding limousine. Chris watched Brian, saw the limousine and thought of Neil's life. His less successful life.

Chris and Julie had gone to Neil's wedding at a large winery in Red Hill that looked like it was a set from some Julia Roberts' movie. Green trees, lots of people in white and nice music. Julie and Chris had sat up the back next to a fat actor from a television show about forensic investigators.

'Neil designed his beach house,' whispered Julie to Chris. 'He wanted ceiling mirrors in his bathroom.' Julie giggled. Chris looked at the fat actor. The fat actor nodded back. Chris nodded and smiled.

'I wonder if this man knows that I know he has ceiling mirrors in his bathroom...'

Chris Andersen also wondered if it was kosher to share a client's wishes with friends. What were the ethics?

Brian Keith had almost overhauled the ball as it raced towards the boundary. He bent and picked it up. It was an inspiring effort on a hot Saturday afternoon, especially when you were getting hammered.

'Oh good lad, Brian. Good lad!' yelled Chris Andersen.

Brian picked up the ball and kept on running. Over the boundary line. He hadn't quite been able to pull it off. He stopped and looked back towards Chris and Chris could hear the hoots of laughter from the Trinity benches.

'Well done, Brian,' he boomed. 'Well done, good chase.'

'When did he tell you that?' Chris whispered to Julie.

Julie looked back and smiled, 'When I RSVPed. I asked who else was coming.' She nodded to the fat actor, who was now looking at them sideways out of the corner of his eyes. 'You should see what he wanted in his toilet.'

Chris Andersen laughed. The fat actor shot him another little look and Chris suddenly felt sorry for him.

Brian walked back and stood in the field. Chris watched him and the actor's face faded away and Neil's danced in front of him; at his second marriage. It was at a beach house he designed. Not the fat actor's, but a pretty impressive one nonetheless. Neil was very proud of the house and spoke more about its sense of space and life force than about his new wife. In fact, Chris could only vaguely remember her – he thought she had red hair and had giggled a lot.

They weren't invited to his third wedding. Nobody was. Neil got married in New York to a woman they never met. That didn't last either. He wasn't married at the moment but he had come to the barbecue with a tall blonde woman who was dressed in the clothes of a woman who was much younger than Neil. Sadly, she was the same age. She hadn't talked to many people at the barbecue, she stood on the verandah in her high-heeled boots, flipping through some magazines about school uniforms.

Neil blew her a kiss and then sipped his beer. He dipped his fingers into the water feature and wriggled them, sending little splashes across the pond.

'They haven't really made the most of the space they've got but it's not too bad.'

Chris Andersen looked at his chunky bottle of Vic Bitter and then said to nobody in particular, 'I don't really know why you choose to do up your house...you really let yourself in for it...when you consider all the shit you go through.'

'Oh, I don't know,' Neil said and smiled as he flicked his fingers dry. 'People turn their focus to their homes at times of uncertainty in the world because hopefully in their own home they can have some order, some control.'

Neil, by way of example, pointed with a very expensive imported beer at the home next door, which was being renovated. 'You see, their garden is a great example because they've obviously bought the home from an older person. Now the older person has had time to tend the garden and create something in some sort of form...you can see that the maintenance would be pretty high.'

Chris Andersen thought of his own garden. He had bought his house from an old lady who had loved roses. At the auction, when he was signing forms in the little kitchen with the deodorant-drenched real estate agent, the old lady had smiled at Chris and spoken to him very sweetly, 'Can you just promise me you'll look after the roses? Especially the white ones.'

Chris Andersen had nodded solemnly. Two months later he'd mown over them by mistake. He thought that Neil might have some sort of point. He sipped his beer again.

'So the garden is really beyond them, see, the old plants that require a lot of effort. What they're doing is completely right, they're reclaiming their home, making it work for them.'

Chris thought Neil sounded like a bank commercial. He looked across the fence and saw a backyard that was half covered in concrete. The bricks were obviously to be stencilled in later.

'By covering their backyard in cement?' Chris asked. 'They're doing the right thing?'

Neil nodded. 'Yes, mate, they're reclaiming control of their life. That's why you renovate.'

Chris Andersen looked at the expensive beer in his friend's hand. He realised that he had been to many barbecues with Neil and that Neil always had such beers in his hand.

Was it just architects? Years ago it had been a pale Mexican beer in a clear bottle that had looked like wee. Then, as Neil had become more successful, there had been a succession of Japanese beers. That was when Neil had been working on lots of shopping centres in Malaysia. He now specialised in the dark-green bottles of the Euro grove beers. Ones with labels of old men with moustaches in fedora hats drinking in villages.

It struck Chris that the label looked like it was a colour plate from a Sunday school book. Neil was drinking a 'Christian gangster drink'.

It also struck Chris Andersen that there were three things wrong with what his friend was saying. 'Neil, that is bullshit...'

Neil laughed. 'You think so?'

'Yes, I think so... Jesus, if you want order and control in your house you do not renovate, especially if you have children and dogs and chooks and whatever new pets have been found...'

'Yeah?' Neil said and smiled, but it wasn't a smile that looked happy.

'Renovations are a fucking nightmare. You live through them, just.'

Neil smiled again and rolled his beer in his hand, apparently that does something to the ale and the fermented bits and pieces in the bottom of the bottle. Or that's what Neil had told him.

'People are not renovating homes because of the threat and uncertainty of modern life. They do it because property values are going up, interest rates are low and reinvesting in your home is financially prudent. Depending on which witchdoctor-cum-financial adviser-cum-voodoo man you are listening to at the time.' Chris took a healthy swig from his Vic.

'Whatever you reckon, old mate,' Neil said. 'But my clients love that sort of guff.'

Neil finished his expensive beer and plucked another from a bathtub filled with ice and went to admire the sausages on the barbie. Chunky, warty-looking things that didn't come in a plastic wrap but in a brown paper bag from some deli in a market that reeked of good taste. Neil had brought them.

'They won at the Melbourne Show three years running, apparently...gold medals,' he laughed as he told them.

As he did, one of the warty gold-medal winners promptly spat out and burnt him. Chris Andersen laughed. Quite loudly and much to Neil's annoyance. Who says there's no justice?

Renovations drive people insane. Chris Andersen knew that. People start out with a budget and end up with a paper chase of quotes, bills and bank statements. You suddenly find yourself moving in a new circle of people, 'hardware people'. These are other renovating folk whose paths you cross at the local Bunnings or whatever other DIY hardware shop you choose to loiter at. People who all nod sagely as the aproned shop assistants point to this knob and that fitting then go and hide down another aisle and have whispered conversations on their mobile phones.

Chris Andersen saw one man at the local Bunnings five times in one day. The first time they just noticed each other. The second time they smiled at each other. The third time they laughed, albeit in a rather forced manner and the fourth time the other man was almost in tears. 'Where's the devilled washers? Where? I don't even know what they do, let alone what they bloody look like... Do you know where they are?'

The fifth time they almost hugged as they staggered out for what they said would be the last time.

Well, my renovation was going to be different, Chris Andersen told himself. He had people he knew and liked doing the work and what's more he was going to help out.

He had little or no idea of what to do but he did what he did with a great deal of enthusiasm. He broke panes of glass and put holes in walls, doors and frames…and this was just making the coffee.

The people who actually did the work on the renovations were all known to Chris. Chris had met Nick, the builder, through the review panels at the Board of Works. He liked the same music Chris liked, could build, was honest and enjoyed a joke. The only thing wrong with him was the fact that there was only one of him. Bitter Kevin was an electrician. A bitter one. He was a friend of Nick's. Nothing was right in Kevin's life and everything about the job reminded him of his ex-wife. The floorboards: 'She liked spotted gum.' The nails: 'She used to crucify me, mate.' The way Chris made coffee: 'You make it too strong… Like her. She hated instant.' He looked at the coffee with smouldering hatred. 'I love International Roast,' he snarled.

Chris Andersen's long-suffering friend Rob Orchard helped out on the weekends. They listened to the football and had a few beers as they worked. Chris would break things and Rob would mend them. It was very pleasant.

Rob was the type of man who would just turn up to help. No questions, no fuss. He helped all his friends with their renovations. After a particularly hazardous effort at hanging a piece of ceiling plaster, Chris Andersen asked him why. 'Dunno. You're my friends and it's a good thing to build a home. Good thing to be a part of.'

Chris Andersen looked down to fine leg, down by the fence, to see Rob Orchard swaying slightly with his head tilted to one side.

Chris smiled. Rob was listening. He might as well stay down there at fine leg.

He was alright, was Rob. He was funny, in a good way. After a week of driving people around he'd turn up and be happy to put up with the chaos. Chris also knew Rob Orchard hated lifestyle shows on television. He thought they were for people with no imagination. People who think they have more money than they have and more time than they have. 'I don't know why they just don't pick up rubbish off the streets. We'd all be happier. Instead they want to live in a house that's exactly the same as the one next door, which is exactly the same as the one on the telly.'

Maybe we live in a time when people don't look outside their houses, thought Chris Andersen. Don't look outside – you might find something really important to renovate, like a community, a way of life, a social fabric. No, just put a new bathroom in, a new parents' retreat. Build up the walls in your house to shut out everything else.

What could bridge that gap? That gap between the lifestyle renovation and the world outside, our new uncertain world? Well, let me tell you, thought Chris Andersen, that a red-haired building inspector and ten millimetres can.

Chris Andersen looked at him. 'Why, does it matter?'

The red-haired building inspector looked at Chris Andersen. 'It's ten too high. Someone might trip. Trip and sue the council.'

Chris looked at him. 'No one has ever tripped on that step. It's been there four years.'

He looked at Chris Andersen. 'I may believe you. That could be true. But, matey. Who would have thought that people would drive jet aeroplanes into big tall buildings?'

Chris Andersen blinked. He couldn't really believe what he'd heard.

For a start, nobody says jet aeroplanes anymore. Only dead actors in old black-and-white movies that play at three o'clock in the morning on the ABC. But to stand in his house with a step ten millimetres too high and invoke the awful day that people 'drove' planes into 'big tall buildings' was too much. If this bloke and his yellow tape had just said that regulations are regulations, that would have been okay. But to play the fear card, to play George W. Bush's 'World of Uncertainty', all for the sake of ten millimetres was too much.

Depressed. This is the world we live in. Chris looked at the red-haired building inspector. The red-haired building inspector looked at Chris Andersen.

'What if I fixed a strip of carpet on the floorboards at the bottom of the step.' Chris Andersen asked slowly.

He looked at Chris. 'Yep. I can live with that.'

Well, good for him, thought Chris Andersen. We all have to live with something and Chris Andersen had to live with paisley carpet on the floorboards.

Chris stopped at the top of his run. The world of uncertainty. Of fear. What's there to fear on a day like today? Maybe the Trinity batsmen and Brian's fielding. But really, what is there to fear? Uncertainty had always been with us, only before it had worn different clothes. We're buying into it, thought

Chris. He looked at his son, Lachlan. His son clapped a little in an attempt at encouragement.

We are all buying into it, why do we fear...life? He thought of the review panels at work. People so suspicious of each other. He shook his head. Line and length.

Chris Andersen looked away down the pitch and ran in. He delivered the ball and Dougie, the Trinity opener, brought his bat down on the ball like a sealer brings down his club on a baby harp seal. Another four.

No one moved save for Dougie, who gave a little nod down the pitch to Chris.

'Thanks for that,' he said with a smile.

Chris Andersen smiled back, and as he did the wedding limousine did another lap around the oval. It was time for a spell in the slips.

He kept Tim Two going at one end and let Tim One have an over or two. Chris sauntered over to the slips.

'Matt, have a spell in the covers,' he said. He trudged over to where Matthew Halley had stood in the slips and he threw his head back and breathed in deep. Matt Halley skipped past tugging his pants.

Livey snorted, hawked and spat. Then started to stretch like Merv Hughes entertaining the hill.

'Well, you had a couple of close ones there,' he said.

'Yeah... I think we're in for it.'

'Yeah, no luck,' Livey said.

'Well, my dropped catch was harder than yours, you fucking meat-ripper,' Chris Andersen declared.

He turned to Michael Martin. 'How you travelling? Good to be back in the colours of the mighty fourths?'

'Just as long as we don't have to appeal in any other languages, I should be fine.'

Livey clapped his gloves together, squatted down and let rip with a bit of advice. 'Come on, come on, fellas, pressure's on, come on, young Tim.'

He then let rip with another bit of advice, from his arse.

'Livey, you're farting like a two-stroke,' Chris Andersen said.

'It's doing what it's meant to be doing. I'm thinking of appealing in arse-speak.'

Tim One's first ball fell just short of a length and then disappeared out through point to the boundary.

Livey farted his thoughts.

'You appealed for that?' Chris asked.

'No, mate. I see you're not familiar with the language. I'll translate. "That's alright Timmy, that's alright!"' yelled Livey.

'You're as high as a Frog, Livey,' said Michael Martin.

'Can't help it if I've got a Johnny Cash.'

The ball came sadly back from the boundary and landed in Livey's gloves. He tossed it to Chris Andersen, who passed it around a variety of hands until it reached Tim One. The boy stood at the top of his mark.

'What's Johnny Cash got to do with your farting?' said Chris.

'Had Indian last night. That place on Barkly Street...'

The slips and keeper went quiet and Tim One let the ball go. He was fuller in length this time and he was a bit quicker as well. The tall batsman went to play, but the ball raced onto him. He jerked his bat down hard and just managed to keep the ball out.

'Bowling!' said Livey and Chris in unison. Nobody added their voices to the call.

If it had been a different game and a different team, the talk wouldn't have gone on. But it was the fourths and Chris Andersen wanted to know more about Johnny Cash. Michael Martin did too, because this type of conversation was of the moment. Cosy, blokey banter. He had missed it. If Chris Andersen wasn't going to say anything he would, but he needn't have worried.

'Yes, you had Indian...'

'Yes, Tandoori Palace. Very tasty. Went in there and asked for a vindaloo that'd melt a plate.'

'Yes.'

'Got one.'

'Good for you.'

'Knocked it back, had a few drinks and Bob's your uncle.'

'And Johnny's your Cash.'

'Absolutely...woke up this morning with a massive case of Johnny Cash.'

Chris Andersen looked at Livey like he was mad.

'What are you talking about?'

'Johnny Cash.'

'Yes.'

'The man in black. Woke up this morning with a "Ring of Fire". A burning ring of fire.' He farted.

'That sounds more like "Folsom Prison Blues" to me,' said Michael Martin.

From where he stood, Rob Orchard heard Chris Andersen laugh. He turned his head away from the house and looked over to the slips. He smiled.

He liked it when Chris Andersen laughed. He thought a man like Chris should laugh a lot, especially today because Rob Orchard didn't really want to bowl and if Chris was happy, then that would mean he could stay down here by the old brick house at fine leg.

He turned his head away from the game and listened.

It was unusual for the fine leg fieldsman to remain unchanged. The idea is that the position is usually reserved for the resting bowler, for fine leg is deep in the field and not that busy in terms of ball chasing and exertion. So the bowler who has just bowled trundles down and huffs and puffs and spits a bit and rests.

On any other ground that would be the case. But Rob Orchard had made this position his own. The bowlers knew that it was his and even when the ends changed and the field was supposed to swap, he stayed there. Fine leg becoming a very deep mid-on. He stayed there.

It was unusual for a player in the field to turn his head away from the game as much as Rob Orchard did, but then he was listening. He had spent many hours listening.

He had first stood by this spot eight years ago. Eight years.

He had just moved into the area. Just begun driving the bus. Just begun to settle.

He hadn't played cricket for years and had only turned up at the club to play because he was tired of sitting in his flat there by Yarraville Gardens. He had seen on telephone poles little signs saying 'Players wanted for the Yarraville West Cricket Club'. He had remembered the signs as he lay on his bed and one Thursday he'd gotten up and gone to the ground. There he had met a big man who had yelled a lot but had kind, sometimes anxious, eyes. His name was Chris Andersen.

He was told by this man to roll up on Saturday afternoon at Bull Oval in his whites.

So he had and so he had continued to do for the past eight years.

He had found friends and a belonging. And he had found the house here at fine leg.

The first time he noticed the music was when he had just finished his first over for the club. He was hot and a little puffed and had to bend over with his hands on his knees to suck in some air. Then he had heard the notes. The plucking of strings. The tuning of an instrument. At first he had concentrated on the game. Then he turned to see where the sound was coming from. A large round window on the lower floor at the rear of the house at mid-wicket. He could see that it was raised, but the bushy fence hid what was inside.

Still the tuning went on. Slowly and uncertainly. Sometimes with an unevenness, followed by the murmuring of voices.

One voice, a soft deep voice saying over and over, 'No, no. Again. Once more.'

Then the plucking of the notes would start again. The calmness of the voice was at odds with the occasional explosion from the wicket.

But it was the sound that was made by whoever was plucking the instrument that captivated him. Sometimes it would call from the window, so rich and pure.

There would be a quiet exclamation from the voice and a kind tone. 'You see? Can you hear? Can you hear it speak?'

That first time it went on for nearly an hour. Simple plucking of a stringed instrument. Once, in between a series of sharp twangs, came a note of such warmth that it stood out from what had gone before. He hadn't realised that he had listened so intently.

It was only when he heard his voice that he understood he had listened. 'There, that's the one! That's a beauty.'

There was a silence and then the soft voice said, 'Well there...there, Sarah, you have an audience.'

The plucking went on a little longer and then it had stopped.

Soon the noise was that of a piano. Scales up and down. Then a guitar and then a trumpet. The window was shut by this time.

After the game, his first game, Rob Orchard had sat and had a beer with his team.

'The house at fine leg?' he asked Chris Andersen.

'Yes, the brick one?' said Chris.

'There was music coming from it, people playing instruments...'

'Yes, it's a music teacher's house.'

'Yeah.'

'Yeah...bit noisy was it?'

'No...no. It was kind of nice. It was nice.' He sipped his drink and smiled.

Chris Andersen looked at him. 'Well,' he said, 'you'd better come and play again so you can listen some more.'

They had had a couple more drinks.

For eight years almost every second Saturday for most of the summer months he had fielded at fine leg and listened.

Rob Orchard had listened to Reggie, a heavy-handed piano thumper who had pounded away for nearly two summers, and whenever he was questioned by the quiet voice as to, 'Why do you make the same mistakes when you have been shown how not to make those mistakes?' he would invariably answer, 'My Mum says I should come and play so I can get into a good school.'

He stopped thumping one Saturday and Rob Orchard never heard him again. Rob supposed that Reggie must have got into his good school.

There was Lauren, who torturously worked her way through a year or two of flute and laughed when the quiet voice would say, 'Oh, Lauren!'

Kwy was a guitarist who would play his scales and carefully step his way through intricate pieces. Occasionally he let rip with some manic riff and would stop suddenly.

Rob thought that perhaps the quiet voice had come back into the room and caught Kwy as he rode his fingers up and down the fret bars, for the scales would start again. Rob Orchard smiled. He was sad when Kwy and his riffs weren't heard anymore.

Sometimes Rob Orchard had stood there and the window had been closed, so the muffled sounds of the students would strain within the room as if trying to break free. Sometimes it was good, especially if Colin and his trumpet were there, squealing off keyed snatches.

But Rob Orchard knew that window would open and she would play. He wondered why sometimes. Why had she never closed the window?

She had started with plucking the strings and gradually worked her way through those Saturday afternoons with Rob Orchard, headed tilted to one side, listening there behind the leafy fence.

Her first piece of completed music had been 'Twinkle Twinkle Little Star'. Haltingly she limped through it. Rob stood there willing her along. Some of the draws of bow on string sounded like the slow low moan of a cat.

The few final notes fell from the window and she had finished. Then there was silence.

Rob Orchard spontaneously applauded.

'That's the girl! That's a girl.'

The players from the pitch looked over to him. A sulky batsman who wore all new equipment but was playing like a donkey stepped away from the crease.

'Come on, come on. Not while the batsman's facing,' said a fat umpire. He then wandered halfway down to fine leg to inform Rob Orchard he had been placed on report for conduct unbecoming.

Sadly, the umpire didn't realise he caught Rob Orchard's bus. He missed it three mornings in a row that week.

Rob nodded and the fat umpire waddled back to his position behind the stumps.

Behind him he heard the soft voice. 'Now, stop, Sarah. Stop. You must start somewhere. You must start somewhere. Stop now.'

Rob Orchard faced the game. He watched the bowler roll his arm over and the ball plopped onto the wicket and sponged slowly off into the keeper's gloves. The batsman had no idea and there were a few calls from the slips that wafted down to Rob.

He couldn't make them out but he heard the chorus line of the slips laugh. He didn't really care. He didn't look around but all his concentration was on the window. He could hear the sound of tears.

'Still, be still. I'll fetch a drink for you. Now be still,' said the soft voice.

Rob Orchard wasn't going to say anything, and there was a silence that fell across the ground. He wasn't going to say anything, but then again he heard his voice.

He faced the cricket and spoke loudly enough so she could hear, 'I wasn't laughing at you... I wasn't... I was listening... I was listening.'

He didn't even know if anyone was there. He could be speaking into the air.

'I... your music... some of the notes... were so... they were alright... no they were beautiful. Don't cry. Please don't cry... And don't stop... don't stop. I think it was pretty okay that piece you played.'

Somewhere over by mid-wicket an old dog barked.

How long does it take to get a drink? he thought.

'Don't stop. Please...don't stop...just try again...and you know...oh...'

'How's he!' came a shriek from Chris Andersen.

The fat umpire raised a podgy finger and the well-dressed rabbit tucked his expensive bat under his arm and walked off swearing to himself.

The players gathered in the middle of the pitch and slapped the big bowler on the back. Rob Orchard started to jog in. He took a few steps and then he slowed, a smile crossing his face. He heard playing from the window.

Faltering and halting but the tune came and it carried him across the ground until he reached Chris Andersen. He slapped him on the back and smiled.

'Twinkle Twinkle Little Star!' he yelled. The players laughed.

When he walked back to his position the tune was still playing. He smiled up at the window. By the time her lesson had finished the playing was surer and stronger.

'Little star, little star,' he said to the window.

There was no reply. He had never heard her voice. He had never seen her. But he had heard her play. Over those eight summers she had become surer and stronger.

He learnt that the instrument she played was a cello. He learnt the names of the pieces of music she played and he learnt the names of the people who composed them.

Each time Rob would field down at the fine leg boundary at Bull Oval he would listen for the window to open. When it did, he would not turn completely to the house but hold his head on one side and softly whistle the first few bars of

'Twinkle Twinkle Little Star'. Moments later the rich strings would complete the phrase.

On this day he hadn't heard the window open yet and he hadn't heard those strings. He looked at his watch. He smiled, it would any time now.

Inside the house a new piano player was attacking the keys. He thought of Reggie and smiled.

He kept smiling as he heard Chris Andersen laugh. Yes, it was good that Chris Andersen was laughing, that he was happy. Chris should be a man who is happy.

Rob Orchard looked at his watch again. If he got a few overs now, he thought, he wouldn't have to worry about nicking off when she plays. Maybe he should bowl now.

He rolled his arm over and called to Chris.

The big man turned and looked at him. Chris Andersen held his hands in question as Rob Orchard rolled his arm. Rob nodded.

'Righto, Rob, you right for the next one?'

Rob nodded and checked his watch as he jogged in from fine leg.

Chris gestured to Lachlan to move to fine leg. As he walked over to his position, Rob Orchard yelled out: 'Now listen, Lachie, let us know if the window opens in that house behind you.'

Michael Martin watched the movement on the field and noticed how Lachlan had nodded at his father's direction and trotted off, his lanky frame looking not unlike Brian's awkward flutterings. The difference was that Lachlan would grow out of this stage.

'That Brian's having a big one,' said Livey Jones.

Michael looked at Brian and at Livey.

Michael knew by looking at Brian that he wasn't one hundred per cent. 'Not quite right' had been his grandfather's term. Almost there, but not quite right. Michael could see that his grandfather would have said that about Brian.

Michael had watched him in the field from the slips. He had tried and had involved himself in the game as much as he could. He appealed only when he thought somebody was out, which was every second ball. There would be silence and then a shriek from Brian that would hang there and die in the air.

Some of the Trinity players would yell back, laughing usually.

Michael saw that Christo would look over and scan what the actions of the Trinity players were. If it was just laughter then he would more than likely do nothing, but sometimes words would be offered.

'Dickhead,' came wafting out onto the ground after one of Brian's appeals. Sure enough, Chris Andersen's voice would boom: 'Well done, Brian...good talk, matey. Good stuff!'

Michael Martin waited through a few balls. The batsmen had fallen into a lull, no doubt tired by their own excess, so for a while all was quiet. Rob Orchard was a pleasant bowler to face, so they were taking their time.

'What's Brian's story, Christo?'

Chris Andersen looked across to the on side of the ground and moved Tim One wider. He turned back to Michael.

'Brian is good. He's a good man... Just a bit special.'

Livey laughed.

'He's not the full quid, Marto. He lives down in Newport with his mum. He just turned up at training one day, caught the wrong bus. He got a bit upset.'

'More than that, the poor bugger,' Livey added.

'So he stayed here for a bit and had a go. Calmed him down and then he remembered where he'd written his address.'

'Where his mum had written his address,' said Livey.

'I rang her up. She was in tears and so I dropped him down there and the next Thursday he was back at training.'

'Only this time he hadn't caught the wrong bus,' Livey said. 'He's been here ever since. He's alright, Brian. He has a go... He's alright. I don't mind it when they laugh, you know, it's hard not to...'

A ball trickled out to Brian and he picked it up and threw, a hard strong throw, right into the healthy arse of Matthew Halley.

'Ohhhhhhh!' screamed Matt Halley and he moved like a dancer from the old *Don Lane Show*. His arms pointed one way as his legs went the other. '*Ohhhhhh*!...you fu...' he turned and saw that it was Brian who had thrown the ball.

Brian was holding up his hand and trying to mouth something. Matt Halley stopped what he was saying and laughed a little.

'...ck...okay...good throw, Brian, good throw...just sing out and let me know where it's going!'

Livey couldn't help himself. '*er Vor Hann*! *Er Vor Hannnnnn!*'

Matt Halley turned to the laughing slips cordon with a pirouette. 'Fuck you,' he mouthed and smiled.

'Yes,' agreed Chris Andersen. 'It's hard not to laugh but you know you don't want people having a go at him. So you know, go easy.'

Michael Martin nodded. He felt strangely comfortable and he realised that he hadn't felt the need to take any pills. His thoughts hadn't raced away and he hadn't thought at all of the things that would often come.

He heard Chris beside him.

'Why does he keep looking over to the playground?... Brian!'

Michael Martin looked to see Brian pointing, or was he waving? As soon as he heard Chris Andersen's voice he stood still and looked towards the big man.

'Brian, keep a watch, mate...keep a watch...concentrate, there's a lad.' Chris held his thumb up to Brian.

'Lachie!' Chris yelled suddenly, 'Move a bit finer.'

'Hope Matt'll be right to dance,' said Livey.

'He'll be right,' Chris said.

Michael looked over to Matt Halley. He was stretching, with his billiard-table legs stationed into the ground and bending over with a flat back.

'I thought he was a teacher,' Michael said.

'Oh, mate, he is, but come Thursday he's away off teaching all sorts of shit in the ballroom at Yarraville.'

Michael looked at Livey.

'Modern. Tap, bit of ballet, jazz, classical ballroom...he's a wizard...It all looks the same to me.'

'Yes, Matt specialises in *Countdown* video clips,' Chris Andersen said and smirked.

'You'll see for yourself later on, Marto,' snorted Livey. And then for good measure he farted.

'I walk the line,' said Michael Martin.

Chris Andersen looked down at the grass before him. He wasn't thinking of Johnny Cash or Livey's arse-speak.

He was thinking of *Countdown* and video clips and he thought about what he'd seen at the pool this morning. The video screens with the rap singers, the muscly sunglass-wearing rappers. 'Put a cap in your ass.' He thought about the teeming pool. The different colours. The rainbow of people. All together under the roof.

He looked around the oval and saw only white. The white of the cricketers. All were the same. All basically the same.

So this is why he noticed the difference on a Saturday.

Take away the white clothes and we're all the same. Take away the rainbow colours and we are all the same.

Chris Andersen looked past the houses that ringed the oval and saw the flats. He knew in there, in these flats, were the families who perhaps would have been down at the pool this morning.

The families that made up the melting pot. Twenty-odd men, dressed in white playing with a little red ball surrounded by all that diversity. All those cultures. And we all look the same.

Beside him Livey farted and the ball padded into his gloves.

Well, fuck, thought Chris Andersen. That's what we're supposed to do. We all look the same. That was the thing; we all look the same but what goes on underneath?

There's the thing.

Just the same things that went on underneath the people in the flats and the people in the pool and the people on the other side of the planet. He supposed, as he scratched his testicles in that languid way cricketers do, that understanding this is the problem.

He thought of the pool.

'Livey.'

'Yep.'

'Livey, what happened to Hush? That band Hush?'

As he asked the question, he thought that Dougie was starting to get a little tired and was trying to reach for his shots rather than move. In doing so, he was hitting in the air. He signalled to Tim One to drop back a bit at mid-off. As he did that, he suddenly knew why he had thought of Hush. He was thinking of his brother. Of Tony.

Thinking of the things that go on underneath.

'Hush,' Livey said in a considered snort. 'Hush did okay for a while... Les Gock, he was the guitarist and ended up making millions writing jingles. God knows what happened to Keith Lamb. He was the lead singer who used to thrust out his satin-covered crotch.'

'How the hell did you remember their names?'

'Dunno,' said Livey. 'You can never tell when information will come in handy.'

Michael Martin stared at nothing in particular and remembered how conversations in the slips would start and stop at random. The communication without anchor or direction. It was not unlike passing the time with strangers at bus stops and doctors' surgeries. But there was a difference.

These were bits of conversation that came from the deep, quiet well of reflection and comfort. Namely, arsing around in the park playing cricket. But sometimes the water drawn from the well can be tainted with that awful toxin of self-reflection and truth.

'I've a girl named Boney Moroney,' said Chris Andersen.

Livey laughed.

Chris closed his eyes and thought of Tony laughing and reading on the couch. How he stared his father down so Greg could watch this band called Hush, whose guitarist made money in advertising and whose whooping permed-haired singer ended up God knows where.

Chris thought of his son. Lachlan was so much like his Uncle Tony. You can never tell how it's going to fall.

He remembered the pool and the laughing African women and the tall, languid men walking in their homeboy outfits.

'Africa...what was Africa like there, Marto?' Chris Andersen asked his old friend.

Michael had half-expected this question. Why wouldn't somebody ask him? He had gone there. Dr Michael Martin. He'd gone there.

What had it been like?

His big loud friend had asked him. He might be interested. He might be just passing time in the slips. Well, that would make two of them. What a question to ask to pass the time.

'It was...it was something I won't forget in a hurry,' he said softly.

He thought he had said it simply. Neither man beside him said anything in reply. Perhaps they were thinking of other things to pass the time.

Rob Orchard stooped and then knelt. He retied his bootlace and as he did so Michael closed his eyes and felt the heat, the stale baked smells. He closed his eyes and saw the faces and the eyes.

He was about to open his own when he felt a big gentle hand fall on the small of his back. A few gentle pats.

He turned and saw Chris Andersen looking at him with a level gaze. The big man smiled a little and nodded gently. Compassion comes in many forms, but a six-foot-three cricketer was not one that would be expected by many. Least of all by Michael Martin.

It caught Michael by surprise. Had he given himself away? He felt a tightness in his chest. A burning in his eyes. For a moment.

What had his grandfather said?

'It's a terrible thing to see into a man...and it can happen anywhere.'

Michael Martin remembered that his grandfather had always said that when they had played cricket together here at Bull Oval. 'It can happen anywhere...in a slaughter-room. On a cricket field, in a bar... Anywhere.'

Even in the slips, thought Michael Martin.

Chris Andersen knew enough of life to know the way Michael answered meant there was a story that might need listening to or one that might need forgetting. He was unsure why he had patted him, but something told him that it was the right thing to do. It was something that Tony would have done.

Chris thought again of the pool and of his son Lachlan, reading there on the bench. They were so alike.

He asked without thinking, 'Have you read *To Kill a Mockingbird*?'

'Oh, mate, you are going the lucky dip today, aren't you?' Livey said and laughed. 'From Boney Moroney and Hush to Harper Lee and *To Kill a Mockingbird*.'

'I'm working to a theme here,' Chris Andersen said before asking, 'Who was Atticus Finch?' If Livey knew the book and presumably the author of the book, Chris Andersen had every right to be ashamed of himself.

Michael Martin took a sharp intake of breath. 'Atticus,' he said.

The ball crashed from the bat and went out to the boundary. Still, thought Chris, he was hitting up in the air.

'Atticus Finch! Mate, he was Gregory Peck!' said Livey.

'Atticus,' Michael Martin laughed as he said it.

'He was the lawyer, the father. And he was the fella who stood up to the town when they wanted to hang the black bloke…and his kids thought he was a joke…and then…' Livey took a breath to put a gloved index finger to one nostril and with an explosion of air cleared out the one left open.

Chris Andersen finished off the description, 'And then the kids didn't think he was a joke because he turned out to be a hero.' He looked at his son.

'No,' said Livey, 'he turned out to be Gregory Peck.'

'You know this?'

'Fuck you, why can't butchers read books?'

'Atticus Finch,' Chris Andersen said to himself.

'Atticus, that's the name of the bloody dog.'

Chris Andersen was going to ask Michael Martin what he was talking about after the next ball. But then it happened.

Dougie reached forward once too often and even though he got hold of it, he didn't get onto it. The ball flew high and Tim One ran in a few steps to take the catch. It was the first wicket and the calls were more in relief than in the celebration of the hunt.

Dougie trudged off happily enough and accepted the applause and the 'Well playeds' from the Yarraville West Fourths.

Rob Orchard wiped the sweat from his brow.

Chris Andersen slapped him on the shoulder.

'Well done, Bus Man! You want to go back to fine leg?'

'Do you mind?'

Chris Andersen laughed. 'No, I wouldn't ask if I did. Your job is done here.'

'Twinkle twinkle,' said Rob Orchard.

'And you, Tim One, well done. Tim Two, now you've got to take one just for the sake of symmetry.' Chris Andersen gave Tim Two a phantom punch to the stomach.

'Christo, do you mind if I choof off to mid-wicket?' Michael Martin said.

'Had enough of Livey's arse-speak?'

'Yeah, too much of a good thing.'

Chris Andersen nodded. 'Hey, watch out for that dog.'

Michael laughed.

Matt Halley stood rubbing his backside.

'How's the rump, Matthew? Hope you'll be able to front up for bowling,' Livey wheezed.

'If my captain needs me I'll be there. It was a good throw there, Brian.'

'Yes, he didn't miss, did he,' Chris Andersen said.

'Pretty easy target though,' said Livey.

'You know, I think I liked you better with your meat hat on, Livey,' said Matt.

Lachlan was laughing.

'And you, you're as bad as your father, Lachlan...Hey, that wedding car's been going around in circles,' Matt said.

'Maybe he's trying to find a couple of customers,' said Livey.

'You interested, are you?' asked Matt.

'You're not proposing?' said Livey.

'Right, Christopher, are you ready?' asked Ron Sparrow.

The new batsman was neat and very proper and fiddled with his mouthguard as he batted. He hit the ball even harder than Dougie. He played straight and hit the ball back over the head of Tim Two, but the young man kept his head and bowled a bit fuller. The batsman with the mouthguard misread one ball and nearly played on. He swore through his guard and helmet grille and sounded like a bad ventriloquist, muttering to himself about the shot he had just played.

Every time the ball raced down the ground to mid-on or mid-off the wedding car would circle. It was a bit disconcerting. It looked like some Great White Shark slowly and silently gliding around and around.

Chris Andersen was drifting off again. The Mouthguard was trying to find his range and Chris wasn't concentrating. He thought...Weddings.

It was very hot. And getting hotter. Perhaps that is why he thought what he did. He didn't know.

Weddings. The Mouthguard mis-hit a no-ball and swore again. 'Gloody batard...'

Livey laughed.

Weddings. Weddings can mean many things to men. Different things to different men. Chris Andersen thought briefly of his own. They hadn't had a limousine. Well, not one that big. They had a couple of nice old Valiants and Julie had looked beautiful. He remembered her eyes. Calm and very sure as she looked at him when they stood together.

He was astonished when he saw that look. It wasn't sky rockets and flowers and rainbows. It was two lovely brown eyes looking into his. As he looked into her eyes he thought, Shit, she really wants to be here with me.

Now he realised it was quite incredible that he could have perceived this. He'd been so nervous. But her eyes, they had told him so much. He remembered that look. He flushed a little and picked his nose and spat, just so it wouldn't look like he was thinking of this sort of stuff.

He remembered those eyes and thought, that look is what life is.

Chris Andersen clapped his hands for no reason and jumped a little – one of those bursts of happiness. His heel rubbed and he swore softly.

Weddings. That look was what he remembered most about his wedding.

His father had made a speech and his mum had got a little teary and Julie's parents had been nice and nobody had misbehaved that much, except his aunty, who had insisted on pushing aside the entertainment director at the reception centre up in Essendon. Once she had taken the microphone she took out her teeth and sang a song called 'Denim and Lace'. That was expected.

He couldn't remember Greg's wedding much. His brother had just started to go bald and had actually gone to the chemist shop he was working in at the time a couple of hours before the ceremony and bought spray-on hair.

He looked like he had cobwebs all down his back.

Livey, whose hairstyle was the same then as it was now, said to Chris and Chris' aunty that Greg looked like Spiderman.

This was not the wisest piece of wedding banter because once the seed was planted it grew like bamboo. At about ten o'clock Chris' aunty had pushed aside the entertainment director, grabbed a microphone, taken out her teeth and sang the Spiderman song to the bridal couple.

Poor Greg, he'd gone and got married in the early eighties and back then it was all about hair – and lots of it. And he was losing his. In fact, his hair had all but given up the ghost by the time Chris and Julie got married.

Although he had kept his moustache.

Perhaps it was not so much weddings but the nature of cricket that led Chris Andersen down the next meandering adventure of memory as he stood in his cricket whites on a blistering end-of-summer day.

He heard Julie's voice and, yes, he saw her eyes and he almost laughed as he stood at first slip thinking of how they had lain in bed together one Saturday morning. Lain in each other's arms.

'Cricket...the only reason you play cricket...'

'I play it because I like it.'

'Yeah, and you like it because it lets...'

'You've got lovely hands, Julie.'

'...because it lets you do things you can't do in better company.'

'What do you mean?'

'You're grown men and you chew gum with your mouth open and fart and spit and pick your noses.'

'And look at it.'

'...and look at it and then you can play with yourself in public.'

'It's hardly playing with yourself.'

'Well, what do you call it?'

'Well...it...technically, it might be playing with yourself, but you know...you can't linger too long there – then you're playing with yourself.'

Julie chuckled. Chuckled. Not many women chuckle. And he didn't know why, but it was heavenly. A heavenly chuckle.

'It's adjusting...adjusting. It is a ritual of cricket.'

She had smiled and her hand had slid from his chest and traced softly down.

'Shall I help you to adjust a little?'

Chris Andersen smiled and then he found himself, if you like, adjusting.

Adjusting. The great gift of Ian Chappell to Australian cricket. The art of adjusting. Of scanning the field with narrowed eyes, of holding the bat with the left hand and having it raised to your shoulders while the right hand cups the protective box...and adjusts.

Mouthguard, the bad ventriloquist, got it right and the ball spat off across the boundary. It might be time to give Tim Two a rest, Chris Andersen thought. As he thought that, he caught himself tugging slightly at his scrotum. Through his cricket whites of course.

This was technically the Captain's Tug. Julie had never understood this but it served a greater purpose than the Chappelli Adjust. It was akin to thoughtfully running a hand through the hair or cupping your chin in Rodin's *The Thinker* fashion. It was, he admitted, something that he would never do in court or before the review panels or anywhere where he wasn't wearing cricket whites.

The Captain's Tug, made popular by Allan Border and Mark Taylor. Allan Border had favoured a swift series of sharp attacks with his forefinger and thumb. As if he were tugging in Morse code. Mark Taylor has a more ruminating, thoughtful type of tug. But both, undoubtedly, were great exponents of the Captain's Tug. He must admit that done anywhere else, this form of meditative, reflective, tactical thought would be well and truly branded as...playing with yourself.

The tug suddenly became a kneading and from a dreary cricket game in the suburbs, Chris Andersen's mind led directly to a place he would never have thought to travel.

Perhaps he was just getting old. It was hot and a mind does wander, but cricket creates that stream where linear thoughts won't automatically come on days like today.

There was nothing linear about his next little mind adventure.

Life is full of adventures, milestones if you like. Like weddings. Adventures and sensations that tell us we are alive. Such as having your testicles folded and pressed by a gloved hand to the tune of 'The Way We Were'.

Yes, Chris Andersen's sack of goodies was being prepared for a little adventure. Not a Chappelli Adjust or the Captain's Tug. But the Surgeon's Grip. Chris Andersen remembered being prepared for another journey.

A trip to the doctor for the snip. As he lay there supine, with his trousers around his ankles he suddenly thought of an old Marcus Welby television episode. Marcus Welby was some silly old TV doctor that his Aunty Faye adored. The show was melodramatic and stilted but she didn't care. He could remember having a sleepover one night at Aunty Faye's with Greg and Tony. She had opened a tin of spaghetti, warmed it and served it hot on toast for all of them. As an extra special Friday night treat, they had been allowed to make sarsaparilla spiders and sip them in front of the television.

On the night of the spider and spaghetti-on-toast sleepover a man wanted Marcus Welby to give him a vasectomy.

'Are you *insane*?' Marcus said and his eyes rolled and he thumped his television doctor's desk.

Chris Andersen thought about Marcus Welby as his perfunctory physician went about his task. Am I insane? he thought. Well, it is never comfortable going off to the doctor and having a complete stranger, even if he has the suitable professional letters after his name, fondle your wherewithal. No, it is not high on the list of good things to do in your spare time.

But he was not insane. He was just having a vasectomy. Like thousands of other Australian men, he had decided to have a vasectomy as a form of contraception.

Well, about time, too. Many men have vasectomies for many reasons. In his case, it was only fair he took charge of the question of contraception. Alright, after a talk with Julie, she thought it was only fair he took charge of the question of contraception.

Apparently vasectomy is nearly one hundred per cent successful as a form of contraception. That's what Julie told him.

It is intended to be permanent. It is safe and it doesn't affect sexual pleasure. That's what his doctor told him.

'Are you insane?' That's what Marcus Welby said.

The truth is, it's a relatively painless and quick operation but looking at the greater scheme of things, thought Chris Andersen as he lay with his pants around his ankles, he was about to scratch himself off the list of reasons why he was here on the planet. To reproduce. It was his biological duty. After twenty minutes of prodding and poking and God knows what else he would be a slightly sore dud entry in the reproductive race.

Chris Andersen stood on the Cec Bull Oval and thought of himself staring at eternity with his pants around his ankles. At that very moment he was confronting his own mortality. He wasn't going to breed anymore. He knew he mustn't worry too much, he had to draw strength from Australian history, remember that Phar Lap was a gelding. That is what Chris thought as the over finished and he called out to Matthew Halley to start warming up. He turned to Tim Two.

'Well bowled, Tim Two, just have a bit of a break and come back into it, but well done you...'

'Thanks,' said Tim Two, and he trotted off to the deep. All in the deep now, thought Chris. They're caning us. All in the deep. Not even a drinks break and we've already spread.

'How long to drinks, Ron?' he asked the umpy.

'Next over, Christopher,' said the older man slowly.

The wedding car kept circling and Chris gave Ron Sparrow his cap.

On the edge of eternity with my trousers around my ankles, thought Chris Andersen, and he looked at the wedding car.

'How many people have you married, Ron?' he asked.

The old umpire sucked at his teeth before he answered. 'Quite a few, I suppose, but you know I seem to be burying more these days.' And he smiled, a half-sad little smile.

'Right arm over, batsman,' he said, and Chris Andersen walked back to his mark.

Chris Andersen thought about mortality as he lay there in the North Melbourne Vasectomy Clinic.

His doctor was no Marcus Welby, he was a more frightening vision. A surgeon who was doing weekend surgery and was dressed in a manner that indicated he was more interested in playing golf than attending to the matter at hand. When he slipped on his medical gloves it seemed as if he was slipping on a golf glove.

Chris tried to engage the surgeon in conversation but for some reason he could only think of two things: Marcus Welby and Phar Lap. He chose to focus on Phar Lap.

'Well, I suppose Phar Lap was a gelding and he did alright,' said Chris Andersen.

The surgeon looked at him. Music started to play. It was a version of 'Can You Feel the Love Tonight'. There was a pause while they both considered each other.

'Phar Lap ended up stuffed in the Melbourne Museum,' the surgeon said.

Why was this music playing?

'But he won a Melbourne Cup,' said Chris.

His surgeon nodded sagely, almost a little like Marcus Welby, 'Mr Andersen, you are not going to win a Melbourne Cup.'

Am I insane? thought Chris Andersen as he studied the polite professional who still looked like he'd rather be playing golf. He was full of quite interesting facts, though. About the vasectomy.

Chris Andersen became desperate to chat and so he asked about reversal. Just in case.

The surgeon snorted. 'Oh, I've had a fellow who has had two vasectomies and one reversal. It's not impossible by any means, but it is costly and it is purely lifestyle driven. You don't have any lumps, by the way. It's good to know that everything is as it should be.'

The music changed to 'Love is Like a Butterfly' as Chris Andersen asked the surgeon what a lifestyle driven vasectomy was.

'He left his wife for a younger woman. They didn't want children, then the younger woman got older and wanted children, then he left his younger wife for a younger woman and so the various procedures followed his lifestyle changes.'

For a brief moment Chris Andersen thought of Neil Greene. Neil Greene would do that. Why didn't he just buy a red sports car?

The surgeon said, 'Right, I'm going to carry out the procedure.' His hold on the testicles became the Surgeon's Grip.

This was the moment, then. The music changed to 'The Way We Were'.

Chris Andersen lay there and thought of Chappelli, imagining him peering down alongside the surgeon. Chappelli, with his bat held high adjusting his protector while scanning where he would belt the next ball. He could almost see Tubby Taylor and Allan Border in deep thought just over by the coloured anatomical wall chart of a human body cut into layers, from skin, to fat, to muscle and ligament, down to bone. Tubby and AB taking turns to pull at themselves in the Captain's Tug.

Chris Andersen couldn't help himself. 'This music, is it supposed to relax me?'

'Well that's the theory,' the surgeon said and sniffed. 'Why? Don't you like it?'

By the time the Kenny G-type tones faded the deed was done. He had joined the 'Snip Club'.

He desperately tried to think of other members and could only come up with Dean Martin, the late singer; Phar Lap; and Bob. Bob was a friend of his Mum and Aunty Faye who wore Stubbies a lot.

Barry Andersen didn't like Bob because he always 'Dances a tad too close to the ladies at the Probus Club socials'.

Chris Andersen told himself that nothing much had changed, really. After years of bearing family planning decisions his wife was off the hook.

He flicked the ball in his hand. 'Jesus,' he said to himself, 'this all started with a wedding limo driving through the streets.' And he looked around and saw the wedding car and he started to whistle.

Ron Sparrow heard him and turned to see Christopher Andersen, all fifteen stone and six-foot-three of him, standing there whistling, badly out of tune, 'The Way We Were'. He was smiling.

Ron Sparrow shook his head. Oh well, it's a funny game and it takes all sorts.

As Chris Andersen slowly ran in to bowl, the tune stayed with him and his mind clouded with a mixture of Marcus Welby riding a stuffed Phar Lap in the Melbourne Cup. They were being cheered on by thousands of Chappellis adjusting themselves and an equal number of Allan Borders and Mark Taylors Captain-Tugging in excitement.

Not surprisingly the ball was hoicked high over square leg for six.

# Jessie's Girl

Michael Martin stood in front of the house at mid-wicket. He looked at the fence; it had seemed taller when he had tried to fetch the ball all those years ago. He reached up and placed his hands on the top. A bit taller than him. He guessed it was about six foot. He could pull himself up quite easily.

The grey wooden planking had begun to buckle here and there, and the top of the fence had a splintery weathered feel under his fingers that he didn't remember.

He ran his hands over some of the palings and picked at them as if he were examining the timber for some medical problem. Dr Michael Martin, fence doctor.

He looked at his hands and rubbed little bits of the fence into grey-black dust and then let it sit on his fingers. There was no wind to speak of. So he stepped back onto the field and blew the powdered fence away onto the oval. A bit crumbly but the fence was still fairly strong, it had aged well. Like me, he thought.

Michael closed his eyes behind his sunglasses. He closed his eyes and tried to think of how old he had been when he had perched on the fence and the dog had barked below.

Eighteen, nineteen? Probably nineteen. It was almost the last game he had played for the club because he had started studying medicine. He'd dropped down from the higher grades to play in the fourths and after a season had stopped playing altogether.

Medicine. Carrying on the family tradition. He was the third generation of Dr Martins. His grandfather, his father and himself. Two GPs sandwiching the surgeon, his father.

He thought of them both. He thought of how he had walked around this oval with them. He wished, for a moment, that his grandfather was still alive. He might have understood, thought Michael. He might have understood. He'd been through a war or two, so he might have understood.

He looked out across the oval. The heat rippled the air and made everything distort just a little. He saw Brian standing and waving to Lachlan Andersen. Lachlan seemed to be trying to placate him. Then he heard Chris Andersen's booming voice. 'Eyes on the ball, Brian, eyes on the ball. Lachlan! Just leave him be!'

Michael Martin shook his head slowly. It was where Brian was standing, on the far side of the ground by the old scoreboard that didn't work. That was where he had waited with his grandfather.

One early evening after a Sunday visit to his grandparents, Michael had walked with his family around Bull Oval.

All of them, the old doctor, his son the surgeon, and his grandson, young Michael, who was thinking about following in the family professional line, they all walked in each other's footsteps on that early evening, slowly ambling around Bull Oval

Two pleasant but yappy dogs belonging to Michael's grandmother trotted with them. The rest of his family walked close together, laughing at one of the little dogs sniffing the arse of a bigger dog. The other yappy dog sniffed around the old doctor's feet.

Michael Martin came and stood next to his grandfather and the old man stared out across the oval, so Michael wasn't sure for a while whether the old man was actually talking to him.

'It's a thing, an awful thing, sometimes, to see into a man, to share a secret. It can happen anywhere, you know... And it doesn't just happen because you're a doctor and it's your business to deal with people, young Michael. It can happen anywhere, on a bus, on the cricket field, at work.'

Michael Martin moved closer to his grandfather. The old man gently flicked at the yappy dog with his foot.

'Cec Bull. Old Cec Bull...he died out there, out there in the middle of the ground, dressed in his best. Died right out there. On the night they named the oval after him.'

The old doctor laughed as he said the name, 'Cec Bull. I used to work with him...while I was at university...down at the meat works in the slaughter-room.'

The old man laughed again. 'Not bad training for a doctor, the slaughter-room, better for your father, he's the surgeon of course. But Cec Bull, he was the head slaughterman.'

The small yappy dog walked in tiny circles, then pinned its ears back and looked over its shoulder and bent its legs. It began to poo on the ground.

'Oh you bloody thing, oh, you're as high as a Frog. It's your grandmother feeding it all these treats.'

The old man looked at a spot on the oval and said softly, 'As high as a Frog.'

The old doctor turned and looked directly at Michael Martin.

'Sometimes, when you look into a man, you can see his secret, what he carries with him, deep inside. It can be awful but you know, Michael, you know it depends on the man. A good man can take a terrible secret and turn it into a better life.'

The old man paused a second and then continued, 'Old Cec Bull... well, at least he had an oval named after him. Come on, young Michael, let's catch up with the others.'

Michael Martin rubbed his fingers clean. He wished he could have spoken to his grandfather. He could have told him of the things he'd seen. Of the things he started to see now. The eyes, the dark eyes filled with nothing. Staring at him and then a look of such kindness. He stopped. He pulled his hands into tight balls. Anything. Think of anything else. Without being fully aware he turned to the fence, gripped the top and pulled himself up. He stared into the backyard of the house.

It could be any backyard; he could remember nothing of it. There was a bit of decking that looked like it had come from a kit and some outdoor furniture and some plants that seemed to belong in everyone's backyard. The yard had been done over.

There was a fishpond, or should he call it a water feature? Whatever you might like to call it, there was one. Directly below him. He peered down and three or four big fat carp drifted lazily through some weedy-looking plants.

Michael could see himself and the bright blue endless sky reflected in the water. He stared.

'Are you right there?' said a woman's voice.

He looked up and saw a woman framed in the window. She was made up, he could see that. Her hair had been done, quite extravagantly. She had bits of foliage in her hair.

Her facial appearance was at odds with what she was wearing. An old T-shirt and baggy shorts. She held a glass in her hand. A champagne glass.

'Um... I was...looking. I'm sorry...the dog, well a dog used to live here... Sorry.'

The woman half-smiled and he nodded, not knowing what else to say, and he climbed down and walked back onto the field.

Michael Martin felt like an idiot. He looked back at the pitch and saw Chris trundle in and drop one on line. Mouthguard, the ventriloquist, went down on one knee to slog sweep the ball square. But he'd misjudged Chris Andersen's pace, or lack of, maybe Chris'd given him a slower ball. In playing the stroke Mouthguard reached too early and was already halfway through the shot when he hit the ball. He must have had a good bat because even though he got under it the ball flew high. It looked off the bat like it might have cleared the fence but the batsman had got under it.

Michael knew that because he saw it, he saw it. He was sharp, Michael Martin, you could tell that from what he did next. He was sharp, even if he was deadened a little by the white pills from the dispensary.

He made sure where the boundary was in relation to his feet and widened his legs slightly. With his hands up in front of his face, the way a photographer might study a subject, he traced the arc of the ball high into the air. He moved slightly to his left and in a bit.

Michael's eyes followed the ball into the sky and, even though the sun shone fiercely for a moment into his eyes, he never lost the track of the ball. He brought his hands up even more, cupped them and caught the ball softly.

Neat and precise. A wicket. Chris Andersen exploded and clapped his hands.

'Martooooooo! Well caught. Well done, you! Marto!'

Livey stood up and pointed to Michael Martin with a gloved index finger. Michael Martin waved a little.

Matt Halley said something Michael couldn't understand so he thought it must have been Norwegian and gave the same little wave. Brian was still shrieking and Mouthguard mumbled indecipherable unpleasantries as he stormed off.

Michael threw the ball back to Livey, a flat hard throw that fell just shy of the keeper, bounced off the ground and zipped into his gloves.

Ron Sparrow called for the ball and announced drinks.

The players trudged off in a gaggle to where the ice-cold Staminade and water sat under the awning of the clubrooms in the square foam watercoolers.

Michael took a few steps in the direction of the clubrooms and then stopped. Her voice stopped him.

'Good catch... Marto.'

He turned and looked up at her. She was almost smiling. He looked at her for a bit and then walked back to the fence and rested his hands on the top.

'I don't know why I jumped up like that before, sorry. It was just that I was trying to remember the dog's name. I'd been thinking about it all morning and... well, I just wanted to...'

She looked at him.

'Atticus. I wanted to see Atticus' backyard. I came here once before... for a cricket ball and Atticus didn't want to give it back.'

She stared at him for a moment and then broke out laughing. She had a nice laugh, thought Michael Martin, and it made him smile.

'Atticus,' she was laughing a little less as she spoke. 'Well Atticus is down there somewhere, underneath that palm, I think. Good old Atticus.'

They looked at each other.

'I thought it was you,' Katie Spencer said.

She studied Michael. How long ago had it been? It had been years since Atticus had died and he was ancient when he went. She heard a booming voice. That was his friend. The big noisy one.

'Marto! Drinks!' came the cry from the tall man underneath the awning of the clubrooms.

Katie Spencer looked down and watched as the cricketer below turned easily and held up his hand to his friend. He was quite graceful still, thought Katie.

She remembered him.

Her sister, Donna, had been the first to notice him. He was the one that Donna and her friends would talk of while they lolled about on the swings of the playground when they wanted to talk about boys or maybe even smoke.

Donna and her friends let Katie come along one afternoon and as they pretended to be engrossed in the cricket in order to check out the younger players so they left Katie to her own devices. She spent her time on the monkey bars. One at a time she gripped her way across the grey steel structure. Then two at a time. She wondered about trying for three and then thought better of it.

Katie did what every child does when they play on the monkey bars. She decided to hang by her legs upside down.

Katie was hanging upside down and she got that feeling in her head, that mad rushy feeling when the blood, or whatevever it might be, runs, no gallops to your brain.

After she had got used to that feeling the view made her giggle. Donna and her girlfriends sat in a tight scrum, all trying not to show too much interest in that dark-haired cricketer. They were clumped together on the roundabout and to Katie they looked like an upturned cupcake.

Katie watched the cricketers, but they didn't move. She righted herself and they still didn't move. Then she went upside down again and still the cricketers didn't move. They looked like the pieces of ice that grew in her father's beer and crab fridge which creaked its business out in his shed. Little stalactites that hung from a green roof. And did nothing.

'Katie! Katie, don't do that without shorts...we can see your undies!' cried Donna. The other clumps of cupcake laughed.

Katie plopped down onto her feet and steadied herself on the bars. Still the white strips of ice did nothing. She felt like having a lemonade icy pole.

Then suddenly there was a crack and one of the stalactites started to move. He had dark hair and was slim. He could run fast and laughed easily with a big loud man who acted the same age as the dark-haired cricketer but looked like all the older men who played.

They were both chasing a little red ball and the dark-haired man was winning. He ran right up to where the girls were sitting on the roundabout and he picked up the ball before it hit the white line. He threw it back easily, a long, hard, flat throw.

He smiled at the girls, who were pretending they weren't looking. The girls giggled. He had a nice smile.

But he was still a stalactite. Katie Spencer had no idea why anybody would choose to stand still on a hot day and then suddenly chase a little red ball. It wasn't long before she left the monkey bars and went to play on the swings again. The cricketers faded away into the landscape, like some old concrete gnomes in the front yard of one of the houses around here.

Katie Spencer swung high up into the afternoon and felt that rush in her tummy. She liked the swings. She spent the rest of the visit to the cricket swinging hard, so at times she felt like she was launching into the deep blue summer sky. Even though some of the white figures would occasionally do something or shriek sometimes, she had little interest in the game.

As she looked down at Michael Martin, Katie Spencer had another sip of champagne. In the background the wedding car glided by. She drained the glass.

'You winning?' she asked.

He looked up at her and she remembered how the girls had loved the colour of his eyes. Today they were hidden behind his sunglasses.

'No,' he said slowly, 'we are not winning. It's not even close...' He trailed off.

'Is it fun?' she asked.

He laughed a little before he answered, 'Now that's a question.'

Katie thought of all the Saturdays she had spent in the room where she now stood. She thought of all the afternoons that had dripped through her fingers with the cricket stalagmiting and garden gnoming in the background while she had lived her life.

She thought of the last time she had seen him, perched up high on the fence, laughing. His loud friend laughing at him and with him. Atticus going off his nut.

'He liked the balls,' she said.

'Sorry?'

'Atticus. Atticus, the dog whose name you couldn't remember. He loved chasing balls. I think he wanted you to throw it.' She looked at her watch, she really didn't have that much time left. That car came early. Trust bloody Mum, she thought.

'He looked like he had a keen taste in cricket-player meat,' said Marto.

'He was alright, just having fun...like you. You're having fun, aren't you?'

'That's the idea...' he said slowly.

She saw him looking at the palm in the corner.

'It was a long time ago. You up on the fence.'

'Yes,' he said.

'Have you been playing cricket all that time?'

'No...no, I stopped playing for a long while after that,' he paused and looked back out at the oval. 'First time I've played in years.'

She looked at him. She had often heard the cricket going on in the background as she grew up. She could remember hearing the loud man, either laughing or yelling. She suddenly realised that when she thought of this house one of the sounds she associated with it was that man.

She remembered one Saturday. That Saturday her mother and father and sister Donna had gone out to the big Highpoint Shopping Centre up the road to buy Donna some clothes for her graduation and Katie was left at home to study. Dale Carter had rung up and asked if she wanted to go out. To walk around the shopping mall at Highpoint.

'They've just done up the food court...there's a McDonald's there now...' She had said no but without thinking about it she asked him over. Dale and Katie had been an item for most of that last year in high school so it wasn't unusual for him to call up and ask her out – but it was unusual for her to ask him over.

She quite liked him and he wasn't that bad looking. He didn't have much of a chin, but then none of the Carters did. But he was nice and they trusted each other and he wasn't as much of a goose as most of the other young men she knew. He was the only one who smelled nice. She liked the way he smelled.

Anyway, over the year they had gone out they grew to have an understanding. They decided if they were going to do 'it', it being the 'it' that plagues the minds of most young people sooner or later, then they would do 'it' together.

Katie knew why she was asking him over. For some reason, something told her that now was the time for 'it'. It was a beautiful day. It was time.

There was a pause down the end of the line.

'I've never seen a McDonald's in a shopping centre before.'

'Dale!' Katie Spencer said. 'Do you want to come over?'

There was a silence and then Dale forgot the uniqueness of the marketing strategy of fast food chains.

'I'll be there in a tick.'

As they had bounded up the stairs to her bedroom both had started laughing. If you're going to do 'it' then it might as well be fun as well as a little furtive.

They took care and fumbled with each other and when they kissed they banged their teeth but they held each other and slowly moved together.

Katie Spencer looked up once and from her angle Dale seemed to have absolutely no chin whatsoever but she quickly put this out of her mind. Despite the awkwardness, it really wasn't bad.

She caught her breath and felt warm and comfortable and Dale held her and looked down with gentle chinless concern.

'Are you okay?' he said.

Before she could answer she heard a familiar voice. A loud voice that cut across the hot beautiful day.

'Howwwwwzaaaaaaatttt!' It was the loud man.

She took a breath and smiled. 'Not bad,' she said slowly.

Katie Spencer laughed again. She didn't even know his name. Marto's friend. She was going to ask him what the name of his friend was but stopped herself.

She didn't really need to know, just let him be the loud man who runs around Bull Oval every second Saturday during the summer.

She smiled again. Dale Carter would be there this afternoon. Dale and his wife. She hadn't seen him for a while, but he was still nice and gentle and chinless. It would be good to see him again.

After 'it' they hadn't lasted much longer as a couple, Katie Spencer and Dale Carter, but they remained friends. When they had finished high school, Katie had gone off to university and Dale had gone off to a factory that made tubes.

Couples. Katie Spencer had been a member of a few since then, none too serious, but her mother had liked Ryan, the engineering student, very much.

Unfortunately, Ryan ended up liking women, or as he put it, 'girls' who didn't 'argue so much', which basically meant women, sorry 'girls' who had a brain and an opinion they didn't use or voice.

Long after she'd broken her mother's heart by telling her that she and Ryan were over, Katie had bumped into a man at an accounting conference. Dominic. He was hanging around the biscuit tray and they had laughed because she had pinched the last Monte Carlo biscuit. He was a bit podgy, but really who wasn't? They made each other laugh and he was quite handsome if you looked at him in the right light. Katie Spencer smiled to herself. The right light. Who really cared?

They had been together for nearly six-and-half years and then he had gone and asked her to marry him.

Katie Spencer heard her mother's voice behind her. 'Come on, Katie, it really is time to get the rest of it on.'

Michael Martin watched as the woman at the window turned and said into the room, 'Okay, Mum.'

Katie turned back to Michael and started to give a little wave. Michael thought she was about to go and stopped her with a question. 'Your T-shirt. Do you remember it? You walked down the steps and called to Atticus and you never said a word to me...and you had a T-shirt on that had a face on it, somebody's face. Who was it?'

Katie Spencer knew she should go, but she wanted to stay a little longer. Somehow, she thought, this is what she should do on this day. Remember, a little.

She was surprised that she was able to remember the T-shirt. It was probably because of the connection to her nanna. Like an uncoiling spring her memory shot forward and before she could stop herself she announced, with a clarity and certainty that was acutely embarrassing, the name of the face on the T-shirt.

'Rick Springfield. It was Rick Springfield,' she said.

Michael Martin looked at her and laughed.

'Rick Springfield?'

'Yes, Rick Springfield. It was a birthday present from my sister,' Katie said.

Donna had given it to her with an offhandedness that belied the true importance of the gift. It was 1981, and her sister had given her a T-shirt with Rick Springfield's face on it. It was as close to heaven as anyone could have taken her. She knew this was important because she had seen Rick Springfield on the television. She had seen him and his guitar and his carefully pleated trousers and pop star pout.

She hugged Donna very tightly and when she put the T-shirt on she felt very grown up. Even though she knew that it was an iron-on transfer from *The Sun* newspaper it made no difference. Katie loved her Rick Springfield 'Jessie's Girl' Hitmaker T-shirt.

She was wearing it the day she heard incessant barking from the backyard. She had been lying on the floor of the sunroom, colouring in a competition from *The Sun*'s Kid's Page. She was colouring a picture of Captain Stubing from *The Love Boat*. He was almost bald on the television show and he was supposed to be almost bald in the colouring-in competition, but she had decided to give him some hair. Katie Spencer was admiring the way the orange Texta she used to give Captain Stubing a mohawk was bleeding in with the blue of his skin, when she had heard the barking.

She held still for a while and when the barking went on for a little too long she stood and stepped over the orange cordial her Nanna Bev had made.

Her parents had driven Donna to a netball carnival and so her Nanna Bev had popped over to look after her for the afternoon. Her Nanna Bev always brought over orange cordial.

'It's much better than that fizzy stuff your mum gives you and your sister,' Nanna Bev said. Katie Spencer thought it was funny the way Nanna Bev always complained about Katie Spencer's mum, Nanna Bev's daughter. But she supposed that was just the way grown-ups were.

Nanna Bev always made her cordial much too strong. It was good that her nanna liked to watch television because that meant Katie had plenty of time to tip the sweet orange liquid in the sink or garden and as she stepped over the drink she thought that investigating the barking would also give her an opportunity to do a bit of surreptitious pouring.

Her nanna's voice rang out above the television. 'Katie... Katie, what's that dog barking about, dear? I'm just watching a Rock Hudson cowboy movie.'

'I'll check, Nanna Bev,' Katie Spencer said as she slowly picked up the glass of orange cordial, walked to the back door and peered out. That's when she saw the cricketer perched on top of the fence laughing and Atticus jumping up and down. Atticus was pushing the wet cricket ball with his nose.

'Nanna Bev... Nanna Bev, there's a cricketer after his cricket ball and Atticus is barking at him.'

'Oh, hang on, Katie...' there was a gunshot and loud music. 'There you go! Rock got him. Now, Katie, just go fetch the ball and come back in... You remember what I told you.'

'Yes, Nanna Bev,' said Katie Spencer as she walked out the back door.

She walked down the stairs.

She wore her Rick Springfield 'Jessie's Girl' Hitmaker T-shirt.

She called the dog. 'Atticus... Atticus!'

The dog lolloped over to her as she poured her orange cordial into the pot plants on the stairs.

The cricketer with the nice eyes looked at her and smiled questioningly before laughing. She looked at him, and then took the ball that Atticus had in his mouth, walked up to the fence and handed the cricketer the ball. She didn't say anything, just turned, walked back up the stairs, into her house and went back to her *Love Boat* colouring competition and Captain Stubing's orange hair and blue skin. Nanna Bev was cheering on Rock Hudson as he shot the bad guys.

And I didn't win the contest, thought Katie Spencer.

'I wasn't allowed to talk to you. My nanna told me not to,' Katie Spencer said.

'Why?' he asked.

'Because of some old cricketer. Some fellow she saw at a church match years ago.' She blushed as she remembered what her nanna had recounted many times at family dinners. Nanna Bev called it the Cecil Bull Doodle Incident.

'There he was up in that little scoreboard hut weeing out the window and there was the reverend yelling up at him. I swear I had no idea what it was at first and when I knew, well, what do you do? Really, I'm amazed in a way that I ever had children. I'm sure your granddad missed out on a bit of business because of Cecil Bull... and after he was finished he bent down and looked through the window and he smiled... got the fright of my life. I screamed. Cricketers... and they call them gentlemen.'

After narrating the incident in minute detail Nanna Bev would look at Katie and Donna and wag her finger. 'You never talk to a cricketer, you girls, you just never know.'

'You just never know,' said Katie Spencer to the cricketer with the sunglasses. They both laughed.

'Well,' said Michael Martin, 'thanks for solving those few mysteries. Is your Nanna Bev still alive?'

'Yes, well sort of. She's not very well, anymore... she's in a home... she's not really with it. But we'll give her a piece of cake. Mum thinks she'll like it. To pop under her pillow... to wish on...' Katie trailed off, she really should get ready.

'Cake?'

'Wedding cake. I'm getting married today. Came back last night to spend my last single night here... so we've both come back after being away.'

'So that's your car that's prowling around?' asked the cricketer.

Katie nodded. 'My mother ordered it early.'

The cricketer smiled and said, 'Right, mums can be like that.'

They were both silent and then Katie said, 'Hang a bit.' She ran through her bedroom and down the stairs. Past her mother, who was changing her earrings and talking with her sister Donna and Aunty Carol about how much the function centre had cost but how it was worth it.

'Katie! Where's your dress? . . . You're not in your dress.'

Past her father who was having a drink with the photographer.

'Hello, love!' he said as she passed.

Katie Spencer ran out through the sunroom, down the stairs and across the decking to where the cricketer stood. She balanced on the fishpond and stared into the cricketer's sunglasses.

'Take off your glasses.'

'Sorry?'

'Just take them off for me. I'd like to see your eyes.'

The cricketer took them off. They were still the same blue. But they had travelled, those eyes. Perhaps she may have had a little too much champagne but she smiled at him.

'Those eyes have seen some things, haven't they?' she said.

He squinted and looked back at her. 'Have a great wedding and good luck.'

'You take care . . . Marto.'

Michael Martin watched her run back up to the door and saw a woman standing at the top of the stairs looking down at them.

He stayed where he was a little longer and then turned. There were still a few minutes of the drinks break left and he started to trot over to the clubrooms. As he trotted he started to think. Memories don't take long to move you away from what you are doing. Something can last a few moments but span a lifetime. But Michael Martin knew that memories meant a life lived.

He put his sunglasses back on and put the woman in the window out of his mind. But one thing leads to another. Whatever happened to Rick Springfield?

As he got closer to the clubrooms he heard Chris Andersen's voice booming at Brian. And he thought, maybe today is a very good day.

# One Man's Treasure

Chris Andersen was holding a large foam drink container and was yelling at Brian to hold his plastic cup steady. Chris would never think he was yelling as he talked to Brian, but he was. Anyone there would say so.

'Still, hold it still, don't wave it about.'

Brian was looking in Lachlan's direction and so, as he had done for most of the morning, Chris Andersen spoke to Lachlan as well. Well, he shouted at Lachlan, 'Lachlan!'

What that was supposed to communicate was anybody's guess. But Lachlan Andersen looked back with a steady pair of eyes and walked closer to his father.

'He's worried about that woman over at the bus stop.'

Chris looked at his son as he poured the green Staminade over his boots.

'Bastard.' He looked down at his shoes and back at his son. 'What woman?'

'That woman…that woman…at the bus stop. At the bus stop. She can't speak…she doesn't know.'

Chris Andersen looked at Brian and something flashed across his face. Just for a moment Brian looked a little frightened and then he turned his head to Lachlan. Chris felt somehow he had stuffed up. Why did he always feel that somehow he had stuffed something up?

He hated it when Brian looked like that…he looked at his son and asked, 'Have I been yelling?'

His son looked at him but didn't reply.

'Right, okay.' Chris nodded and put the drink container down. Lachlan hoped his father didn't clap his hands.

Chris Andersen clapped his hands.

'Righto. In here. In here. Everyone in.' Chris Andersen counted his players and looked up to see Michael Martin trotting slowly in from mid-wicket.

'Marto… Marto… in here,' and he clapped his hands again.

Michael Martin walked the last couple of paces and joined the rough little circle that was the Yarraville West Fourths.

'Right. Rob?' Chris Andersen pointed a big hand at Rob Orchard.

'Brian seems to think that woman over there at that bus stop might be in a bit of trouble. If she's waiting for a bus…well?'

Rob Orchard looked over towards the bus stop. The 220 didn't run on a Saturday and he knew that the only other bus that went past that stop only started running in the early evening. Rob Orchard thought a little and looked at Brian, and he smiled.

'You're right, Brian. She'll be waiting there for a while.'

Lachlan looked at his father.

'She's been there for a long time...since I got here...she doesn't know,' Brian stopped abruptly.

Chris Andersen gave him a slap on the shoulder.

'Right,' said Chris. 'I'm sorry, Brian. I'm sorry, mate. You've been trying to tell me about it and, well, there you are. I didn't listen, so I'm sorry.'

Chris Andersen said, 'I'm sorry,' loud enough for the Trinity players to hear. A few of them turned to see him patting Brian's shoulder. Rob Orchard looked down at the ground and smiled. He waited a moment.

'And, Lachlan, I've been...baking you a bit, too. And I'm sorry as well,' Chris Andersen said and he clapped his hands.

Rob Orchard smiled wider and he looked up at Lachlan. The boy gave a small nod of his head and went a bit red.

It wasn't only the music from the house at fine leg that made Rob Orchard feel good about playing cricket on a Saturday.

Chris Andersen picked up the drink container and some plastic cups and then asked Rob Orchard, 'Do any buses run today around here?'

'Down on Barkly Street there's a full service on the hour,' he said.

Chris nodded and indicated for Michael to follow him. 'Marto, can you come and give us a hand?'

Michael looked blankly at Chris Andersen for a moment and then shrugged his shoulders and followed.

Ron Sparrow was putting on his white umpire's hat near the toilets when he felt Chris' big hand gently tap him on the shoulder.

'Now, Ron, give us a few extra minutes would you? We just think that somebody might need a bit of a hand. Might have to walk them down to Barkly Street... Only take a tick.'

'Well, you've still got a couple of minutes of drinks.'

'Won't take a tick, Ron, give us a few extra will you?'

Ron Sparrow took his hat off and sat it down on a bench.

'Well, it's hot enough for a double break. Off you go.'

Ron Sparrow watched the two men walk off. He was an odd lad was Christopher Andersen, the old umpire thought as he watched after the two.

Michael Martin followed, not quite knowing why, and it took him quite a few steps to catch up to Christo. When he did the big man turned slightly to him and asked, 'You find that dog?'

'Well, I found where they buried him. Under a palm tree.'

'Well, that'd be a good a thing to be buried under, I suppose, if you're a dog.'

'I suppose.'

They walked through the gates of the playground and onto the road. 'Christo, what are we doing?'

'This woman,' Chris Andersen nodded his head in the direction of the woman at the bus stop.

The two men stood opposite the bus stop. A woman sat on the seat in the hot sun. She sat with her eyes closed, and they could see she was holding something in her arms.

It was very hot.

'She African?'

Michael stared ahead. 'Christo, you are not going to ask me to converse with this person in African are you?'

'Mate, get a grip. Come on, she's been sitting here in this heat for nearly two hours. I thought you might just have to check her out if she's a bit crook.' He laughed a little. 'Do you talk African, Marto?'

'Fuck off.'

Chris Andersen laughed a little more.

Michael looked at the woman. She was indeed African. He looked at her and he knew there was always a way to make yourself understood, doctors were good at that, and he had learned how to do it. There was always his bad French, more often than not that had worked in the clinics where he had been. He thought a moment.

Michael guessed she was probably from somewhere like Zaire. The way she was dressed in long robes. And she looked quite tall. He looked at what she held in her arms and Michael felt his muscles griping in his stomach.

They stared at her a while and then the wedding limo prowled slowly by with its big red-and-orange indicator flicking. The car slowed and stopped and for a moment the woman at the bus stop was obscured by the car.

The two men saw themselves reflected in the dark windows of the limousine.

They stood there in the dark convex mirror, looking small and dumpy. A bigger dumpy blob of white holding a drink container and a sunglasses-wearing finer blob beside him.

The car slowly moved off.

Uwimana Malanda opened her eyes. The big car was rolling past again very slowly. It was the clicking that woke her. She knew as she heard it that it belonged to the car, for she had heard it before many times during the morning. That long morning she'd waited for the bus in the sun.

Yes, she knew that it was the sound the big car made when it stopped to turn, but the sound was one that led her mind to the sounds of the old rifles being cocked by young boys in uniforms. Boys too young even to know how to playfully aim the weapons at people as they walked the streets into the markets. The sound didn't frighten her, but she couldn't stop thinking of the boys. Some she had seen growing up in the town's outskirts. Some she knew. They would point the rifles at her and laugh. Those boys. Their eyes. How young they were. Instead of a rock or a stick or a ball they played with the long heavy rifles that lay in their laps.

Uwimana didn't want to think of those boys and what had become of them, so she opened her eyes.

The bus must come soon.

The big car moved away and then she saw them. She blinked a bit and then held her eyes shut for a few moments.

Two of them, staring at her from across the road.

She looked at them and the young boys with the ragged military uniforms gave way to the two men in white. Staring at her.

She shifted where she sat on the bench and they moved towards her. They frightened her much more than the young boys with the guns ever did. These men in white. She didn't know who they were. What they would want. She knew they were playing some sort of game. Like the one on the bus this morning. The one who kept looking at her and saying things she didn't understand. Her English was bad, she knew this, her husband told her so. But even she knew that the man in white's words didn't make much sense.

And now these two, from the game played in the park. She moved slightly and she felt him move.

Michael Martin placed a hand on Chris Andersen's arm as they crossed the road. 'She's got a baby.'

Chris looked at him and then smiled at her.

'Hello... Hello. We're just from across the road. One of our friends, Brian, the tall man who saw you this morning, was worried about you... You've been here a long time in the sun...' He smiled again. He offered up the drink and the plastic cups. 'Would you like a drink?'

She stared at them and her bundle made a noise. A little cry.

A small arm reached out from her robes and she tucked it back in again.

The big man with the drink container smiled.

She didn't smile back. She didn't know what they wanted. Did they want her to drink?

She was thirsty.

She was very thirsty.

'No,' she said in her best English. 'No thank you.'

The big man stopped smiling and turned to his friend. 'I don't think she's got much English, has she?'

Michael Martin looked down at her. He thought that his bad French might do better.

'Do you speak English?' Chris Andersen said.

She jumped. He had a loud voice, this man, but she thought she knew what he meant.

'No, little English.'

He nodded.

Michael Martin took off his sunglasses and bent a bit closer.

'Do you speak French?' he said in his staggered French.

She looked into a pair of very blue and very worn eyes. I know the look in those eyes, she thought.

'Yes,' her French was much better than her English. Her husband did not like her to speak in French but she would smile and hold him and say she spoke it better. Then he would smile and he would sit her in front of the television and make her watch the television shows. He would sit with her and they would laugh as they tried to understand what was being said.

Those eyes, she thought, those eyes look sad.

'Right, she's got French.'

'See, you do speak African,' Chris said and laughed.

'Christo!' said Michael.

'Tell her about the buses not running here on a Saturday. They run down on Barkly Street on the hour.' Chris Andersen was nodding and smiling.

Michael smiled slightly and told her in French about the buses.

'Not running today on this street.'

She sighed a long, gentle sigh. Not running today. She had asked her husband if he was sure this bit of paper he had given her was right and he had smiled and assured her it was so. Men.

She felt her son move and she looked down.

The man with the blue eyes asked after her child. He was a doctor, he said. He was worried about the two of them sitting in the heat. It was a dry heat that would sneak up on people who weren't used to it.

She stared at him a moment and then she opened her arms and offered her child to him.

She had no doubt he was a doctor, she had seen people like him before. A kind practised smile and an easy manner. And soon he would give something to her son to play with.

Michael Martin looked at the child. A little boy, perhaps about eighteen months old. He grizzled a bit and so he gave the boy his sunglasses to play with. The little boy grabbed them in a pudgy hand and Michael looked at the child in a manner that was thorough but swiftly done.

Chris Andersen watched his friend. He's very neat, thought Chris, he's moving like the way he took that catch. Very neat.

Michael turned to Chris.

'He's alright, a little uncomfortable but fine. Give him a little water, Christo.'

'Tell her we'll walk her down to Barkly Street if she likes, she'll be able to catch a bus if she's quick.'

Michael Martin asked the woman if she wanted them to show her where to catch the bus.

She looked from one man to the other. 'I gave him some grapes,' she said to Michael Martin.

He smiled. 'I know. We were just worried for you, the other man, and the tall one before, he was worried you didn't know where you were. We're just trying to help.'

She looked at him and smiled. Yes, they were just trying to help. She took a cup of cool water in the plastic cup. It was clean water. She held the cup to her son's lips and he took hurried thirsty sips.

She had said to her husband she would go to the market down in Footscray, to walk around and then meet him at the station. She had directions drawn on a piece of paper. If she caught a bus now it would be good because she would be in time to meet him.

The bigger man spoke. 'Tell her it won't take long, it's just down the street.'

Michael told her and they waited as she stood and gathered her string bag and steadied her son. Together they walked across the road. They walked down the street that ran along the edge of Bull Oval, the street that the wedding limousine had turned down.

The woman walked slowly but with sure strides and Chris Andersen noticed that she was taller than Michael Martin. He also noticed that Michael was very quiet.

'How long has she been here?' Chris asked Michael.

Michael asked her.

'Two weeks,' she said. Two weeks she had been living in the flat that her husband had organised for them. 'He has lived here longer; I only just arrived,' she said. She did not want the men to think that they had no home or that they had so little. She was proud of her husband.

Michael Martin told Chris Andersen what she had said.

Chris laughed a little to himself, he was asking how long she had been at the bus stop, but she did not need to know that.

'Well, two weeks, it takes two lifetimes to make sense of bus timetables over here,' Chris Andersen said. And he fell quiet for a bit and they walked on past the oval. Brian waved to them. Chris waved back.

Uwimana Malanda saw him waving. She said in French to Michael Martin, 'I didn't know what he was trying to say, your tall friend.'

Michael nodded. 'Sometimes he is hard to understand. I don't know him that well.' He pointed to Chris. 'He knows him well, I think.'

Uwimana Malanda looked at the man with the blue eyes; he had put his sunglasses on. These two, she thought, looked like friends. The big man who limped a little and this man. The big man let the other be silent but she noticed how the big man would look every now and then at his friend.

She spoke again. 'Your game is an odd one.'

Michael smiled. Chris looked at him. 'What did she say?' he asked.

'She was commenting on our game.'

'Tell her I'm fielding because I lost the toss,' said Chris Andersen.

Michael smiled a little more. 'She says it's an odd game.'

'Well, maybe it is. But you know it's a little like a bus timetable... you'll suddenly understand it one day and everything will become clear. I'm sure her boy will understand it,' said Chris.

Uwimana Malanda looked at Michael Martin.

Michael Martin looked back at her. 'He says that the game is like a bus timetable...'

She laughed and smiled. 'Yes, you have an odd game.'

'My friend thinks your son will understand it one day, it takes a little time.'

She listened but didn't say anything.

She liked this country, she thought. Her husband did. But there were things to get used to. Like bus timetables and odd games and all these things on the pavement.

All morning, while she had been waiting for the bus, she had seen people throwing things, good things they seemed to her, out onto the footpaths. So many things. And the big car they were walking past, why did it drive around and around?

Chris Andersen looked down at the bonnet of the limousine that was now parked outside the house that backed onto the oval. The car had two dolls on the front of the bonnet, a Barbie doll and a GI Joe. The female doll was in a wedding dress and the male doll had a scar down one side of his head and his big plastic jaw locked in grim Marine determination.

Chris Andersen looked at the dolls and thought of the boot camp Wobblies at the gym that morning.

'She's getting married,' said Michael Martin as they walked past. He said it again in French.

Neither of the other two said anything. Uwimana Malanda thought how white the doll looked, how yellow her hair and how white the little dress she wore. White. She looked at the two men in white clothes who walked with her.

They stepped around a washing machine and some garden furniture placed on the footpath and she said, in English, 'So much...many things. So much.'

Chris Andersen and Michael Martin looked at her.

'Hard rubbish weekend,' Chris said and then he thought and added, 'Well, I don't suppose you can really translate that... Just stuff... things people don't need anymore... it gets picked up...'

'So much things,' she repeated.

Chris Andersen looked at the street, this street where he lived. It was littered with many things. He didn't know exactly where she had come from, this woman, but he knew that she didn't grasp the concept of what she saw. And he realised he didn't either. He suddenly felt a little defensive.

'Tell her it's just stuff, looks wasteful and it probably is, but you know... this is a good country.' He smiled and waved his drink container. 'A good country... not perfect but a good place.'

Michael Martin wondered why Chris Andersen had bothered to try to explain, but he told the woman what his big friend said.

She smiled at Chris Andersen.

'Not a great country, and that's good, great countries want to run around proving they are great countries. No, it's a good place this... good to try things... good to have a life... by and large... I hope you'll be happy... and you know... thanks for coming.' I have no idea what I am talking about, thought Chris. He nodded to the woman and tripped over an old rake that someone had left out.

Michael Martin said roughly what Chris had said and Uwimana Malanda nodded.

How lovely that someone would thank her for coming to live here. She knew it would not always be easy, but for the first time that morning she felt like she belonged. Like she was welcome.

She knew it would not be easy and there were things she did not understand, there would be people who perhaps did not want her here, but this big man in white made her feel better. She smiled.

'Thank you,' she said in English.

'Well, there you go,' said Chris Andersen. He still felt a bit defensive, for they had passed a rather large pile of rubbish, outside a comfortable but messy looking home.

Chris Andersen looked at his home. He looked at his pile of rubbish. There was another man looking at it; from the front seat of an old Ford station wagon. He saw that their own car wasn't in the driveway. Julie must have taken Moira off somewhere. He kept walking. She was right, he thought, this woman is right, there is so much stuff. So much shit on the streets. All the effort that went into making it, selling it, giving it, and now disposing of it.

They walked on until they came to Barkly Street. Chris looked at his watch. 'You should make it, there's still time.' He smiled despite his foot being a little more than sore.

Michael Martin pointed at a bus that was slowly crawling up Barkly Street. 'You still have time,' he said in French.

'This one goes into Footscray,' Chris Andersen said, and this time Michael didn't have to repeat.

The woman nodded. 'Fotts...sray Foots...sray,' she said softly.

The bus lurched closer and the two men stood aside, the bigger one holding up his hand clutching the drink container.

The bus pulled to a halt by the metal sign. The doors gushed opened and the air-conditioned interior hummed invitingly.

'There you are, that's a bit cooler for you,' said Chris Andersen.

Uwimana Malanda got out the card her husband had given her and placed it in the ticketing machine. But just before she took it out she looked back at the men.

'Thank you,' she said again in English. She thought of the man in the sunglasses and she thought of the boys in military uniforms and the guns sitting in their laps. She thought of their eyes. Their eyes were the same. They had seen things that eyes shouldn't have to see, she thought.

So she added in French to the man in sunglasses, 'Be kind to yourself. Thank you.'

He didn't say anything. The big man waved. She sat down and cuddled her son.

She looked out the window and the two were moving off back up the street.

Before the waste had angered her. But now, even though she didn't understand it, she smiled and kissed the head of her small son and said to him softly, 'A good place, a good place.'

Hard rubbish, thought Chris Andersen. Hard rubbish.

The man in the station wagon was still there near his house. Chris had seen him earlier that morning. When they had gone down to the pool he had seen him looking at his pile of hard rubbish.

It was the fan, thought Chris Andersen. He was looking at the fan.

'That's my pile,' said Chris to Michael Martin.

'Sorry?'

'My rubbish, that's my home.'

Michael Martin looked at the rambling house, half-brick, half-weatherboard. It looked like a nice home. He looked at the rubbish. It looked like a nice pile.

'Good rubbish, Christo,' he said.

'Yes,' said Chris Andersen. As they walked on he looked sideways at the man in the wagon. 'He's after the fan,' he said almost to himself. Michael didn't bother to reply and kept walking.

He'd been prowling around the streets for a good while, but this time he looked like he might mean business. That is what Chris Andersen thought. It looked like it was a big decision for him.

He was serious alright. Chris watched as the man unbuckled himself and heaved his large frame out of his station wagon. He was still unsure. He stood looking down at the fan.

Chris Andersen looked at the man staring at the old fan that he had placed on the pile of discarded treasures. Why on Earth would you deliberate so long over rubbish?

He had bought that fan about five years ago, from a man in an electrical store. He had a name badge that said 'Dwight'. Dwight had a lisp and a very bad toupee. Chris Andersen wondered what had happened to that man. Their only connection, the fan, was now on the street. Dwight's fan lay there tempting the man with the station wagon.

How many times was this scene played out around municipalities and suburbs right throughout Australia? Hard rubbish day. The day when ratepayers and renters, home owners and millionaires can pile their unwanted hard rubbish out on the nature strip in front of their homes and wait for the council to remove it.

So many peope throw out so many things. So many broken dreams and good intentions. You only have to look at the amount of fitness equipment that decorates the nature strips at hard rubbish time to see that. Thigh crunchers, abdominal flexers, even the mighty bullworker can be seen gathering dew on suburban lawns.

Those dreams of six-pack stomachs and bustling muscles seem achievable when demonstrated on television, but it seems that realities set quicker than instant glue for some and out go the fitness tools.

And televisions. By the hundreds. Big old fake walnut jobs with names of corporations long-evaporated by mergers, rationalism and time. Thorn. Rank. Pye. Fallen gods of the lounge room.

It is oddly touching seeing those old tellies outside with the rubbish. They stand stoically, almost like pets, on their four squat legs. Their blank tubes reflecting the coming and going of the streets.

Chris Andersen thought of the time he had stopped to look at a washing machine on one hard rubbish day. It was outside a house in one of the more exclusive and leafy Melbourne suburbs. He had become increasingly embarrassed as he was poking around. This was where Julie had grown up. This was where his girlfriend and wife-to-be had lived. She knew these people and they would know that he was her boyfriend. They would see

183

him and tell her. Or worse still, they would tell Julie's mother. Even Chris Andersen knew some of the people who lived here.

He decided he needed a washing machine and this one looked alright. He opened the lid to check it out properly only to find the machine was chock full of what, in the politest term, are commonly known as 'marital aids'. All sizes, shapes and colours. He slowly closed the lid and stared down at the virginal white enamel of the machine. Out of the corner of his eye he thought he saw some movement at a window. A curtain being hurriedly drawn. He slowly walked back to his car. He was blushing. After a few moments he said to himself 'Guess whose Mum's got a Whirlpool'. He drove off through the streets trying not to imagine the contents of all the washing machines he saw.

The best thing he'd ever found was a poker machine. It was turfed on the side of a street. Royal Flush it was called. He was with Livey, walking back from a pub one night. Livey was so taken with it that he coaxed Chris Andersen into helping him take it home for 'me shed'.

They struggled and lugged the Royal Flush over three suburbs and two bus routes to place it proudly in Livey's shed.

The thing that amazed Chris Andersen was that nobody seemed to notice that these two boofheads were wobbling around with a poker machine. Indeed, the only recognition they received was when a bus driver charged them extra for 'the pokie' because he'd thought that 'it was the only time he'd ever get a bit of money from the bloody things'.

Chris Andersen had known people who had picked up mounted heads of animals, a wedding dress and a suit of armour. Not from the same pile of rubbish, of course.

Once, coming home from work, Chris narrowly rescued his new set of golf clubs from the hard rubbish pile in front of his house. He asked why they had been thrown out. Moira, who was three and a half at the time, said she had 'thought that our rubbish wasn't as good as the neighbours', so I wanted to add something special'.

There's an interesting thought. People being judged on what they throw out. Hard rubbish as a status symbol.

What would people think of my rubbish? Is it good enough to look through? Well, the big bloke was still looking at Dwight's fan. He thought of Dwight again. Chris Andersen remembered he spat when he spoke. Dwight assured him that the fan was a bargain.

In the afternoon heat Chris watched the big bloke bend down and scoop up the fan. He shook it and seemed satisfied. He tucked it under his arm and stuffed it and himself back into his station wagon. And went on his way.

Chris and Marto walked past the wedding car and back onto the oval and Chris Andersen suddenly remembered that Bull Oval had once been a tip.

'Jesus, that's where all the rubbish goes. All the shit we forget. We bury it... And then we play cricket on top of it.' He laughed a little and looked at Michael Martin. 'Come on, Marto, we'll get this thing over with. Matt Halley, you're up!' he yelled.

Michael Martin followed quietly behind. Maybe we don't bury it deep enough, he thought, although he didn't say it.

# The King Bowls

A game of cricket, in its strictest sense of classical clichéd description, should ebb and flow like a tide. There should be swings and roundabouts. You should take the good with the bad.

Ron Sparrow threw the ball to Christopher Andersen. Well, thought the old umpire, there hadn't been much ebbing and flowing. The swings had no roundabouts and from the Yarraville West Fourths' viewpoint there had been a grain of good to take with the sacks full of bad.

It was now very hot and that quiet, which is a characteristic of park cricket, began to fall.

Standing there in the middle of the oval on that hot summer afternoon, Ron Sparrow thought of how quiet it was out there. There was the talk and the noise of the players, but that was only close in. The slips and perhaps the cover fieldsmen. Yarra West always seemed to chat amongst themselves. It was out there in the outfield that the quiet would settle.

He looked as Chris Andersen threw the ball to the chunky little right-armer called Matthew Halley.

The new batsman was taking guard. He asked for middle and Ron Sparrow gave it to him. The new batsman was the scorer for the Trinity team and so a new scorer had to be found amongst the Trinity contingent.

If the new scorer had any sense he wouldn't ask the name of the bowler. But most people who have never scored before or who are relatively new to the whole idea of filling in the cryptic sheets will cling to the set routine of the scorer's guidelines. Namely, to ask for the bowler's name when the new over commences.

This should be a pretty straightforward system. Cricketers by and large are a relatively conservative lot and closely adhere to what the appropriate behaviour should be. But there are some teams that, in a time-honoured tradition, will always give in to the temptation to, as the great expression readily describes, take the piss. Though these same teams will remain deadly serious in their endeavours on the field.

Ron Sparrow knew that the Yarraville West Fourths were just this side. He called out to the batsman, 'Right arm over, batsman.'

The batsman nodded. Matt Halley came and gave him his hat.

'What are you bowling, Matthew?' asked the old umpire.

Matt Halley smiled. He looked down at Livey. 'What am I bowling, Livey?'

Livey snorted. 'Give us a bit of the Kenny Loggins-cum-Kevin Bacon, mate.'

Matt smiled at Ron Sparrow. 'Right arm over *Footloose*, Ron,' and he wiggled his shoulders.

Ron Sparrow stared back down at the wicket. I do hope the scorer doesn't ask the name of the bowler, he thought.

There was silence and then came the plaintive call of a new scorer. 'Bowler's name?' cried the caller.

It wafted across the sun-baked oval. It didn't help that the scorer had a lisp. Ron Sparrow heard Chris Andersen and Livey Jones laugh.

'Holt, Harold,' cried out Matt Halley and he rolled the Rs of Harold in his best Henry Higgins voice.

There was silence.

'Thank you,' yelled the scorer.

There was a bit of laughter from the Trinity benches.

It was just as well that Ron Sparrow wasn't watching. He hadn't seen *Footloose*. *Footloose*, a pinnacle of bad hair, tight stone-washed jeans and weird-nosed American actors.

*Footloose*, the height of the eighties. *Footloose*, the story of a dance-loving teenager with an odd nose from Chicago who shifts with his family to a small Midwestern town with a strict code of moral beliefs. Namely, no dancing and no rock and roll. What exactly rock and roll meant in the 1980s was anybody's guess but here in the small Midwestern town the teenager from Chicago falls in love with another teenager with a funny nose from the small town with moral beliefs. Together they teach the town how to live! And dance and rock and roll. Whatever that may mean in the context of 1984.

'Oh, yeah, come on Harold, let's have some *Footloose* line and length!' cried out Livey Jones. '*Footloose*, Christo, a golden moment of cinema from 1984!'

'1984,' repeated Chris Andersen. 'That is a fair while ago . . . I was twenty in 1984.'

Twenty, and he was peering through a washing machine in Mont Albert packed full of dildos. He didn't share this thought with Livey but he laughed.

'1984,' he said again.

'Yes, mate, the Orwellian *1984*. Old George Orwell might have thought he wrote about some scary shit, but his *1984* and Winston Smith had nothing on the jeans Kevin Bacon wore in *Footloose*.'

Chris Andersen laughed. 'We are doing well. We've had Kenny Loggins, Winston Smith, Kevin Bacon, Harold Holt and George Orwell all mentioned before the first ball after drinks.'

'What are you saying, mate? Are you saying butchers shouldn't bloody read?' snorted Livey and he farted for good measure. 'Let's go, Harold!'

Ron Sparrow could hear the talk and the laughing. 1984. A long time ago, thought Ron Sparrow. I would have been on the reserves up in Queensland. A long time ago.

Yes, it was just as well Ron Sparrow hadn't seen *Footloose* and it was just as well he couldn't see Matt Halley, for if he had he would have had absolutely no point of reference for what a stocky, epically high-panted humanities teacher with a goatee beard was actually doing when he came in to bowl.

Matt Halley went back almost to the straight boundary and then he started his run-up. It was in this forty-metre run-up that Matt managed to make a great statement about the ludicrous inanity of a whole decade.

He flung his arms this way and that, pivoted on his toes and shook his head. He did something particularly odd with his face and eyes that drew a moan of recognition and an appreciative round of applause from the Trinity benches.

Matt Halley was *Solid Gold*, the *Countdown* dancers and even a little bit of Tony Bartuccio and the *Saturday Show* rolled into one stocky piece of human bravado. He finally arrived at the crease with an almighty piece of Kevin Baconing that made even Livey Jones nod in admiration.

The batsman took a step and although he smiled, he belted the poor little red sphere inside out for six.

'You should have stayed on that Chinese submarine, Harold,' came a cry from Trinity.

'I don't really think I'd want to do that again, go to *Footloose* land,' said Matt Halley, with his hands on his knees.

'Go a different decade, Harold,' sang out Livey Jones, as the ball was returned to the bowler. It rolled close to Matthew Halley and stopped, the way a fearful dog might behave.

'Oh come on,' said Matt, clicking his fingers at the ball. 'Come on, come here. Anyone got any suggestions?' he asked.

From out at mid-wicket Michael Martin had something to offer. 'Go Rick Springfield.'

Livey Jones looked out to Michael Martin. 'Rick Springfield, this'll test him,' he said.

Matt Halley laughed again then stood stock-still and rubbed the ball across his groin the way Rick Springfield played his guitar in his clip for 'Jessie's Girl'. All pout and bad masturbatory wrist and arm action on the strum. Just for added value Matt Halley threw in a hyperactive knee bend.

Livey Jones turned breathlessly to Chris Andersen in the slips. 'You can almost see the pleated pants, can't you? You'd have to pay that one!'

Michael Martin laughed. A big laugh. He hadn't expected to and that's what made it even better.

Matt Halley stopped Rick Springfielding and pranced in what people took to be a Mick Jagger leg break.

The batsman tried to hit the ball too hard and he only managed to bring his bat through too quickly and push the ball backward of square leg for a one.

This brought the opener on strike.

Matt Halley bowling as Harold Holt got hit for two fours. Chris Andersen muttered to Livey Jones that, 'Maybe I should get Ben Chifley to bowl.'

'Couldn't do any worse than Harold.'

Matt Halley looked to Ron Sparrow. 'How many left?'

'I'll be kind and tell you it's one.'

Matt nodded and looked at the ball. He rubbed it on the back of his bottom and winced. He'd rubbed it on the part of his bottom that had been hit by Brian's wayward throw. He changed cheeks and then looked pleased with the shine that he managed to achieve.

'Give me the King.'

Matt Halley looked up. 'Sorry?'

It was Ron Sparrow. He'd made a request. 'Give me the King. Give me a bit of old Elvis.'

Matt Halley looked at the umpy and squinted a bit.

'Vegas or pre-Vegas, Ron?' he asked.

Ron Sparrow knew he really shouldn't be encouraging this sort of behaviour but it *was* the last game of the season.

'You've only got one ball left so you better give both.'

'Right,' said Matt Halley.

He turned and spoke to the batsman, who had remained unsmiling through the over. 'My idea is to start with a bit of *Blue Hawaii* type movement and then bring it on home right through the decade from *It Happened in Rio* to *Charro*. Okay?'

The batsman looked at Matt Halley. 'Dickhead,' he said.

Matt Halley laughed and strutted back to his mark. He tugged his pants a bit higher and wobbled his legs a little. Then he wobbled them a lot and ran in, wobbling his legs even more, and adding an odd leering with his lips. He also managed to elicit and cajole some wriggling from his hips. What he bowled he couldn't tell you too much about. He just let it go somewhere out the back of his hand.

The ball pitched on a length and moved back towards the batsman, and if he hadn't been in such a hurry to bully the stocky little bowler he might not have tried to hit the ball as hard as he did.

He didn't move his feet, unlike the bowler who hadn't been able to keep his still, and he tried to push through the shot. He got a nice thick edge on the ball and it cracked into the stumps.

'Bullshit!' cried Livey incredulously.

'I'll take that as an appeal then,' said Ron Sparrow.

'Thank you, very much,' Elvised Matt Halley.

'You're a dickhead, Holt,' sneered the batsman as he walked.

'That's no way to speak to a Prime Minister,' Matt Halley said as he took the slaps on the back from his teammates.

'The batsman has left the building,' added Livey.

Chris Andersen shook his head. 'It's a bit sad, you know, that bloke thinking your name is Holt.'

Livey called out to the departing man, 'Hey, mate, you've just been bowled by a fella who's been dead for forty years.'

The batsman looked back and then muttered a few words to the incoming batter. Dougie yelled out from the Trinity benches, 'Well bowled, Harold!'

Matt waved back.

He turned to Chris Andersen. 'Christo, you want me to keep going?'

'Yes, do you mind, Harold? We'll keep you going for a while. I've got two left so I'll bowl myself out and we'll share the rest. Brian, you feel like a bowl?'

Brian shook a little convulsively. 'Oh, Christo...'

Chris Andersen looked at him and held up a hand. 'It's alright, mate...you'll be right. I just thought you might want to have a go.'

Lachlan looked at his father and at Brian. Brian slowly nodded. Lachlan started to say something but stopped himself in front of all the people. He looked at his father and he knew that his father was thinking about something else.

Chris Andersen shook his head. 'I can't believe that fella thought you were Harold Holt.'

'Oh, come on, it's a long time ago,' said Matt.

'Yeah...' said Chris.

'People forget, Christopher,' said Ron Sparrow, holding out his hand for the big man's cap. 'People forget.'

Chris Andersen stood for a few moments and looked at the old umpire. 'Did you vote for him? For Harold Holt.'

'Right arm over, batsman,' Ron Sparrow said to the batter. 'Yes, I did as a matter of fact, even if he did bowl like Elvis Presley.'

'Bowler's name?' the scorer called out.

'Fraser, Malcolm,' cried Matthew Halley.

'Thank you,' the scorer replied.

Dougie laughed. 'It's Chris Andersen, you dill...he's the captain.'

'Thank you,' the scorer said again.

Chris Andersen limped back to his mark. Jesus, even old Mal Fraser. Everyone forgets. Has to happen to all great men. Would you call them great? Well, everybody knew who they were when they mattered. But to be forgotten. That's a little sad. To be forgotten. And then he saw her. It was only yesterday.

The way she had sat on the review panel, all pressed suit and attitude. She hadn't recognised him. He was forgotten.

'Thatcher's fascist thugs hands off Malvinas,' he said as he spread his field. The first time he saw her was nearly twenty-three years ago. She stood by a small card table that was covered with ordered lines of pamphlets. She was packing the pamphlets into a backpack and had a bundle of International Socialist newspapers by her feet. Chris Andersen was heading off for a beer with a mate.

He and his mates would go down into the city to the Tenants Hotel, where lots of students would go drinking. He had often passed the card table covered with multi-coloured pamphlets. Usually there was a small, odd-looking bloke, who Chris knew slightly from an elective humanities tutorial, looking after the table. Garth. Chris found this slightly amusing because Garth was a name that seemed completely unsuited to him. Little bits of spittle would gather in the corners of Garth's tight mouth when he spoke, which was quite often. He spoke with great excitement in a high, torn voice. He looked emaciated and half mad.

The table belonged to the International Socialists and even though Chris Andersen was hardly a Liberal, he never could bring himself to flip through the pamphlets on the table. Garth wouldn't help matters, either, when Chris tried to pass with a blokey nod of greeting, 'Not interested in the truth? Not surprising,' Garth would say and spittle would fly from his mouth.

'Wanker,' Chris would say under his breath.

He moved Tim One to short mid-on and then back again.

Lachlan, watching from deep mid-off, knew his father was thinking about something. Chris Andersen waved his arms about and moved Tim One back to short mid-on.

He started running in and then lost his run-up. He stopped, held up his hand and walked back to the top of his mark. As he did he moved Tim One back to a deeper mid-on. Yes, thought Lachlan, his father was thinking about something.

He was. He was thinking of that day when there was no Garth behind the International Socialist card table. Instead, she stood there.

The afternoon light streamed through the trees on Swanston Street and a streetlight shone above her even though it wasn't yet dark. She looked like she had stepped down from another planet.

Chris Andersen stopped and stared. It was her attitude as much as anything else. She stood there almost daring people to laugh, to mock. Funnily enough, nobody did. For some reason, Chris Andersen thought of the woman from *Heart of Darkness* on the banks of the river. The way she stood staring after the boat carrying Kurtz away. Standing there with her arms outstretched.

Fuck, thought Chris. I haven't even had a beer yet and I'm thinking about stuff I've read in a humanities elective. This could be serious.

She was holding out a pale blue pamphlet. In that light it matched her green eyes beautifully. He didn't know what to look at, her eyes or the pamphlet, so he looked at both.

He stared into those green eyes and then looked at the face of Malcolm Fraser. He wasn't sure if he was in love but Chris Andersen knew that if he looked back at those green eyes he might find out.

This time he kept his rhythm and the batsman played and missed.

'Good bowling, Mal Fraser,' Livey cried out. The boys didn't want to let a chance for a running joke go by.

It was one of those moments when attitude and atmosphere and something in the universe all collide and something in your brain tells you this is it. Well, maybe it was. Your brain can sometimes bullshit you.

I must tell Lachlan that, Chris Andersen thought, and that your heart is different from your brain.

He could have said something really witty and clever, instead he came up with, 'Where's Garth?'

She looked at Chris Andersen with her green eyes. 'Garth's running late. I'm filling in.'

'Need a hand?'

Chris Andersen's mate snorted, 'Get real,' and he walked off into Tenants Hotel.

'Are you interested?' she asked

Chris only had the pamphlets to go on and he hadn't really read them. But he knew Malcolm Fraser was involved somewhere.

'I've always had time for Malcolm Fraser.'

'Malcolm Fraser?' Her green eyes narrowed.

'Yes...' He stared and had no idea what to say. 'As an International Socialist.' He tittered a bit and she thought he was trying to be funny.

She nodded and they stood together handing out bits of paper that lionised Senator George Georges, and demonised poor old Malcolm and Maggie Thatcher and Ronnie Reagan and just about everyone else. He shuffled through the pieces of paper; a purple pamphlet had Allende on it.

'I admire him so much, he was a brave man.'

'Yeah,' he said. Even *he* knew who Allende was and knew he was a brave man.

The next ball was wide and the batsman left it for Livey Jones to take. Well, that was the theory.

She looked at him and weighed him up; Chris Andersen looked at her and was completely swallowed.

His next ball was straight and just short of a length. The batsman probably thought about a pull shot, but that was after he padded the ball back down to Chris Andersen. He practised the shot but Chris paid no attention.

Allende. He stayed when he could have run. He stayed. She had never said why she thought Allende was a brave man. Chris looked down at the ball. It mattered to somebody, didn't it? That sort of courage, to stay when you could run and then to die for something you believe in. Maybe Allende didn't think about it until he had to. And today nobody, thought Chris Andersen, nobody would probably remember him – well not here.

'Who do you admire?' she had asked.

And he had stared back at her. Sadly he heard a voice and knew it was his own.

'Allan Border,' he said, staring into her eyes.

She looked at him and then smiled. But not at him. She looked through him, past him. Garth had turned up. And he came over to the card table and bent down and kissed her. 'Come on, Gwen,' he said.

What was worse was that she kissed him. And her name was Gwen. 'Do you mind handing out the weeklies, brother? We're a bit late for a meeting,' Garth rasped. 'Just cry out the banner headline, that'll let people know what the story is.'

Chris Andersen had just looked at him. Garth. At the spit gathering in the tight little corners of his mouth.

Garth looked back at this big boofheaded law student.

'Well? Well? What don't you understand?'

Gwen looked at Chris Andersen.

'Just read the banner headlines. See? "Thatcher's Fascist Thugs, Hands Off Malvinas!"'

'You want me to yell that out?'

'"Thatcher's Fascist Thugs Hands Off Malvinas!"' said Garth, the spit building up. I have seen dogs do that, thought Chris Andersen.

'You want me to say that in the street?' asked Chris.

'Are you worried about that?' Gwen said.

'No, nobody seems to be paying any attention.'

'That's not the point. The point is that it is said,' Garth replied. So he said it again.

'"Thatcher's Fascist Thugs, Hands Off Malvinas."' He yelled it and nobody paid any attention.

'What are the Malvinas?' he asked.

'The Argentinian name for the Falkland Islands,' said Garth.

Chris Andersen bowled a ball that was straight and the batsman whacked it onto the bat and it rolled to Matt Halley.

The Falklands War... There always seems to be a war somewhere, thought Chris Andersen. And people forget them too.

The Malvinas.

'Well,' said Chris Andersen. 'Well, why... isn't Thatcher democratically elected? Aren't the Argentinians run by the military? A junta... they're the sort of fellas that killed Allende.'

Garth looked at Chris Andersen. 'It's not that simple. Just yell out the banner headlines.'

'I don't think people will buy many,' Chris said.

'They are fucking handout papers,' said Garth.

Chris shrugged. '"Thatcher's Fascist Thugs, Hands Off Malvinas,"' he said. Nobody paid any attention.

Garth and Gwen walked away to their meeting.

He packed up the card table and popped the pamphlets in a bag and left them in a neatly stacked pile on the pavement underneath the streetlight.

As he walked away he turned and glanced at the pile. Sighing, he walked back and started to fold the pamphlets. Then he yelled in a strong clear voice. '*Daily Sun*! *Daily Sun*! Get your *Sun* newspaper!'

People who had hurried by before stopped briefly and bought the paper without looking. The afternoon rag.

It didn't take long until he had enough to go to the pub and buy himself several drinks.

And he never saw Gwen again, until yesterday.

Until that afternoon in the review panel. The jewellery she wore around her neck and wrists could have paid off the mortgages of lots of people. She was dressed in a suit, her hair lashed back in a bun.

As Chris Andersen delivered the last ball of his over he heard her voice and saw her green eyes pretending to be hard and shrewd, so he didn't really notice how the ball very nearly sneaked under the bat.

She didn't get unions, she said. She had forgotten Chris Andersen.

'Bowling! Bowling!' clapped both the Tims.

He nodded his head vaguely. She's probably forgotten a lot more as well.

He thought of Garth and how he had laughed at a funny little man with a tight mouth who wanted his idea of the truth told in the street and he thought of a man called Allende who chose to stay and died when he could have run and lived. And of Malcolm Fraser and of Harold Holt and everybody who had ever been forgotten.

He thought of green-eyed Gwen. And he felt a little sad.

After bowling an over like that, where he had beaten the bat, drawn false shots and had the batsman beaten inside out he felt a little sad.

What was it that woman had said? An odd game. An odd game.

Then Chris Andersen laughed. Who had he admired? He looked at nobody in particular. 'Allan Border,' he said and laughed even louder.

During the next hour or so many prime ministers of Australia bowled. Stanley Bruce, looking a lot like a young under-17 called Tim One, bowled some pretty lame deliveries in his second spell and got carted by batsmen who threw the bat at anything. Tim Two, renamed Ben Chifley, toiled away manfully but got similar treatment, even though he managed to pick up the wicket of the Trinity scorer, who gave him a nod for well bowled but added that he should lay off the pipe-smoking.

The boy looked a little perplexed. Ron Sparrow smiled and told him Ben Chifley smoked a pipe a lot.

The boy looked at the umpire.

'That's what probably did him in the end. He wasn't a bad fellow, though.'

The boy nodded.

'Look him up in a book, mate,' said Livey Jones. 'He was a good one, Ben Chifley, good on the big picture, big heart.'

'What about mine?' said Tim One.

'Stanley Bruce,' Ron Sparrow said and winced. 'Well, he wore spats. If you don't know what they are you can find out about them in a book.'

'Yeah,' Harold Holt said in agreement from the covers.

'You saying butchers don't read?' said Livey.

Michael Martin came in and bowled a few left-armers. He was dubbed Gough Whitlam.

'Thank you,' said the scorer with a resigned tone.

'A leftie!' Harold Holt said.

Michael Martin didn't really look that interested in the game anymore as he was plastered to all points of the compass.

He had a slow, precise action but didn't really try to do too much with the ball.

Chris Andersen looked at him. 'I'll have to sack you, I'm afraid.'

'Well, you're the man to do it, Mal,' said Livey Jones.

'Yes. It's time,' said Chris Andersen.

Bob Menzies, looking a lot like Rob Orchard, replaced Gough. He wasn't treated with much respect and Chris Andersen stood next to his wicket-keeper and folded his arms.

Menzies' lack of success could have been put down to the fact that Rob Orchard had been waiting almost all of the first innings to have his whistled first few bars of 'Twinkle Twinkle Little Star' answered.

He had waited and no answer came. Perhaps, he thought, she won't come. But she had to today. It was the last game of the season. He began to worry a bit. After all, he did owe the house by fine leg so much.

He had seen Chris Andersen waving to him and he had turned and waited before he moved towards the bowling crease. He'd been listening to a boy called Max having an introductory trombone lesson. Rob Orchard looked at his watch, about five minutes to bowl an over and this lesson had nearly gone its half an hour. He had run in and been given the ball.

'Bowler's name?' came the expected cry.

'Menzies, Bob,' yelled Livey Jones.

Rob Orchard had got through the over as quickly as he could and even though the batsman took to him he finished roughly within his time budget. He returned to the fence line and Max was still farting his trombone up and down the scales, sounding for all the world like Livey Jones.

A double lesson, he thought.

Rob Orchard felt a pang of disappointment. It didn't really matter if she didn't come, he told himself, but it would be a bugger. Yes, it would be a bugger. This game was almost gone and the day was still hot and it was getting on. Getting on. He was a man who ran his life to schedules and he was always searching out clocks or glancing at his watch.

Rob was constantly measuring away the minutes of his life. Be at a street by 7.55, wait at the stop for the minimum amount of time so a steady travel flow for a trip could be established but give the maximum amount of time to the customer to get on the bus.

Someone, somewhere, in some office determined the maximum amount of time that a customer had to get on a bus was twelve seconds. Twelve seconds. When the time was up, off you went. He was supposed to look at the clock on his dash and leave when the twelve-second period was up. Invariably, people would be launched down the aisle of the bus, grasping at the hand straps. Sometimes they were sent lurching into other customers.

Sometimes Rob Orchard could make out some sort of driver retribution if a person had been rude or unpleasant, or just seemed to be deserving of a bit of justice. He would tap the accelerator before the twelve-second mark and send people bouncing on their bum.

But Rob Orchard was careful. He knew that these things, once started, can lead anywhere.

He had done that occasionally to a bad-tempered woman and look where that had ended up. The bad-tempered woman worked at a rather antiseptically sinister building with long dark glass windows in Spring Street. She once accused Rob Orchard of being lost.

The fact that Rob was lost had nothing to do with it, drivers got lost all the time. Not epically lost, but sometimes your mind drifted and a turn went by and all of a sudden you knew that this route wasn't where you were supposed to be.

When that happened, you didn't need some twerp yelling at you, 'You're lost!'

This is what the bad-tempered woman did. 'You're lost,' she said loudly from the first row of seats.

Rob Orchard didn't say anything for a moment. He'd been thinking of Vaughan Williams. How soft his melodies were and, on a grey day like today, how warm they made him feel. They probably were a little too accessible and people who really knew music would sniff at them. But he had been introduced to Vaughan Williams by Sarah and the quiet-voiced teacher by the house at fine leg. He loved having something to sing in his mind and to hum while he drove.

Yes, he liked Vaughan Williams.

But now he was just trying to think of where he was and how he could get back to his set path. He looked at his dash clock. He looked ahead. He saw he'd just entered a street that had become one way.

'You're lost, aren't you? It's alright for you... I haven't got this time to waste,' said the bad-tempered woman. She had a very sure sounding voice. She, thought Rob Orchard, is a person who likes telling people what to do.

'Just trialling a new route,' Rob Orchard said. Nobody else had even bothered to look up to see where they were.

Rob turned down an even narrower one-way street that led back to his set route.

The woman sniffed and said, 'Lucky... you were lost. Simply not good enough.'

Rob looked back at his dash clock and saw that he was only a minute down.

The woman almost smiled at Rob. 'I know you were lost, I know.' After that day, whenever the woman got on the bus she would look at Rob Orchard.

'Going to get lost today?' she would ask in a tone that was almost polite.

Throughout the trip Rob Orchard would catch her staring at him in the mirror and he would look away. When she did it once too often Rob Orchard gave her the twelve-second treatment.

Rob checked his mirror and saw the woman wasn't holding the hanging strap. He pressed the accelerator pedal just under the twelve-second mark and the bad-tempered woman went bumping off into a pole. She turned and looked at the mirror, Rob's eyes met hers for a moment. The woman stared back.

The next morning the woman was readying herself to sit when Rob Orchard beat the twelve-second mark again. She was bundled into the seat and bounced back and forth like a doll. She looked up to the mirror and saw Rob's eyes looking at her again. Rob held her eyes and raised his eyebrows in question.

'Enough?' was what the look communicated.

The bad-tempered woman didn't sneer, but looked a little longer and then tidied herself.

The next morning as the bad-tempered woman got on she stopped by the driver's window on her way to validate her ticket. Rob Orchard didn't look at her and only turned when he heard a slight, almost embarrassed tapping.

The woman had put out a flat, square package wrapped in brown paper. Rob Orchard took it and then looked up at her but she had hurried off down the aisle to claim a seat. He looked at her in the mirror but she did not return his glance.

After the bus had emptied in the city and the bad-tempered woman had walked away into the crowds of people, Rob Orchard unwrapped the package. It was a compact disc. A recording of Vaughan Williams' 'Lark Ascending' and his Sixth Symphony.

Rob Orchard stared at the compact disc. He had been humming a movement from the Sixth the morning he had driven off route. He turned the compact disc over and saw a small scribbled note.

'Enough,' said the note. There was a P.S. 'What do you think of Elgar?'

Rob sat for a bit longer and instead of having a small break and drinking tea from his Thermos and reading the horoscopes and form guide, he darted out of the bus. He had enough time to do what he had in mind.

The next morning the bad-tempered woman got on and went to validate her ticket. She was stopped by what she saw by the driver's window.

Rob Orchard had slipped through a small rectangular package wrapped in brown paper. He held it with his fingers but looked ahead. When he felt the package move he let go.

Rob looked at the bad-tempered woman as she found a seat. She didn't look up but slipped the package into her bag. He watched her during the trip but couldn't tell whether she had opened the package. More people got on and he lost her behind the passengers in the aisle.

He never saw her unwrap the package containing a compact disc of Elgar's 'Cello Concerto in E Minor'.

He had fussed so much when he had run into the music store. There were four versions to choose from, and so he had listened to snippets of each and had closed his eyes and thought of which one made him think of Bull Oval and the house at fine leg. He chose Yu-ning Lee, and ran back to his bus.

He arrived at a stop and some of the people in the aisle moved out the side door of the bus and, just for a moment, for only a few seconds, Rob Orchard saw, reflected in the mirror the bad-tempered woman smiling, looking down at something she held in her hands.

More people got on and stood in the aisle and he lost her in the mirror. In those minutes Rob Orchard felt like giggling or laughing and he felt acute pangs of nervousness and even fear, as if he had made a fool of himself and then he would almost giggle again. There is a saying, 'Catching your breath' and that is exactly what the bus driver did. He caught his breath and hoped for the best and looked in the mirror.

Then...there she was standing almost behind him, and she was smiling. She moved closer to the driver's box and the bus halted at a bus stop. Longer than the twelve seconds that somebody sitting in some office somewhere decided was the amount of time to give passengers to get on and off a bus.

The bad-tempered woman and Rob Orchard looked at each other and he smiled.

'I did get lost,' he said.

She laughed. They stared for a little longer and he said, 'Catching the bus tomorrow?'

She smiled and she nodded. 'Of course,' she said. He watched her as she walked through the people in the street and she turned and smiled again before she disappeared into the white building with the long, dark windows.

Rob Orchard smiled and then he looked at his dash clock. He'd been there for nearly half a minute. He put his indicator on, put his foot on the pedal a little too enthusiastically and eight people in the bus almost fell on their arses.

Rob Orchard and the bad-tempered woman, who he came to know and love as Maria Dimitriou, had been together nearly three years. He had discovered she really wasn't that bad-tempered and they had been happy in the company of each other's arms.

He always felt that he owed Sarah the cellist so much more than he had ever given her. He had stood and listened to the music and learned about what she played and he had listened and learned from the quiet voice of her teacher.

He knew that other students he had listened to and liked had come and gone and he knew that Sarah would one day move on. She'd go and play her music somewhere else.

Rob Orchard looked at his watch. The innings would finish soon. Then lunch. The break between innings. Sarah usually played before the break. Max's trombone moaned on. He suddenly wished he could have told her how much she had given him. He wished he had already thanked her. He would today. That is, thought Rob Orchard, if she plays.

He had that on his mind as he ran and bowled, so that is probably why Bob Menzies got carted around the ground.

The Trinity total had climbed to well over two hundred and fifty runs and it continued to accumulate in the dying overs before lunch. Livey Jones gave the gloves to Matt Halley and came on to bowl as Billy McMahon. If it were possible, he was a worse bowler than Billy was a prime minister.

'Why the fuck couldn't I be Keating or Gorton or Hawkie?' moaned Livey.

'I don't really think it would be fair to them to have you bowling in their name,' Chris Andersen said. 'I believe Billy McMahon suits you down to a tee.'

'Piss off,' snorted Livey and, just for a change, he farted.

The batsman laughed and Livey turned to him. He turned around and farted at him. Over his shoulder as he walked back to his mark he said. 'Go on, smartarse, hit that for four.'

The men around the wicket laughed. Even Ron Sparrow smiled. From down at deep mid-on, just down by the fence, Lachlan Andersen could hear the laughter. It floated in the air and died just short of him. It was as if the laughter was never really meant to include him or be for him, only for the men in the middle, in the engine room of the action.

Lachlan would play cricket in the juniors and would watch the other players, how they all wanted to bat or to bowl. To be close to the wicket, to be a tangible part of the action.

He enjoyed that as much as anyone, but it was out here in the deep near the boundary that he found himself. Out here watching, listening to the laughter and a joke from the middle die before it reached him. It looked like fun, the way they were laughing in the middle, even though the runs were coming too fast.

He knew that there wasn't really much you could do when you were two men short, a cricket field was a big place and two men down left a big hole.

The Yarraville West Fourths hadn't won a game all season. They had come close and had drawn a couple because of rain but they had not won a game all season. There was no doubt they were losing this one, too. The way things were going they would probably lose outright. His father hated that.

To fall short of the run total set by the opposing side was okay, a part of cricket, but to lose all your wickets twice and fall short of the total was something that Lachlan Andersen's father never liked.

He would yell most likely and be bad-tempered for a while and then he would start to laugh and become himself again.

Lachlan looked at his father. He wished his father would listen more, see more. Brian had wanted to bowl, he had been so excited at the prospect he could hardly contain himself. But perhaps his father was right, it might not have done Brian any good to be belted around the park.

Lachlan could still hear the Trinity team members laughing at Brian occasionally and the big fast bowler from grade cricket would sometimes prop up on an elbow and moan, 'It's not your fault, Brian.'

Sometimes people laughed. Sometimes they didn't. Perhaps they didn't hear, or pretended not to. Lachlan knew that Brian heard every time they said it, because he would look over to Lachlan and he would smile and nod.

Lachlan knew his father heard and he wondered slightly what he might do, and then he wondered what Atticus Finch would do.

He was old enough to know that people like Atticus Finch didn't really exist and he thought that he could never imagine anybody doing what the character did in the book. Standing in front of the people of the town where he lived telling them how to live and what was right and what was wrong. He couldn't imagine anyone doing that anymore than he could imagine anybody fighting with light sabres and going in search of magical rings.

The ball suddenly streaked out in his direction and Lachlan Andersen felt that surge of mild fright and apprehension that happens when the game in the middle stretches out to the fielders in the deep.

As the ball came closer, he heard someone call, 'Yours, Lachie.' Well, thought Lachlan Andersen, whose else would it be?

Don't muck it up, even though we are getting thrashed, don't muck it up. He turned his body side-on to the ball, knelt on one knee and cupped his hands. His body covered the trace of the ball just in case it jumped up off the ground.

The ball came closer, a red ball skimming across the green of the oval. Closer and closer. It smashed into his cupped hands. He felt his hands sting and as he picked himself up and threw the ball back to the bowler, his right hand tingled from fingers to the palm.

'Well fielded, Lachie,' Livey Jones cried out.

His father raised a thumb to him.

Lachlan Andersen didn't nod back, that's not the thing to do, not for a normal bit of fielding.

'You've got a good arm for a young fella!' said a voice.

He looked around and saw a man walking slowly around the boundary with a small boy. The man held the boy's hand.

Lachlan nodded and smiled.

The man smiled and squinted past Lachlan and at the pitch. 'How are you going?' he asked.

'Getting flogged,' said Lachlan.

'Oh well, it's not a bad day for it. Have a good one,' said the man. He walked on with the boy.

Lachlan looked after them.

'Yes, they're playing cricket...Come on, the playground's over there...' said the man to the boy. The boy sang and pointed.

Lachlan watched for a little while and his fingers still stung. He rubbed his hands and walked backwards to the boundary line. Out in the deep. He liked it out in the deep. By himself, out in the deep. Out here in the deep there was so much space and time seemed to stand still or drift any which way.

Sometimes he would close his eyes and listen to the sounds of cricket in the park. He could hear the vague and intermittent chat from the middle and the occasional peal of laughter.

He could hear the droll prolonged tones of the batting side lounging around their benches. They were winning, they were confident, untroubled.

He heard the fast bowler from the District Grade most of all.

Lachlan knew he was making jokes but he couldn't quite hear, although he heard 'walkabout' and 'brudder' and 'Abo' mentioned, so he guessed that the fast bowler was making fun of the father and the little boy who were walking around the boundary line to the playground.

They were Aboriginal.

Lachlan knew that beyond that chatter, if you listened really carefully, you could find that layer of noise, that symphony you could hear as you stood on Cec Bull Oval playing cricket.

A plane flying overhead, banking noisily into Melbourne Airport.

The music from the house where Rob Orchard stood, the odd explosion of an instrument.

A baby crying.

A lawnmower from some backyard.

A car driving past.

The small boy calling out to his daddy.

Dogs barking.

A bang from the shunting trains down at the railway.

Someone singing in a foreign language.

And the fast bowler mimicking it for no reason.

Some laughter.

Sometimes all he could hear was the sound of flies.

Lachlan liked to hear the orchestra that surrounded him in the deep. Now he could hear himself, his own breathing.

He was puffing a bit and his hands still stung. A cricket ball is hard and sometimes it can come to you very quickly, it can interrupt thoughts you may have sailed away on. That's why he liked it out in the deep.

Alone, beneath the big empty sky that seemed to have no lid, no top. Lachlan looked up and smiled. That's what Brian had told him once.

He called to Brian.

Brian looked over. 'The sky, Brian, what do you think of this sky?'

They both looked up, up into a blue sky that seemed to stretch forever. Well, it stretched for as long as it was blue and then it became black and there was space and there was, whatever there was.

'This is a sky with no lid, Lachie,' sang out Brian and he raised his arms above his head and stretched and he laughed. 'I can't touch the sky!'

Lachlan smiled. His father yelled. 'Lachie! Brian! Come on, come on. The game's down here!'

They nodded and Lachlan looked over to Brian. He was looking at Lachlan and wiggling his fingers and mouthing, 'Can't touch the sky.'

Lachlan looked back to the pitch. From out in the deep it seemed a long way away. In the background he could see that the playground was starting to fill up with children. Families from around the streets, from the flats nearby, were starting to walk down. They would reclaim the park from the cricket.

He could hear the children talking as they walked on their way to the playground.

Lachlan looked at two girls on the roundabout and he remembered how much he liked the roundabout when he was a kid. He loved lying on his back on top of the roundabout and looking at the sky.

A blue sky with no top, no lid, is a scary thing when you think about it too much.

What is above me? Around me? There was a time when Lachlan thought that people lived up there.

His nanna said that one Christmas when he was a little boy. He'd gone out to the backyard after he pinched an extra cracker, because he wanted to find another little water pistol in the middle of the cracker cylinder.

He had thought he could hide behind the big rubber tree and break the cracker open. But he had found his nanna there first. She was crying a little and had a drink in her hand and a hanky.

She turned when she heard Lachlan.

'Oh, hello. Come on, come here for a cuddle.'

He wandered over, trying to hide the cracker, but then he saw she was reaching for it. 'Come on, let's pull the cracker, darling...darling Lachie.'

She was crying. Her eyes were all black.

'Nanna's a little upset, sweetie, a little upset,' she said and she took the end of the cracker.

He held his end and waited to pull but she let go and said, 'Nanna is just thinking about Uncle Tony...he's not here... and you didn't know him... Uncle Tony.' She smiled at him.

'Uncle Tony is...' She seemed not to know what to say. 'Uncle Tony is up there with the angels...' She broke off and then grabbed onto the cracker again and pulled.

'Uncle Tony's up there,' she patted him on the head and sniffed a bit and walked quickly back into the house.

She had won the water pistol and had taken it with her. She was upset. Lachlan could see that.

That day Lachlan turned his eyes up into the blue sky. A brilliant blue sky. Uncle Tony's up there. And he went back inside to try to find another cracker.

He never heard anybody else offer anything about his Uncle Tony. He had seen pictures and trophies but really all he could remember was that blue sky. He knew Uncle Tony had died. Up there.

A part of him had always thought that blue skies meant death. Blue skies turn into black. Black turns into space and vacuum and satellites and then just...space.

It was a little scary, a little odd, for even though he liked to be alone out here in the deep he didn't like that feeling of being completely alone.

Perhaps that is why people invent things to explain away the nothing, the blackness, the space. Like Nanna. Up there.

He heard his father's voice.

'Lachlan!'

Much like before the ball raced across the grass and he did as he had done before and cupped the ball in his hands, but this time as he got up he held the ball tightly a little longer before he threw it.

He threw the ball in.

Brian sang out, 'Good throw, Lachie.'

He smiled.

'Last ball of the innings, last ball,' cried Livey Jones. And he Billy McMahoned a beauty. A ballooning, fat, masochistic full toss that just screamed to the bat, 'Hit me!' And the bat did just that and a bit more.

The ball flew high over Brian's head and flailing arms for six.

Six off the last ball. Trinity's benches broke out in applause. The end of the first innings. The end of the first forty overs. Three hundred up off forty overs. Three hundred.

'That's lunch, gentlemen,' said Ron Sparrow, gently lifting the bails from the wickets.

Lunch, thought Rob Orchard. Lunch and she hasn't played yet.

Lunch, thought Lachlan. I wonder if there'll be cold pizza.

Lunch, thought Michael Martin. A little pill would be good.

Lunch, thought Chris Andersen. Lunch and they've scored three hundred. Outright. Outright defeat.

Lunch. Ron Sparrow waited near the pitch for Brian to bring the ball to him. He watched as Brian walked towards him.

Brian held the ball in his hands. He held it as if he were about to bowl. His fingers running along the worn seam. The ball had been so shiny and hard at the start of the innings. The Kookaburra gleaming gold on the face of the deep-red leather.

Brian felt the worn leather ball. This ball had been alive once he thought. It had been a cow.

He stopped gripping it so tightly.

He liked cows. He liked to go see them at the Melbourne Show. He liked the smell of them, the dairy cows. They had nice big eyes and were warm to touch. So big.

All those big cows and this thing that used to be a cow... he held in his hand.

He was walking now and he thought about cows. He liked them. And he knew he liked sausages. He felt a bit sorry. Poor cow, he thought, and held the ball quite gently. Poor cow. He mooed a little and patted the ball with his other hand.

He knew it was just a ball. But he thought he owed it to the cow to remember what that ball had once been.

He looked up and saw the umpire. He gave the ball to Ron Sparrow.

'Thank you,' Ron Sparrow said. 'Lunch now.'

'I've got sausage sandwiches,' Brian said. He walked happily towards the clubrooms humming to himself.

The old umpire trailing not far behind could have sworn that the tall awkward lad was softly mooing to himself.

# Secrets

The players milled about aimlessly, as people do who are waiting for food. They attended to the usual pre-lunch necessities – the checking of bets that may have been placed on that day's races, the skiving off around the corner to have a fag, the checking of messages left on phones.

Trinity had given Yarraville West Fourths an almighty hammering and so they lazed about like old plantation owners from the Deep South, waiting for their banquet to be presented. They laughed easily and a little too loudly for the liking of Chris Andersen. An outright defeat, that's what ran through his head. They all think they're going to get an outright over us and we've got to feed them, too.

The fielding team, Yarraville West, trudged back to the clubrooms and followed their own set practice of commiserating with each other as they rummaged in bags and kits for nothing much in particular and then headed into the rooms to prepare the lunch.

Lunch was really more like a big afternoon tea. Some clubs went to a lot of trouble and care and some clubs did what they could. Yarraville West did what they could.

The trestle table was draped with a plastic tablecloth that had the pattern of woven rope printed on it, as well as the saucy remnants of other home-game catering efforts.

'Oh shit, somebody didn't wash the tablecloth,' Livey Jones said.

'Don't worry,' Matthew Halley said. 'Just cover it with a couple of plates.'

'You're all class,' muttered Chris Andersen as he walked to the big fridge where the lunches were stored.

Chris reached in and grabbed two more drink containers and saw Michael Martin's bottles of Coke and Mars bars sitting on top of a rather dubious collection of pizza boxes.

'Jesus, we haven't just brought cold pizza again, have we?'

For some reason known only to themselves there were times when the remnants of a week's pizza activity found their way to the cricket lunch-break table rather than the bin. This was one of those times.

Tim One said that he had brought two packets of chocolate biscuits and Tim Two said he had jam doughnuts.

'Come on, Christo, Rob would have brought some sangers,' Matt Halley said. 'Some of these are gourmet pizzas, you know.'

'How old are they?' Chris Andersen asked.

'Well, that doesn't really come into it. Age becomes elastic when you are talking cold pizza. It's been in the fridge.'

'How old are they?' asked Chris again.

'Half the marinara is a leftover from last night, there's a bit of a supreme from . . . I think earlier in the week . . . and I can't vouch for Livey's,' Matt Halley said.

'Where's your gourmet pizzas? Which box are your gourmet pizzas in?' Chris Andersen asked.

'Well, the supreme was a gourmet . . .' Matt stopped when Chris pulled out a pizza box and opened the lid.

'That's not a gourmet pizza . . . it's got that shredded ham, that pink shredded ham on it. Gourmet pizzas don't have shredded ham,' Chris Andersen said.

'It became a gourmet pizza after ageing in the fridge,' Matt Halley replied.

'Look, you can't just have all this cold pizza, it doesn't look good,' Chris said.

'I've got proper gourmet pizza,' said Livey Jones. And he flipped up a lid on one of the pizza boxes.

'Oh, come on,' Matt said and laughed.

Chris Andersen looked at the pizza. He looked a bit longer.

'You put tinned spaghetti on it. Is that tinned spaghetti?' he said, looking at Livey, and Livey Jones nodded. Chris Andersen continued, 'You have put tinned spaghetti on your pizza.'

'On my Hawaiian pizza.'

Christo shook his head. 'Is that the same pizza or is it a couple of different pizzas thrown together?' he asked.

'I like to think that this pizza with tinned spaghetti, and it's name-brand spag, mate, none of this home-brand stuff, I like to think this pizza represents a coming together of . . .' he paused.

'Yes?' said Matt. Chris Andersen looked on and Livey paused a little longer.

'Of different bits of pizzas,' Livey finished. Then he poked Chris Andersen with his pizza box. 'Okay, Captain, where's your pizza?'

'Julie's bringing down a tray of fruit, so no pizza, just a tray of fruit.'

Rob Orchard shuffled past with his carefully cut egg and lettuce sandwiches. Rows of sandwiches cut into neat little triangles.

'She played yet?' asked Chris Andersen.

'No, not yet,' said Rob Orchard as he peeled the plastic wrap off his sangers.

Brian came loping in with a plateful of cold sausage sandwiches and some lamingtons.

'Your mum make those, Brian?' Chris Andersen asked.

Brian shook his head. 'No, she did not, but she bought them with me... I like shopping with Mum.' He laughed a little as he spoke.

Chris Andersen patted him on the back. 'Then you're a good man,' he said.

The motley crew of Yarraville West Fourths brought the food out to the self-satisfied plantation owners and spread it out on the table so it covered the stains from the last home game.

Michael Martin straightened the tablecloth and as the food was placed down on it, he pulled his hand away and looked down at the red sauce sticking to his fingers. It had a coagulated feel to it and he rubbed it between his fingers before he reached down and grabbed a paper napkin printed with smiling sausages and hamburgers wearing sunglasses.

He rubbed the sauce off his hands. His fingers were sticky. It was very hot and his head felt empty.

Michael looked at the food, if you could call it that, that was placed on the table. Cold pizza, biscuits, chips, some volcanic-looking doughnuts, neat little home economics triangular sandwiches, big square sausage sandwiches, lamingtons and, courtesy of him, a bag of Mars bars and some bottles of Coke.

'A meal fit for a king,' Livey Jones said.

'On a bad day,' Matt Halley added. People laughed, including the plantation owners from Trinity.

Chris Andersen didn't smile as he placed an ice-cream container on the table. He clapped his hands.

'Now, just before you dig in, here's the container for the umpy's fee. Just pop your five dollars in there and we can look after Ron Sparrow.'

'Pop in a bit extra and he might look after us,' Dougie, the Trinity captain said.

There was more laughter from the plantation owners.

'Like we'd need it,' muttered the fast bowler from the higher grades.

Chris, Michael Martin noticed, didn't laugh. His jaw tensed and his eyes flicked to the fast bowler. Poor old Christo, thought Michael, but then, if Michael Martin was being honest about it all, he didn't care that much about winning or losing. He didn't really care that much about the food. He thought he might go wash his hands and open up the bottle of pills he had stashed in his pocket. Michael was worried about what thoughts might fill his empty head.

'Pretty interesting looking spread we've got here,' one of the Trinity players said to Chris Andersen. 'Lot of work's gone into those pizzas.'

Michael Martin looked down at the garish collection on the table, already being fingered by the players.

'Oh, who cares, I'm starving. I'll eat anything,' said a beefy plantation owner.

'Oh baby,' said another.

Michael looked at the smiling sausage on the napkin, it was winking. He remembered standing behind barricades watching food supplies be delivered to a mass of starving people, people who hadn't seen food for weeks. The military peacekeepers had told the medical staff not to do anything, not to interfere, to stay behind the barricades.

Some of the people moved as if in a dream and others moved like frenetic insects, like the desperate people they were. He remembered standing against the barricades looking at them. He didn't know what to feel.

A Russian doctor who smoked like a chimney and drank even more came over to share the view.

'You're Australian, aren't you?' he asked as a fight broke out between three men over a sack.

'Yes,' Michael said.

'Australia,' inhaled the Russian, 'Australia...you know I have been to Australia once. In the seventies. I go with a group of doctors. To look at your hospitals. We are taken to a show, you call it, a show with tractors and rides and all sorts of things...a...'

'A fair like a big agricultural fair?' Michael Martin said, as one of the men fighting over a package was pushed to the ground.

'Yes...' said the smoking Russian. 'Yes... it was an outing. We were taken to this fair and we went to a hall.' He paused and inhaled a massive drag of his cigarette.

The man on the ground who had fought over the sack tried to stand. He was clinging to the sack, but he had no strength. He fell and clutched at the hard dirt.

'And in this hall was food. Not just food, but fruits I had only ever dreamed about. Pineapples and strawberries and mangoes... mangoes,' he said incredulously. 'So much fruit, beautiful fruit. There was so much and it was laid out... laid out in patterns. At first I couldn't see why the people had placed the pineapples in with melons, and berries in with apples.'

The man on the hard dirt looked like he was trying to moan but no sound came out.

'And then I saw that this fruit made a picture, a rough, odd picture of a kite... of a boy holding a kite.'

The smoking Russian shook his head. 'So much food and you made pictures out of them, not even good pictures I might say.' A long stream of smoke blew from his nose.

'I asked the man showing us what would happen to the food and do you know what he says?' The smoking Russian smiled. 'He says... throw it away, mate.' The Russian tried an Australian accent... badly.

'I almost felt like crying. Australia... It must be nice to come from a place like that. Where you can make pictures with food. Australia.'

They said nothing more. Michael Martin could almost see the Hall of Agriculture at the Melbourne Show. He had always thought the fruit and vege displays were daggy.

The man on the hard dirt wasn't moving much anymore and the other two men struggled on against each other and stumbled off into the crowd, throwing weak arms at one another.

They were told not to do anything, they were told not to interfere. They looked at the crowd of starving people as you might look at a dull pond.

The sounds of the cricketers eating and a bottle of Coke being opened echoed inside his mind. Michael closed his eyes, even though he wore sunglasses. He knew where this was heading.

He knew now, as he knew when the smoking Russian told him of the bad fruit pictures, that there were people with nothing in Australia. You didn't have to go to Africa to find starving people. But it didn't matter anymore. He got up and walked towards the toilets, it was time for a pill.

As he turned to go he saw the wedding limousine. It turned by the playground and a window at the back came down and an arm pointed out.

'She's giving us a wave, look,' somebody said. Some of the players waved back.

Michael Martin stared at the car and the waving arm. He guessed it was him she was waving at. But he found he couldn't wave.

She was right. His eyes had seen some things. He raised his arm but realised he was in the shadow of the awning so she couldn't see him. He suddenly felt old and a little tired, but he also knew where it was heading. He rubbed his fingers and his hand again with a paper napkin. He rubbed as if he were trying to push something from his skin, to brush something away.

Michael turned and walked to the toilets and as he did the wedding car moved slowly on and the hand stopped waving. The window went up.

Katie Spencer's father, Murray, tapped her gently on the arm.

'Don't get yourself messed up, Katie... your mum will go spare, it took long enough to get you ready.'

Katie Spencer didn't say anything and kept waving.

'Who are you waving at?' her father asked.

'Oh, just... anybody.' She laughed a little. She couldn't see him. All the cricketers were gathered around under the roof of the clubrooms.

'I hope they do okay,' she said.

Her father found it difficult enough trying to say something to her without her playing silly buggers and talking about the cricket.

'Hardly, they're the Yarraville West Fourths... they're getting hammered, I'd say.' He sounded more gruff than he meant to. He didn't want to get too mushy, he didn't want to cry in front of her.

Murray Spencer held his daughter's hand. He clutched it tight and he felt a burning in his chest. He was driving with her to her wedding and even if she wasn't a little girl anymore she was still his daughter. He went to say something and his voice broke. He tried again and she turned to him.

'Katie,' he said slowly. 'Katie... I know the fella you're marrying is a good boy... and you've been together for a bit –' His daughter went to interrupt but he held up a finger on his other hand. 'Just you listen... you're my daughter, my girl, and nobody will ever be good enough for you. Nobody.' And he held her hand and gently kissed it and he wound the window up.

'Now, just keep yourself nice.'

Katie Spencer held her father's hand and watched as the cricketers disappeared from view.

It was a time for fathers.


Barry Andersen rolled his car into the car park and then heaved himself from its comfortable seat and walked toward the Bull Oval clubrooms. As secretary of the club it was a part of his duties to drop around to the team playing at home, to check how the game was going and see if they needed anything.

It was a pleasant enough job, tooling about and having a bit of a chat and he always liked popping in to Bull Oval because Chris and Julie lived just down the road. He liked to drop in, he liked to do that, to catch up. To see how the kids were. He liked doing that, just to see if everything was alright.

Lachlan was playing, and he knew that he might get to see his grandson bat. He liked to see the boy bat.

Barry moved slowly but he moved that way because he chose to. Yes, it was good to make sure. To see if everything was alright.

Livey Jones was the first to see him ambling across the car park. He had just eaten a piece of his Spag Hawaiian and he was washing it down with a plastic cup filled with Coke. He saw Barry Andersen and was about to tell Chris, who was standing next to him but with his back facing the oval, but then Livey thought he might knock back the fizzy drink first and then tell him.

Unfortunately for Livey Jones, when Spag Hawaiian meets the still bubbling contents of the night before's lamb vindaloo and then is doused with bubbly caffeine, the best efforts at communication are dealt a severe blow.

By the time he had stopped burping and spluttering, Chris Andersen had disappeared, proclaiming as men often do without any real need that 'I'm off for a leak.'

In truth, Chris wasn't just going to have a leak, he was busting. He was limping and he was getting narked off with the probability of an outright defeat. He hadn't had time to go to the toilet because he had walked that woman and her baby down to Barkly Street to catch that bus. So Chris fairly stomped into the small toilet area, pushed open the door and bumped into Michael Martin just as he was unscrewing the cap of the little white plastic bottle.

The impact of an increasingly bad-tempered Chris Andersen sent the little plastic bottle flying onto the floor.

'Sorry, mate,' Chris said.

'Oh shit,' said Michael. He could see that not all the little pills had spilled out of the bottle but he didn't fancy picking up the others off the toilet floor.

Chris looked down at the little white bottle and then looked back at Michael.

'You right?' he said.

'Oh, yeah, I'm great,' said Michael Martin.

It was a moment when somebody needed to be clearer about what they actually wanted to say, but that is not something that men are always that good at.

Michael wanted to forget or, at least, just dull things a little, that's why he reached for the plastic bottle. Chris Andersen wanted to pee. That is all. He needed to pee. That was his one intention at that moment and he didn't have any other purpose. So when he entered the toilet and saw that Michael Martin was there he was narked in that way that a person needing to go to the toilet is narked.

It was okay, though, he'd scoot around outside and have a leak amongst the banksia trees. But then Chris wondered if Michael Martin had finished and so he asked him, 'What are you doing?'

But it was the way he asked him. It was an open-ended question: 'What are you doing?' When it was asked it could refer to almost anything.

'What are you doing?'

When you think about it, it is a question that covers a whole horizon of subject possibilities and how it is answered depends upon the person of whom it is asked.

Michael looked back at Chris. 'What am I doing?' he repeated slowly, and he said it as if he were asking himself the question.

'What am I doing?' he said again.

Chris Andersen looked at his friend. Chris wanted to pee.

'Just trying to forget, I think. Yes, I think that's what I'm doing.' Michael stopped and met the eyes of Chris Andersen. 'You know...' and he shrugged.

'What?' he said.

'You know, Christo...you know... I want to try and forget that shit happens...that bad things happen to people...for no reason and, well, they just happen. Just want to forget it for a while.'

Chris bent down and picked up the pill bottle.

'Well,' Michael continued, 'I can't forget that things happen, that's just life, isn't it, Christo? I just try to forget some of those things... That's all...you know what that's about, don't you, Christo?' Michael Martin said.

'I don't, I just came here for a piss,' he said.

Michael stood up and held out his hand. Chris Andersen gave him the small white bottle.

'I wouldn't worry about those ones on the floor,' Chris said.

Michael smiled. 'You are a good bloke, but it's not just walking somebody to a bus stop...you know life isn't about stuff like that.'

Chris Andersen stopped worrying about wanting to pee and he looked at Michael. 'What do you mean?' he said softly and he placed his hand gently on Michael Martin's shoulder. 'Michael?'

Michael didn't know what he really meant and he started rubbing at his hand. Suddenly he heard himself speaking and once he started he didn't want to stop. As he heard his voice he knew where it would lead.

'I've just seen stuff, you know. People have seen worse and function with it okay. I've seen things...I've given people immunisations for one disease knowing that they'd be dead of something else in another week or two. I mean, it doesn't make a lot of sense, really, but...' Michael could see where this was heading and rubbed his hand.

His mind went back to that clinic on the border and that one man. And his eyes, that man's eyes.

'I've seen people die before, you realise. I have seen a few... and a lot who didn't. But there was one man...one man... and he came into a clinic station on the border. He'd lost his family, he was the last of his family. Most of the time you just tried to treat them, make them as comfortable as you could. There was so much cholera, people living on top of each other. The water wasn't clean and people were riddled with disease.'

As he told Chris Andersen he saw the man's eyes, dark eyes, and how on that last night those eyes wouldn't leave him. He was delirious, Michael supposed. He was dying.

'And I knew that if I gave him something to calm him down, to make it easier for him, then it would...be good, I suppose...and I went over to this guy, and I was going to give him some morphine and he just grabbed my hand.' Michael held out the hand he had been rubbing. '...and he held my hand and he looked at me and you know, he wasn't delirious. He didn't want anything to make him better. He wanted to speak, he wanted to remember.'

The man had little English but had enough to make himself understood. His grip was strong for a man who was so weak and his eyes, his eyes looked almost apologetically into Michael Martin's eyes, as if to say sorry for taking up too much time. But this man had wanted to speak and he decided Michael was the one to hear.

He and his family had walked for weeks to get to this camp. His wife had died first, she was already weak from carrying the child who had died when he was born, the man said. She had been a good wife and a good mother. You must know she had always done all she could, but she grew weak and was so sad. The man's son died next, he told Michael Martin, the boy was good, he was a boy who was sometimes lazy, as boys can be, but he was a good boy and he was a good son and made the man feel proud. The man said his daughter had died only two days from the clinic. He had carried her. She was quiet, his daughter, but she had always helped when she could and he only carried her when she could walk no further. He had carried her, singing to her, said the man, and she had died as he sang.

The man looked at Michael. 'They were my family, and now I am dying. I tried to be good,' said the man. 'I tried to do what I thought was right. But now I will die.'

The eyes of the man almost smiled, and a look of unbearable kindness crept from them as he spoke softly to Michael Martin.

'I am sorry. But I have told you of my family, of me… soon I will be gone, but please, you will remember?'

He held Michael Martin's hand and he hummed a little song. He held Michael Martin's hand. And then he died.

Of all the things that he had seen, it was the kindness in those eyes that haunted Michael the most.

He laughed and said, 'It's a prick of a world, Christo. Yesterday I sat looking at some silly bastard's dick when he came asking for a referral to a specialist for a penis enlargement, he wanted to renovate. He wanted to because he wanted to and I signed the referral. It's a prick of a world.' Michael Martin's laugh was a little sharper when he stopped talking.

And then he looked into the eyes of his big, bad-tempered, loud friend.

Chris Andersen's hand was still on his shoulder. 'Listen, Michael, I can't begin to imagine some of the shit you've seen and this fellow's wanger yesterday seems bad enough.' Michael laughed. Both men did.

He listened as Chris Andersen went on, 'And maybe you can take these things to help you get through, maybe,' he tapped the little white bottle. 'But don't give things away. Don't forget just 'cause it's hard. That man, the man who held your hand, mate...he gave you the last thing he had. He gave you his life and that is...well, fuck...that is something. You're a good man, Michael, and if it makes it easier...you know. You've told me. I'll help remember.'

Michael Martin looked at his friend and wondered how such an awkward communicator could possibly earn his living as a lawyer. Then he saw something, or rather heard something as he looked at this big boofheaded broken-down fast bowler and the understanding in his face. He heard his grandfather. 'It's an awful thing to look inside a man and see through him. To see his secret. It's an awful thing but a good man can take that secret and turn it into a better life.'

Michael Martin felt something. Perhaps he had felt it for longer than he knew, but could never explain. He felt ashamed. Ashamed that a man, a man who lay dying, a man whom he had barely known, had let Michael see his secret and had given him the story of his life so that it might be remembered by someone. It was a secret. A story that was awful, a story of beauty, a story of love and life. It was a story Michael Martin had been given and had tried to forget. He looked at Chris Andersen and went to say something, but this time no words would come. He remembered the kindness of those dark eyes and he knew he would not forget. That he could remember.

He still wore his sunglasses and even though he did he closed his eyes. For the first time in a very long time, in a funny set of clubrooms at Bull Oval, he cried.

He felt Chris Andersen's hand leave his shoulder.

'You'll be right...just don't come out crying because it'll look like we're sooking about the cricket,' Chris said.

It wasn't much of a joke, but Michael Martin tried to smile a bit and nodded his head.

Chris shut the door and turned around to the entrance of the clubrooms.

He was upset. He knew that he was upset, at himself, he thought. There he was a few minutes earlier pissed off about getting beaten outright. Holy Christ, he thought. This life, this world. What the world could do and be.

Chris Andersen saw Lachlan in the corner by the fridge. His son was going through a kit bag and he looked at the boy for a little while. He could have walked on but it was good he didn't because it was a time for fathers.

'What are you doing?' he asked.

His son turned around and awkwardly tried to hide something. It was a glove.

'Lachlan, what do you want?' he looked down at his boy and Lachlan looked back. 'What are you looking for?' he said.

Lachlan slowly brought up the other glove, the old Slazenger batting glove that had belonged to Tony. Chris Andersen looked down at his son and then looked away.

'Sorry, sorry Dad.'

Chris walked slowly over to his son. His son looked embarrassed, almost fearful.

'Sorry,' said the boy again.

Chris Andersen walked closer.


Barry Andersen had finally got the score out of Livey Jones. Matt Halley was of no use because he was laughing almost uncontrollably at Livey's discomfort. Barry Andersen walked into the clubrooms and stood in the doorway.

There he saw his youngest son and his youngest grandson facing each other. There was a darkness in the clubrooms and his eyes took a while to adjust to the interior to see clearly. It was good that he took the time to see properly, for he probably would have walked straight in.

It was good he didn't walk in because it was a time for fathers. And one mother. Julie Andersen had arrived with a tray of fruit and was placing it on the table. Moira wanted to go and play in the playground.

'Just a minute, Moisy. I'll say hello to Daddy and Lachie,' Julie said.

She had seen her father-in-law, Barry, standing still in the doorway and walked over to him.

There they stood and watched.

Chris Andersen had walked over to his son and stood quite close.

'Give me the gloves,' he said quietly.

'Sorry,' said his son again.

Chris Andersen held the gloves. And he looked at them, his brother's gloves.

'These are your Uncle Tony's,' he said.

'Sorry,' said his son.

Chris Andersen looked at his son and realised that Lachlan was genuinely frightened. He thought he had done something wrong. Chris stood there and suddenly he thought of the man holding Michael Martin's hand, of how he didn't want his life to go unnoticed, unknown, to be forgotten. He looked at his son.

'You're not...in trouble, you haven't done a thing wrong. They're just a pair of old batting gloves,' he said.

'They belonged to Uncle Tony,' Lachlan said.

His father nodded.

'We don't talk much about Uncle Tony... It's...a bit...' Chris trailed off. It would have been easy to stop, but he knew he couldn't.

'It's a bit hard,' he said.

'I'm sorry...he died,' said his son softly.

As he said that and stood so still, Lachlan looked so much like his Uncle Tony.

Barry Andersen saw it too, and he turned to go but saw the face of his daughter-in-law looking at him.

She smiled slightly and he nodded and turned back.

'He died.'

'He died in a car accident,' said Lachlan.

'He died, your Uncle Tony, well, he killed himself. He killed himself.' It was so odd to hear himself say it.

'Nanna said he died in a car accident,' Lachlan said.

Chris looked at his boy. Where do you start? he thought, to tell the truth after not facing it.

'When something bad happens, sometimes it's easier to only tell part of what happened. And you know it's not just people who do it, mate. It's countries, all of us can do it and you think you can manage it better, how you feel about that bad thing that happens.'

'Why? Why'd he do it?'

'I don't know. Nobody does and maybe we never will. Who do you blame? We, we all blame ourselves – Nanna, Pop, Uncle Greg, me...Nobody knows. I can't tell you about it all in one arvo, mate. Life doesn't work like that. But you mustn't be afraid to ask about him. Because he was...he was a fine man. He made people feel proud to be with him... but he must have felt he couldn't...'

'Tell people things?' said his son.

'How did you get to be so big?' Chris Andersen paused. 'You're a lot like your Uncle Tony, you're quiet and you read and you think and you make people proud to be with you. Make me proud. And I...well...fuck...fuck... I know I yell a bit and I stomp around and maybe you think that I'm a bit of a tool, but I...held you when you were newborn, your mum gave me you to hold for a bit and the look on her face...If you ever think you're not good enough, just think of the look on your mum's face when you were born. And I know you won't always be happy, because life isn't like that, and it's good to feel bad once or twice, good to take a knock and a bit of a bruise because if you're happy all the time then you're not really living. You'll be disappointed and you'll miss out maybe...but you know, but you know what...You just remember, Lachlan, I love you. You make me feel like I've done something pretty bloody terrific. If anything ever happened...if you ever thought that no one would listen or care or miss you or were worried or thought that nobody would care...well, I'm here. And how I felt that time I held you when you were just a baby...well, you know...' He stopped.

And his son, and his father and his wife thought, Please don't clap your hands.

Chris Andersen clapped his hands. Quietly, it is true, but he still clapped his hands.

He looked at his son. 'I love you just as much,' he said and he gave the batting gloves to his son. 'You keep these. And anytime you want to know something about a fine fella who played cricket like an angel, you ask me...and you know... I'll try to answer. But things like this don't just happen overnight, or in a two-minute chat in a change room when I have to have a fucking slash...but you know. And, mate, please don't tell your mum I swear in front of you... not a great habit, but you know.'

He shrugged his shoulders and punched his son a little playful punch in the stomach.

'We loved your Uncle Tony, we loved him and I guess we love him still. And I'll tell you about him if you want. I promise.'

Lachlan nodded. The two people in the doorway turned away silently and stood outside looking at the remnants of the lunch on the trestle table with the plastic tablecloth with rope printed on it.

They didn't say much. And when Chris Andersen prowled out of the clubrooms he found himself standing right next to his wife and his father.

'Hello, Darl,' he exploded to Julie.

'G'day, Dad,' he said and nodded to his father.

Julie put her hand gently on his cheek and looked into his eyes. 'Hello you,' she said softly.

'Mummy, can we go to the playground now?' said Moira.

'Yes, sweetheart,' Julie Andersen said. 'In a tick.'

Chris Andersen really had to go and pee. He moved a little further towards the direction of the banksia bushes around the side of the clubrooms. His father gave him a little play punch in his stomach.

'How are you?' he asked in his low voice.

'Oh, you know. I'm not doing too well today, Dad, but you know.' He smiled and shrugged his shoulders.

His father looked at him. 'Oh, I don't know about that,' and he nodded.

Chris Andersen had a peculiar feeling of having done something right, but he really wanted to take a leak and his mind wasn't that adept at doing two things at once, so he nodded back and tottered off to the banksia trees.

Julie Andersen took her father-in-law's hand.

'Fancy a stroll to the playground?' she asked.

'Why not... Your husband, Julie, he has his moments doesn't he?'

She smiled and said, 'Yes he does.'

They walked off around the boundary line to the playground.

It was about that time that the sun was beginning to fill the oval in the golden light that the mid-afternoon brings. It was still warm but the heat had started to go out of the day, the light was softening and the big disused silo at the rail siding that had been shimmering earlier like a piece of sunbaked bone, had softened with the sepia drape of the arvo light.

Lunch was nearing an end and Chris Andersen had almost finished peeing in the banksia trees.

Rob Orchard had walked around to the house at fine leg and stood sipping a cup of tea. He wasn't really enjoying it much, not just because he was drinking from a plastic throwaway cup which gave the tea a funny taste. He wasn't enjoying it because she hadn't played.

Sarah hadn't played.

Nobody had played for a good ten minutes. There was silence from the window behind the fence. It would be time to start batting soon.

He knew they wouldn't win and he'd have to bat about five because of all the juniors playing and that meant he should probably go over and listen to what Chris Andersen had to say about the batting order.

He knew he should go but she hadn't played, and he'd wasted most of the change of innings standing over here, holding this cup of tea that didn't taste very nice and burnt his fingers.

Well, it *had* burnt his fingers, he'd been here long enough for the tea to cool. He looked over and saw Chris walk to the front of the clubrooms and clap his hands. He knew that was the sign to leave.

He threw aside the contents of the cup and stood for a little bit and then he started to move off.

And he stopped. People stopped. Heads turned towards the fence at fine leg. Even Chris Andersen stopped clapping.

It was her. It was Sarah and she played a note so pure and sweet, so rich that Rob held his breath.

The notes of 'Lark Ascending'. Of Vaughan Williams. She played and the notes lifted in the air and carried across the ground. As the people listened, the notes became music and the oval moved to it.

Children on the playground stopped twirling on the roundabout and turned their faces to the tune.

It was part lament and part expression of joy. It was a song of goodbye, Rob Orchard knew that as soon as he heard the first notes. As the piece was played he knew she was leaving. She must have come just to play for him, to say goodbye.

As the music became softer and the lament sweeter, heads turned to hear. And as the music became softer still, Rob Orchard walked closer to the fence.

As the music became notes and as the notes became one last single note, there was silence.

Rob Orchard raised his head up to the window and said simply, 'Thank you.'

From the window came the last phrase of 'Twinkle Twinkle Little Star'. It stopped halfway through and Rob Orchard whistled the last part.

There was no need to say anything else. It was time for Sarah to go.

Rob Orchard heard Chris Andersen clap his hands and he turned and walked to the clubrooms. It was time to go and bat and finish the innings.

# The Evening Star

The trestle table was stacked away and the plastic tablecloth was folded up, unwashed again.

By the time Rob Orchard had wandered back to the clubrooms, all he had to do to make the ground ready for the second innings was to help pick up some paper plates.

He bent down to pick up a plate and as he stood up he saw Brian looking at him.

'That was... That was something, that music,' Brian said.

Rob Orchard nodded and smiled. It *was* something and now as he popped the paper plate in the bin he supposed he would have to finish the game. The game that had a score of over three hundred in forty overs with two men down.

Ah, well, you had to do the right thing, thought Rob Orchard.

Michael Martin stepped out from the clubrooms. He had heard the clapping of hands and knew it could be only one person. Chris Andersen. There he was, standing, clapping, like some big loud seal dressed in white.

Michael Martin had run his head under the cold shower, so he was feeling a little fresher than he had for a while. And then he realised, as he looked out at Bull Oval, he did feel just that. He stood and watched as a big boofheaded man clapped aimlessly and occasionally shouted, 'Hurry up, come on, hurry up.'

Michael realised he was in the moment. He was living. He knew as he pushed some beads of water out of his eyes that he hadn't done that for a while.

The light was becoming softer and he could smell traces of salt air on the wind. He felt a little pang of expectation. It would be one of those long, sweet afternoons of late summer. He couldn't remember the last time he had simply lived an afternoon. Felt it, tasted the air and the light. He wanted to embrace that afternoon. He bent down and rubbed his fingers on the grass and then rose and walked out further onto the oval. He saw Lachlan going through his kit. Michael Martin had heard what the boy's father had said to him and so he stopped, not to say much but just to stop and say hello.

'Ready to score a few runs?' he said to Lachlan.

The boy looked up and shrugged.

'Well, we'll all get a bat, that's for sure,' said Michael.

'Guess so,' said Lachlan.

Chris Andersen was still clapping.

Lachlan bent his head down and his shoulders moved up and down, shaking a little.

'You okay, Lachlan?' Michael asked.

The boy looked up. He was laughing. 'That's my father,' he said.

Michael Martin smiled. 'Yes, that's your father alright.'

Lachlan and Michael walked over towards the clapping.

'You haven't got your sunglasses on,' said Lachlan.

Michael ran a hand through his hair and realised that he must have left them in the clubroom. He looked around the oval. It was good, thought Michael, to see things clearly again.

'I don't, do I?' he said and he smiled again.

Ron Sparrow stood halfway between the pitch and the clubrooms. No-man's-land. The domain of the umpire. He heard Christopher Andersen clapping and he must admit he didn't really see why Chris bothered. Three hundred plus off forty overs, that really was a hopeless task. He knew Trinity had dragooned that fast bowler into the team so he could play in the finals. Well, he'll be playing in the finals, thought Ron Sparrow.

The Trinity players stood in a wide semi-circle and practised their close-in catching. They talked and joked and clapped their hands the way a team does that knows the result of the match but, really, if you looked at them, they weren't much better than Yarraville West.

Never mind, there's always going to be winners and losers. Never mind.

He felt the money in his pocket from the players' fees, the bundles of money from the ice-cream container that had sat next to the chocolate biscuits. Ron Sparrow patted it for safety's sake. He patted the bundles and he smiled.

Chris Andersen would always put the ice-cream container next to the food he thought would be the most popular, in this case the choccy bickies, so everyone would be reminded to put the money in.

Ron Sparrow looked at him aimlessly clapping. And then he heard him winding himself up to talk to his team. Well, he had to do it, only right, to make a game of it.

Ron Sparrow had seen how Christopher had told the younger players not to put in the money, that Chris would cover them. And he'd winked at Dougie, the Trinity captain, and both the captains added a bit extra.

They both knew that the money from the ice-cream container wasn't really for the umpire. Ron Sparrow would take the money and drop it off at the mission down in Footscray. It was an old-fashioned way of doing things and probably not all the teams did it, but despite what everyone else thought about the world, these cricketers and their game were still old-fashioned enough to know what community they belonged to.

Ron Sparrow looked at his watch. It was nearly time to start the second innings. Well, it shouldn't take too long.

And then that is when it happened.

Ron Sparrow was looking across the oval and he thought that it might be nice after dropping the money in at the mission if he went and bought a six-pack and a nice Vietnamese soup from down in Hopkins Street for him and his wife. Watch a bit of telly. Yes, not a bad-sounding night, and as he was thinking that didn't sound like a bad night, he saw a little boy run by and go to pick up a ball that had gone through the hands of the practising fielders.

Chris Andersen had stopped clapping his hands and was now supposed to say something. Really, he told himself, he would have liked to have maybe clapped some more and leave it at that. But he knew he should say something. It was the right thing to do.

'Right, men. Right.' He looked at his team. 'Now listen, there are some people who would tell you that scoring three hundred... twelve...' He trailed off. What was the score?

The scorer for Trinity lisped out, 'It was three hundred and eighteen.'

Chris Andersen winced. His team looked at him. It was just a game of park cricket, why did he have to say anything? 'Thank you very much, mate... Right three hundred and eighteen...' He shook his head. 'They did do well, didn't they?'

There were a few titters from his players. He looked at them and he saw the younger players. The two Tims and his son Lachlan. They were young enough to expect something to be said. They deserved to hear some words. But what? What do you say to a group of men and boys playing a game that doesn't really matter? Oh bugger it, Chris Andersen thought, you've got to do the right thing, you've got to say something and make it matter.

'Three hundred and eighteen runs off forty overs... Now there are some people who would say to you that we have absolutely no chance of getting those runs. We're two men down. We have no chance of winning... well...' He paused and eight sets of eyes looked back at him. He didn't falter.

'They would be absolutely on the money. We've got no chance of winning.'

Livey farted.

'Thank you, Johnny Cash.'

Livey farted twice more.

'Well, yes, as Johnny Cash says quite correctly, it's backs-to-the-wall stuff and we've got to have a go.'

Matt Halley laughed. 'Very Churchillian, Christo.'

'Oh bugger Churchill, he's had his quotes on the calendar. Give me someone Australian...come on, give me someone Australian to work with here.' Chris Andersen waved his big hand. 'And don't make it any prime minister of Australia because I've seen them bowling today and none of them can play for shit.'

'Rick Springfield,' yelled out Michael Martin.

'Right, there we go, Rick Springfield. He had a go!'

'Two mentions in one day,' said Matt Halley, strumming his fist in Springfield style. 'Go Rick.'

'Jessie's Girl,' cried Brian.

'Thank you, Brian, yes, "Jessie's Girl". They said Rick had no chance, no chance at all, but he said "I'll have a go"... and...here he writes a song called "Jessie's Girl"...and what can I say? We're all laughing at his expense but really as far as one-hit wonders go... Bradmanesque! To have a go, boys.'

Livey farted.

'Give me another name.'

'Rick McCosker!' called out Matt Halley.

'Right, I see we're working to a theme here. A theme of Ricks. Rick McCosker, hey.'

Matt Halley smiled.

'Well, now, let me tell you, as far as Ricks go... McCosker's my man. Let me tell you, when it comes to the great broken jaws of history, Rick McCosker is at the top,' he roared. 'There's a man you should see on a tin of Milo.'

'With his broken jaw?' asked Rob Orchard.

'Absolutely, with his broken jaw.'

'Stick to law,' Matt Halley said.

Tims One and Two looked bamboozled and Lachlan had no idea what the significance was of Rick McCosker.

'What did Rick McCosker sing?' asked Tim Two.

'Not a bloody thing... and he wasn't that much of a bat, I guess, but he opened for Australia and there is one thing he did do... he had a go... A major *go!*'

'This is very good, Chris,' said Livey Jones, without farting.

'He had a go. He had a go at a hook shot and... anybody?' said Chris Andersen.

'Broke his jaw,' said Livey Jones.

'Broke his jaw. In a Test match, the Centenary Test. But when he was needed... he batted again... Yes!' Chris Andersen held his arms out.

Rob Orchard, Matt Halley, Livey Jones and Michael Martin answered as one, sounding vaguely chant-like: 'Swathed in bandages.'

'Swathed in bandages is right, his head was like a mummy... and the first shot he played when he went out there was?'

Again the four answered the call, 'A hook shot.'

'And if he had wanted to sing, he would have gone okay because he was a man who *had* a go. And if he did sing he would have sung?'

There was a pause this time, and a few stumped faces. Then Brian yelled, 'Jessie's Girl!'

There was applause at that one.

'Give me another name,' said Chris Andersen.

'Ned Kelly,' said Tim One.

'That's a good one, Ned Kelly. There was Ned...surrounded by hundreds of police, with no possible way out...and what does he do?'

'He gets shot in the legs,' said Lachlan.

'And hanged,' said Tim Two.

'Exactly...he had a go!'

'He Springfielded,' cried Matt Halley and he strummed his fist across his groin.

'Jessie's Girl,' yelled Brian.

Then Rob Orchard Rick Springfielded a 'Jessie's Girl' salute in the style of a broken-jawed Rick McCosker.

Chris Andersen laughed and Rick Springfielded back and yelled in the manner of the broken-jawed McCosker, 'Have a go!'

The team laughed and Rick Springfielded with their fists on their air guitars and yelled in the McCosker style, 'Have a go.'

Somehow the cry of 'Have a go' became 'Jessie's Girl!' And then Rob Orchard, for no reason in particular, yelled out 'Spartacus!' but of course he yelled it as Rick McCosker with a broken jaw.

Chris Andersen agreed. 'Yes, Spartacus, a great Australian... there he was looking like Kirk Douglas and the Romans got him and his team was all dusted and done with. When they wanted someone to dob in Spartacus so they could do whatever they wanted to do with people who looked like Kirk Douglas, some bloke got up and he yelled... "I'm Rick Springfield".'

And then Michael Martin yelled out, 'I'm Rick Springfield' and soon the whole team of Yarraville West Fourths were yelling. They were united. They were a team.

Ron Sparrow shook his head and smiled. They're a funny team, but they're a team. Ron saw that the little boy didn't want to give the cricket ball back and he smiled because the boy was a funny little fellow. And the boy's father had to come and take the ball from his hands and throw it back to the cricketers practising their fielding.

The father said sorry, picked his son up and soothed him with a cuddle and a little song in his ear.

Ron Sparrow smiled.

The father and son were Aboriginal and he had seen them walking around the boundary line to the playground earlier.

He remembered the reserves. A long time ago. Up in the north of Queensland where he'd asked to go and the Church was happy enough to send him. He had tried but he couldn't stick at it. The heat and the work and the desperation of it all had been too much.

He was happy to see the father and the son. You see so many different people from all over the place around here that it made him feel good to see some of the originals.

Ron had never felt at home up there in the north, could never reconcile why things were so different. When the Church moved him closer to the houses on the reserve, well he couldn't stay.

The Aborigines had lived with not much and the folks in the office back somewhere in a city were going to build him a nice little brick air-conditioned house. He knew he couldn't stay, and he felt a little ashamed, but he went in to the township to say goodbye.

As he walked around saying goodbye to the various families, he stuck his head into the empty houses. In one the only decoration on the walls was a print of a man sitting on a horse. As he said goodbye to the old woman who lived in that house he looked at the print and nearly cried. The woman looked at him and he held up a hand and said he really must go.

As he walked to his car he kept his eyes to the ground, for he didn't want them to see him, he felt ashamed. He had almost reached the car when he felt a weak tugging at his arm, he turned and saw the old woman. She had followed him and in her hands she held the print of the man on the horse. It had lost one of its corners a little, she must have ripped it when she took it down in her haste to give it to him.

Ron Sparrow took the print and the old woman held his hands and smiled.

The print sits above his desk in the rectory and when he sees it he thinks of the possibilities of people. That a people so dispossessed could be so generous.

He felt like telling somebody that story then, but there was nobody near to be told. Nobody wanted to talk to the umpire. The old umpire stared and watched the father and son walk back to the boundary line.

Then he heard the fast bowler. Chris Andersen and his team had laughed themselves silly enough to have a little silence as they fiddled in their bags for their equipment so they heard the fast bowler as well.

'Go walk about somewhere else...' and he mimicked an Aboriginal blackfella song, almost in the same spot where Cec Bull had mocked the old black man that he and his brothers had thrown rocks at when the oval they stood on had been a tip all those years ago.

It wasn't anything really. Just a bit of smartarseness more than anything else. But Ron Sparrow caught himself. He nearly said something, but he thought it might cause more trouble than it was worth. It was over as quickly as the fast bowler started.

Those that heard said nothing.

The father of the little boy was carrying his son away and wasn't quite sure what he had heard. He stopped and looked. Perhaps it was nothing, but he saw a tall man laughing. He looked at the faces of the men all dressed in white.

Somebody had said something. Maybe. He wasn't sure. But all the same he tightened a little in anger. Such a beautiful day, so fine a touch in the day and yet it had just changed. He didn't know what had happened. But he glanced back.

Dougie gave his fast bowler a look and the fast bowler had the sense to stop. So nobody said anything else.

Best not say anything, it was just a game of cricket, just let it go.

Ron Sparrow bent his head. He'd have a word with Dougie after the game. Just a quiet little word. He could do that much.

They nearly did let it go, except for Brian.

Chris Andersen looked at Brian's face. It was an open face, perplexed at why somebody would casually mock someone walking in the park. And he looked at his son. Chris Andersen had walked with his son here at this oval and nobody had mocked him.

All of a sudden, so many things flashed into his mind. He remembered what an old black man had said to him once in a pub in Warrnambool one fishing holiday. He had sat in the pub watching the day Kim Hughes resigned as the Australian cricket captain.

Chris Andersen had sat there looking at the screen as highlights of the West Indies towelling Australia were shown. These were the days when the West Indies towelled anybody they wanted to, but mostly it seemed, Australia. And mostly they seemed to towel Kim Hughes. In fact, they hammered him. And there he sat, trying to be brave, trying to do the right thing and crack a few jokes with the journalists on the telly.

He looked teary and chubby and Chris Andersen thought, he's going to cry.

A few other punters had turned to the set.

'Oh, Jesus, he's going to bawl, isn't he?'

'Tosser,' said another voice.

Chris didn't like Kim Hughes but he was the Australian cricket captain and he had been towelled pretty badly and, yes, it was a bit weak if you cried, but really he was no more of a tosser than the next fellow.

Still though, he thought, don't cry.

Kim Hughes tried to read a statement. He took a deep breath and had a go and then started to blub. His lip went. Then he went. Literally, he got up and walked out.

That's a bit weak, thought Chris Andersen.

And as he thought that Chris heard a raspy cough beside him. An old Aboriginal man stood slightly to one side. He glanced up at Chris Andersen as he drank from his glass. He swallowed a mouthful and turned slowly to Chris.

'What's he crying about?' said the old man.

'Oh, he's just had to quit as cricket captain of Australia.'

The old man laughed a little. 'Oh, goodo... crying over a game of cricket. Oh well, you can keep it, matey. It's a white fella's game, that cricket.'

Chris Andersen looked at him for a moment and then said with a smile, 'The West Indies have just pasted us, mate, and they don't look too white to me.'

The old man smiled back. 'West Indies? Oh well, you know they're not my people... They don't live here. No, it's a white fella's game alright. Just ask Eddie Gilbert,' and he walked off.

Chris remembered the name and later he asked around and read about Eddie Gilbert. The fastest bowler of his day.

The only bowler ever to knock a bat from Bradman's hands. The bowler who got Bradman for a duck in each innings of a match. Eddie Gilbert.

Never got picked to play for his country. Never. Not because he wasn't good enough, not because he may have had a dodgy action occasionally. No, not because he wasn't good enough, because he wasn't white enough. White fella's game.

He'd bowled like the wind off three or four paces and for his trouble he got shown the door after a few seasons. Sent back to the reserves. And when the men in the boardrooms had decided to send him back, they went and told him he had to give 'their' cricket clothes back.

Eddie Gilbert died a lonely death in a lonely hospital in Brisbane after years of mental illness and alcoholism. But that's nobody's fault, really. Things just happen. Nobody's personally responsible.

Eddie Gilbert. There is a photo of him claiming Bradman's wicket. Those black arms waving up in the air, dancing there as Bradman crouches low.

He died. And nobody really said anything. He died a lonely death.

But Bradman went to the funeral.

Good for him, thought Chris Andersen.

No, nobody said anything, they just let it go.

But when Chris Andersen thought of Eddie Gilbert he thought of the woman at the bus stop and he looked at Michael Martin and remembered the man who had held his friend's hand. And he heard the voice of Gwen, sitting on the review panel with her smart suit. 'Why bother?' she had said. 'Why would you bother?'

Why bother? He stood for a moment and then he said very slowly but quite loudly, 'Why do we bother? Why do we bother to have a go? Why should we bother about a crappy game of cricket on an oval in the western suburbs that used to be a tip?'

'You know that? They used to dump rubbish here, all sorts of bits and pieces. So why bother?

'We bother to have a go because it's a way of saying that we care. We care about what happens here and what is said. We care about everybody getting the right to have a go. We care about the right of everybody, black, white, or bloody brindle to be able to come here on this oval and not to have to put up with somebody saying they shouldn't be here.'

Chris Andersen turned to face the field and the Trinity team all turned to look. The fast bowler held his gaze.

'We have a go, Brian. We have a go because it's actually what makes us a bit better than what we are.' His voice became quite loud. 'We have a go because if we don't, bad things can happen to good people. They may be little things to some people and sometimes we might think it better to shut up and let it go and not say anything. To pretend it doesn't happen, tell ourselves we didn't hear and didn't see and didn't know. We have a go because it's a chance for us to say to people who don't think there's enough space in this world for us all, that you're wrong. You are wrong. To have a go is something that everybody should be able to do, Brian. To have a go. It's what, I reckon, this country is all about – the best of it. To have a go.'

And as Chris Andersen stood there on that oval he thought of his brother. Of a light lost, of a life cherished but wasted at the same time.

'Life is a gift. Life is something...you don't let people waste it if you can help it. And you do that by letting people know they matter. They matter. That's why we care. Life is something that's got to be shared. And the more we share, the more we live. The better we become...by having a go...and, yes, it may be as silly as saying on this ground, our rubbish tip, that everybody is equal and we all belong and anybody who doesn't like that...is a flat-headed tool, or something like that.'

Chris Andersen still faced the fast bowler.

'And we've got to let people have a go, Brian, because there are some of us who just don't think enough, because when they think, they think they've got a right to chip people not because they're bad or they're doing something wrong, but because they're people who aren't like them. They can't let others have a go. And it's easy to let those fellas get away with that...but you know, it is important to tell them they're wrong.'

The father who carried his little boy had heard what the big man said. He had heard things said like that before, and maybe the big bloke could have said them better, but he had said them. The father of the little boy saw a young cricketer who he had spoken to earlier in the afternoon standing near with his head lowered slightly.

'Hey,' said the father of the little boy quietly to Lachlan, 'who's that bloke?'

Lachlan saw the man nod his head towards Chris Andersen.

'That's my father,' Lachlan said almost to himself.

'He's alright...that bloke,' and he smiled and walked off. He turned to his young son. 'Yarraville West, eh? We might have a go next year? We might have a go,' and he walked off singing to his son.

Livey Jones, who was busying himself with finding his box, leant forward and said as he rummaged in his bag, loud enough for Lachlan Andersen to hear, 'Atticus Finch isn't the only lawyer who knows how to make a pretty good speech.' And then he farted.

There was no way they could win, of course, but then that wasn't the point. Cricket is a game that not everyone grasps.

It has its odd place names, its silly mid-ons and silly points and short mid-ons and its square point. What sort of a game has a position called square point? It has its interminable delays. It's a game more watched than played these days, but it's a game that lets a point, whether it be square or whatever, be made and an honour won. You may not win a game of cricket, you can be soundly beaten, but still there's a victory to be had. If you know how to go about it.

There were, of course, obstacles.

It was one thing for Chris Andersen to tell someone that he thought they were wrong, and there were probably quite a few people who thought what he did was a good thing.

But Chris was enough of a pragmatist to know when he started giving the bowler a mild serve that it would have been better if the man had been a spinner. The same thought dawned on the rest of the team when they saw how energetically the fast bowler rolled his arm over in his warm-up.

Fast bowlers. Well, there was nothing for it, you can't pick a fight and then let someone else face up for you.

Chris Andersen opened the batting.

He had planned to put Livey in but then Michael started padding up. He looked like he knew what he was doing, so Chris let him be.

Michael hadn't played in a long time but there is something about the confidence it gives other people in a team when they see a teammate who knows how to handle a bat. Spirits lift when you watch a person like Michael Martin preparing themselves – it is as simple as looking the part.

They know where the thigh pad goes and how to strap it up quickly. Everything that needs to be done is done and done quickly. Everything fits and sits well and is as it should be. It was good the Yarraville West Fourths had somebody like Michael Martin in the team, because, if they were honest, their captain instilled little procedural confidence.

Watching someone like Chris Andersen get ready to bat was like watching a gorilla set an alarm clock. It was entertaining, in a sad, late-night TV way. If you looked through half-closed eyes the big monkey may actually have looked like it knew what it was doing, but more often than not things ended up in pieces. In fact, the only piece of equipment Chris handled with any certainty and confidence was his batting box. The skull and crossbones disappeared down his pants. He shoved it firmly down over his vitals.

'You know, Christo,' said Matt Halley without any irony whatsoever, 'it's the fact that you are shitting yourself so much that makes what you are doing quite courageous.'

'Up yours,' said Chris Andersen in the tone of somebody wishing a loved one Merry Christmas.

So it was that the two openers walked out to the wicket. One left-hander who walked neatly out and the other a big monkey with more bits hanging off him than a badly decorated Christmas tree.

''Tis a far far better thing I do,' said Livey, but at least he didn't fart.

In true ancient tradition neither of the men wore a helmet.

'I'll face,' said Chris Andersen.

'Fair enough,' said Michael Martin. 'Just remember I'm a doctor.'

'Oh, up yours,' Chris Andersen said and laughed.

He went to the striker's end and took guard, and Chris Andersen taking guard was like a gorilla taking high tea. It didn't really make much sense. But he did it anyway, just to prove a point.

His father, Barry Andersen, shook his head and laughed as he stood pushing his grand-daughter on a swing in the playground.

'That silly bugger has never taken guard in his life.'

'You said a naughty word, Pop,' said Moira.

'No, that's not a naughty word, I'm just talking about your dad.'

If you are going to take guard once in your life, thought Chris Andersen, you might as well make the most of it.

He asked for middle and scratched away, marking his spot until something the size of a small canyon appeared in the pitch.

'You thinking of putting a spa in there, Christo?' Dougie muttered from first slip.

Then the beefy little man added very softly, 'Good on you, Christo, you silly sod.' And then he clapped his hands.

'Come on, Trinity, it's the Yarraville West skipper, give him a round. Come on, let's go, Trinity!'

Dougie clapped until all his team clapped their hands together. Chris Andersen looked at Dougie and nodded. He's not a bad bloke, really, thought Chris Andersen, even if he did bat first.

As soon as Chris turned to face, his good thoughts towards Dougie evaporated. A round of applause for the opposition captain. Nice touch, very sporting.

But Dougie had made everybody clap. Including a disgruntled and narked-off bowler, who by now had the added fuel of having to applaud the goose who had been giving him a bake minutes before.

Chris Andersen, despite himself, smiled. He had to hand that one to Dougie.

'Nice one, Douglas,' he said to nobody in particular.

The fast bowler ran in. Chris Andersen could tell by the way he ran he was good. His rhythm was set and he ran in fast and straight.

But it was icing on the cake. Chris Andersen was way ahead on points, the fact that he had said his piece and pissed the opening bowler off was one thing. The reality of coming out to open and then facing him was another. Anything other than that was a bonus.

Oh, well, I've had a go.

The ball spat up from the pitch and leapt at him and he flicked his head away just at the last moment.

He was fast this man, and he was pissed off. He was frightening but he bowled at the man. The slips behind him whistled. The Yarraville West Fourths, all to a man Rick Springfielded, Spartacussed and Rick McCoskered with their fists and jaws and strumming arms.

'Jessie's Girl,' Brian sang out.

Chris Andersen smiled, he turned and said to the slips, 'Well, that's me sighter.'

A few smiled but no one laughed.

The next two balls he played and missed. The fourth he didn't see. The last beat him completely and must have only just missed the wickets.

One over down, thirty-nine to go. He could feel pain in his heel and as Michael Martin played himself in slowly over the course of the next over it became very sore.

Michael put the bat on every ball he received. He didn't move as quickly as he used to in the crease but Chris Andersen could see that he was only one sure shot away and something would click.

The next over was even quicker. The ball seared at the batsman but Chris actually managed to put bat to ball twice. Even gorillas can strike it lucky.

He didn't know anything about the balls but somehow he got the bat onto them. The fast bowler was working up a sweat and he stood at mid-wicket, bent down and rubbed his hands over the wicket like you might see Brett Lee do on the television.

He looked like he knew what he was doing. And he never took his eyes off Chris Andersen. Perhaps he should have.

John Grassi, the groundsman, had used a heavy roller on the pitch and it was amazing, really, that the dog turd dropped by Ted Bright's old dog, Newk, had remained ground into the pitch for so long.

But as the fast bowler rubbed the sweat from his hands on the pitch and clawed at the ground like a wild beast he rubbed and rolled and glued the dog poo all over his hands. He took the ball and tore in. Chris Andersen played and missed again.

The ball went through to the keeper and was whipped very smartly back to the fast bowler.

A ball clutched in a hand draped in dog shit had passed around half the Trinity team and almost in unison they decided to pick their noses or scratch their faces or wipe their eyes. Newk's best effort brought forth oaths and furtive looks and sidelong glances between teammates.

It annoyed the fast bowler so much that Chris Andersen didn't have to play a shot until the third bowl of his next over. Dougie had run down and had words with him. The next ball was full, fast and straight. Chris Andersen's bonus had run out. He played all around it and his wicket disintegrated.

The fast bowler pumped his fist in the air and then winced in mid-celebration as he got another whiff of Newk's gift.

Chris Andersen hadn't made a run but he walked off as if he'd made a ton.

'Well batted, Christo,' muttered Dougie.

Chris walked back to the clubrooms, put his bat down and began to take off his ceremonial protective gear.

'Well played, Chris,' said Tim One.

Chris Andersen smiled. 'He can only bowl eight overs and he's almost halfway through. We'll be right.'

'Yes, you've warmed him up very nicely,' said Rob Orchard.

'Oh, I don't know, Marto looks okay, he might stick around,' said Chris.

And he did. The score didn't move very much but Michael Martin farmed the strike enough to keep things moving. Michael knew how to bat and the longer he was out there the surer the bat felt in his hands and the quicker his feet moved. The middle was where it was happening and although he got a few frights off the fast bowler the other trundlers didn't hold much terror for him.

Even though Livey was a terrible runner between the wickets, he managed to stay for nearly seven overs.

'Sorry, Marto,' he said after yet another near miss at a run-out. 'Two farts means yes and one means no.'

'Yes, alright, I'll keep that in mind, Livey,' said Michael.

After an exchange that sounded like Morse code, Livey finally met his maker.

He pushed a ball almost directly to mid-on. 'No-no... no... no... nononono... ES!'

Michael Martin never moved and he just smiled at Livey as Livey found himself at the same end as Marto.

'There you go,' said Livey. 'One of the glorious mysteries of life, that run-out. Oh well, that's show business.'

He walked off trotting and farting back to the benches.

Every batsman from Yarraville West tried to get in behind the ball. To stay out in the middle for as long as they could. Without even thinking it, they would say to themselves, 'I'll have a go.'

The longer the game went on the more the atmosphere changed. The longer Michael Martin stayed at the crease, the more confident the younger players became.

Yarraville West were two wickets down at drinks and when they went back Matt Halley lasted a good five overs. He took a few balls on the body and counter-attacked as only he could.

He provided a short and entertaining burst of running between the wickets in the manner of Tom Cruise. All pumping arms and tiny, stocky legs going nowhere very fast. Then he decided to take two in the manner of Kate Bush from her 'Wuthering Heights' video clip. This effort even raised an approving eyebrow from the fast bowler. Amazingly, Matt Halley edged one through to the keeper.

Tim One and Tim Two came and went in ten overs and Rob Orchard managed to keep out of trouble for long enough to give them the idea that they might not be beaten outright.

The Yarraville West Fourths watched from the benches and counted down the overs. The seagulls sailed in from the salty river and wheeled high overhead and then swooped down to pick at pieces of doughnuts and sandwiches that hadn't found a way into the bins around the ground.

Barry Andersen wouldn't move from the playground while the team were batting, because it was bad luck to change places. Moira thought that superstition was a good one. She liked the playground and she loved her grandfather pushing her on the swing. She wasn't interested in the cricket.

Lachlan sat with his uncle's old Slazenger batting gloves in his lap. His father gave him a punch on the arm. Lachlan looked up and smiled a little nervously. He looked away and his father patted him again but kept his eyes on the field.

Chris Andersen felt a flick on his arm and looked down.

'Thank you for asking me to play,' his son said to him.

Before Chris could say anything there was a shout, a pause and a cheer. Rob Orchard had been caught.

There are few things that are as long as the walk out to the wicket, late in the afternoon, when the game matters.

Lachlan didn't know why it mattered so much but he knew it did. He could help. He could stay. He could keep the team going. His stomach felt funny and as he got closer to the wicket his legs began to wobble. He almost felt like weeing.

As he walked, the air around him seemed to change. It took longer to move through it. He felt awkward as the knee rolls on his pads banged against each other. He thought the wicket was a mile away and that he would never reach it. And as he walked past some of the Trinity outfielders he heard them cry little phrases of encouragement to each other.

He didn't want to hear, so he looked into the sky. The players on the television often did that. They looked to the sky when they walked out to bat. He had gone to a Boxing Day Test once and he had asked his father why Ricky Ponting had looked to the sky.

'Well, he's been in the dressing-room and as he comes out onto the field he wants to open his eyes a little, just to let in the light,' his father said.

Lachlan had never done this before. But he did today, he looked to the sky.

The sky, he thought, is a big thing and it holds so much. Like life. Now why did I think that? he thought. For no reason, he stopped walking and stared and he saw golden rays of light playing across the sky and the first stretches of pink and orange lazing above him. When he looked down he saw that he stood on the edge of the wicket. He stared down at it. He stared at the strands of rolled grass and black soil and turf; at the cracks of grey. He studied its smoothness, its flatness.

Michael Martin watched as the boy took a deep, sharp breath.

Michael was about to walk down to him when Lachlan did something that made him stop in his tracks. The boy looked up and smiled. A beautiful, wide smile and then he leant on his bat and laughed. Then he nodded and asked for leg and gently made his mark.

Michael Martin knew he didn't have to go down to speak to the boy. He nodded to him and Lachlan nodded back.

Barry Andersen looked at his grandson and did not move.

The first ball he faced moved off the pitch but Lachlan moved with it. He'd gone back and across and his head was still following the line of the ball when the red missile struck the sweet centre of the bat.

Lachlan Andersen tugged at the gloves that were a little too big for him and looked back down at the wicket. There was no need for him to do anything except stand here and see it through.

Lachlan covered the next ball completely and it struck the same sure blade. Barry Andersen still didn't move.

It was the last ball and the bowler placed it a little wider and managed to swing it even more. Lachlan Andersen should have left it, but he knew what he was doing. He kept his head still and followed the ball with his eyes. As the ball started to swing he stepped towards it and drove through it with a flow of the bat that can't be taught. A flow of the bat that is natural.

Of all the shots to play, that off-drive was the sweetest. It took the breath away and the golden light added a lustre to it that made the game shine.

When Rob Orchard saw it he heard the cello again and smiled.

When Barry Andersen saw it he let out a long, slow sigh, as a man might do who has tasted a beautiful wine.

'There's a boy,' he said softly. And then a little louder and with no care for how proud he sounded he said to a young mother helping her toddler into the cubbyhouse, 'That's my grandson out there.'

The young mother had seen the shot and she smiled. It was nice that so many families came here, she thought. It's such a nice place. She was glad they had bought a house close by. It was good to be back, clean and alive. She looked up at the cubbyhouse. It still had 'Our Home' above the entrance.

The young mother smiled again, it was good to be back.

When Chris Andersen saw that shot he looked at his son. 'How'd you get to be so big?' he said to nobody in particular.

Some of the opposition got narky and tried to have a go at the two batsmen. They had already won but they couldn't beat the Yarraville West Fourths. It didn't work. Dougie wouldn't let them.

'We'll get them the way we should, there'll be no showboating out here,' Dougie said. And as he said that he scratched his nose in thought and not for the first time scrunched up his face at the smell.

The intensity of the game drew people to it. As Ted Bright reached for a fig off the heavy tree he sensed an electricity in the air. It was in the way the fielders clapped and ran at the change of the over. The way nobody had moved when that young boy had played that off-drive.

What a lovely shot that had been. He whistled to his fat old Lab when it was played.

'Now, Newky, there's a shot,' and he rubbed the old dog's back. 'We might just stay and watch this one.' Something was up here. They may be the fourths but this was one to watch.

The sharp left-hander had been seeing the ball like a pumpkin. Ted Bright liked left-handers and this bloke was good. But he could see he was getting a bit tired, the old man thought. He's been through a bit.

Suddenly the pumpkin turned into a bullet and burst through Michael Martin's bat and front pad to break the stumps.

Michael Martin leant forward on his bat and swore softly to himself. He looked over at Lachlan. He could have just walked off and hoped for the best, but he had seen the way Lachlan listened and watched.

He walked down the pitch and smiled at the boy. 'Bring him home, Lachie, just talk him through it.'

'What do I say?' asked Lachlan.

'What you talked about this arvo in the field. When you looked at the sky. You'll know.'

And Michael walked off. He didn't know when he would play again, but the sea breeze was strong and the seagulls wheeled high overhead. He was tired and happy.

Lachlan looked up to see Brian lurching out. He tripped twice before he got to the wicket.

The bowler laughed at him.

Lachlan walked down to Brian and told him just to watch the ball. 'Get in front of your stumps and just watch the ball onto your bat. You'll be right.'

Brian gurgled something and then he said, 'I'm going to have a go, Lachie…Never got a run before. Might be me lucky day.'

Chris Andersen looked out at the wicket and saw the two batsmen turn and stare at the Uncle Toby's silo. Lachlan pointed and Brian's eyes followed. Then Brian laughed and walked to the crease.

What the bloody hell are they doing? thought Chris Andersen.

Lachlan nodded and went back to the non-striker's end. The bowler came in faster than he had before. Lachlan looked back to Brian. He stood in front of his stumps with his bat held out in front of him. The bowler let the ball go…at Brian's head. The ball had slipped from his hand and came out as a high full toss that knocked Brian off his feet. The sound of the ball on the plastic helmet was sickening enough.

Chris Andersen was there from the benches. He reached Brian before Lachie did and held him. He took off Brian's helmet and checked him out. Michael Martin wasn't far behind. Rob Orchard after him.

Brian was alright. Just a little scared. 'But I got in front of me stumps,' he said. This made a few of the opposition team laugh. Chris Andersen looked at them.

'Is that the best you can do? Is it?' They stopped laughing and turned away. Michael Martin put his arm around Brian.

'Come on, mate, you don't have to stay out here. Give us your helmet.' He went to pick it up but Brian shook his head.

'Come on, Brian,' said Chris Andersen. 'You've got nothing to prove.' And he began to lead him away. Brian made a gurgling sound and shook his head.

Lachlan looked at his father.

Chris Andersen turned and was about to speak when he looked at Brian. He was about to gently pull him away and then he looked and listened to Brian. There was a pause.

'What do you want to do, matey?' he asked.

'Got two balls to score a run. Never made a run before.' Brian smiled. A big open smile. 'I want to have a go, Christo?'

Nobody said a word. Rob Orchard nodded, picked up Brian's helmet and held it out to him. What Brian did next was something that would make that game one nobody would ever forget. He shook his head. 'I don't need that. He's not *that* fast.'

The bump on Brian's head was as big as an egg. Yet he walked back and took up his ungainly stance. As the bowler stomped back, the umpire declared a no-ball and looked down at the bare-headed Brian. 'Lad's alright,' he said to Lachlan.

The next ball was a brute. How the bowler got it up off that wicket nobody will ever know. It was an old ball and he'd been bowling like a train. Somehow, in some strange way, the ball missed Brian's head. He was still playing the shot he intended to play, and getting tangled up in his pads in the process, when the ball had gone through the fielders and was back with the bowler.

Two balls at the head. The next one was going to be full and fast. 'Brian, watch for the yorker. Keep your bat in front and low.' Lachlan tried not to speak too quickly, but he was excited. The game had taken on a new dimension. People around the oval, who had paid scant attention before, were barracking now.

Lachlan turned to see an old man who was walking an old Labrador yell out, 'Come on, batsman. Come on, young fella. See him off.'

Brian looked around at the people yelling. Then Ron Sparrow spoke. 'It's for you, young fella. The shouting's for you. You right?'

Brian said, 'Oh, yeah... I think I am.'

The bowler ran in and from the other end of the wicket Lachlan could hear Brian muttering to himself, 'Have a go, have a go, have a go.'

The ball was fast and full and low. It would have pitched at the bottom of middle stump. It would have if Brian hadn't started running as soon as the bowler reached his delivery stride. He scuttled down the pitch with his bat held out in front of him. It scraped along the wicket.

Lachlan was relieved to see the ball hadn't broken the wickets. Then he was horrified to see the ball squirt off towards gully. Brian kept running. He wanted that run.

Instinctively, Lachlan took off. He knew that Brian couldn't stop. No, he knew Brian wouldn't be able to turn and regain his ground. But Lachlan couldn't make his legs move any quicker, his pads bumped into each other and if the wicket seemed a mile away when he first walked in, then the batting crease seemed as far away as the stars in the sky. Time seemed to warp and stretch and he thought that surely the wickets must break, surely they must splinter.

Slowly the distance to the crease began to get smaller. He slid full-length with his bat outstretched. He looked up and there was no noise. Even though the stumps were broken there was no noise. Save for a whispered, 'How is he?' from someone in the slips.

Lachlan looked up to Ron Sparrow. Every head was turned to the old umpy. Ron Sparrow had never once knowingly given a wrong decision. Sure, some of the decisions had been incorrect when he was confronted with a bit of anecdotal review and a chat over a beer, but he always called them as he saw them. And this old umpire wasn't going to start doing anything differently now.

The bowler screamed, 'How is he?'

Ron Sparrow seemed not to have heard. Then he turned to the fast bowler. He'd made his decision.

'Not out, you fat bastard,' he roared and flicked the bails off the wickets.

'Game, gents, that's it and well played the lot of you.'

There may have only been a few people watching but the noise they made sounded like the MCG on Boxing Day. Brian had his run. His name was in the books. The old man clapped and his old dog barked.

'Well bloody done! Well bloody done,' the old man yelled.

The boys from the Yarraville West benches danced and shouted to Brian. And Brian? He went and shook the hand of the fast bowler.

At the end of the game they all shook hands. When Chris Andersen came to the fast bowler he shook his hand and held it for just a moment.

'Well played, mate, well played.' He looked at the man. 'And just...you know...think about it, you can tell me to get stuffed and I'm a dill...but before you do...just think about it.'

The fast bowler looked at Chris Andersen a moment and moved on.

The Yarraville West Fourths stood around in a little group before they went about tidying the ground.

'They weren't a bad bunch of fellas. But they took it a bit too seriously,' Rob Orchard said as he and Matt Halley replaced the wire covering to the wicket area.

'Perhaps they were a bit unhappy with the afternoon tea,' said Matt Halley, shooting a look at Livey Jones. Livey studiously ignored the look but readied himself.

'You reckon?' asked Rob Orchard.

'Maybe, but really,' Matt Halley said, 'what's wrong with jam doughnuts and cold Spag Hawaiian pizza?'

Livey Jones farted.

When the oval was as tidy as it need be. When the clubrooms were locked, and stacked, and shut. When the night was coming. The Yarraville West Fourths, shy two of their number, stood in the centre of the wicket, some leaning on the pickets covering the pitch. Others stood with arms folded or hands in pockets.

They stood and said nothing, sharing the last moments of the season.

'What a great game,' Tim One finally said softly.

Chris Andersen clapped his hands. And the season finished.


As he limped home, Chris Andersen looked down at his son.

'Good shot that off-drive,' he said.

'Had a go,' said Lachlan.

'What did you say to Brian out there, Lachie? Out in the middle?'

Lachlan Andersen said nothing for a moment. 'We'll find out if we're lucky,' and he looked at the sky.

Barry Andersen laughed his deep rumbling laugh as they walked home.


In a reception centre in Essendon, Katie Spencer asked the smooth-voiced master of ceremonies if he could play an old song that she liked.

When she told him what it was, he smiled and said 'Now, that's an old song – is there a story behind that one?'

'There's a story behind every song,' and she walked back to her table and sat next to her husband. She laughed at the look on his face. The way he smiled at her in bemusement.

'Katie, why are you playing "Jessie's Girl"?'

She kissed him and didn't say a word.

As Katie Spencer kissed her husband, Uwimana Malanda held her son in her arms and smiled at her husband as they watched the news to improve her English. She laughed as she watched the television and saw the big crowds watching the cricket. An odd game. She held her son tight and thought that he might like to play it one day. She looked at her husband and said very slowly in her best English, 'A good place.'

As she said that a man who had bowled fast all afternoon sat on the edge of his daughter's bed and took down a book from her shelves. He was going to read for her...and as he opened the page he said to himself softly, 'Have a go.'

His daughter looked up and said that wasn't the title of the book.

He smiled and nodded but before he read the book he thought again, Have a go.

In his lounge room Ted Bright sat and poured himself a small glass of Melbourne Bitter and after he had done that he piled up two small plates of potato chips. One for him and one for his fat old dog, Newk.

The old dog sniffed the plate a bit and then chomped down on his treat. Ted scratched the backside of his old dog absentmindedly and stared out through his window at the night sky. Soon the moon would be up. He knew he would look up and wonder that some fellas had walked up there. And as he looked out through the window and sipped his beer, he let out a little chuckle.

'Oh, Newky, that was a lovely shot, that off-drive.' He scratched his old dog and looked to the night.

Was it worth it? He heard his daughter padding along the hallway.

'Daddy, there is someone on the phone for you, he says it's important,' she said.

'Who is it?'

'Brian...he's yelling,' his daughter said.

Chris Andersen put the Dettol away and stood up and opened the door. He took the phone from his daughter and she ran off down the hall.

He could hear Brian yelling as he held the phone in his hand.

'Brian,' he said.

The words from the phone were tripping over each other and it took a while for Chris to calm Brian down. Chris Andersen could hear Brian's mother laughing occasionally in the background.

'What is it, mate?' Chris Andersen said.

'I seen it. I seen it. Lachie showed me how to see it. Go outside and I'll show you. Go outside, Christo, please let me show you,' the words almost sang.

'Okay, mate, hang on,' said Chris Andersen as he limped down the hallway and out through the dining area and down the interior step that was ten millimetres too deep. And he tripped a little on the paisley carpet piece there on the spotted gum floorboards. He hopped a bit because his foot hurt.

Julie sat and looked at him.

'Yes, alright, Brian. I'm going as fast as I can, hang on.' He opened the back door and stepped down off the low verandah and felt the grass cold under his feet. The dew was settling and it felt nice.

He turned slowly about in a circle as Brian shouted to him through the phone line.

'See the big white thing, the Uncle Toby's silo thing?'

Chris Andersen turned and stopped. 'Yes, Brian, I see it, I see it.'

'See Uncle Toby in his red coat and he's touching his hat to the lady?'

'Yes, I see Uncle Toby and the lady.'

'See his hat?'

'Brian, I see his hat... Brian what –'

'Look right above...right above the hat... I seen it, I seen it!'

'Well, I'll be buggered,' Chris Andersen said. There, above the silo, high in the sky. Shining in the early evening, the first star of the night.

'Star bright

'Star light

'First star I see tonight.

'I found my star... I found it.'

Chris smiled. He called to his family, for them to come and join him. One by one they came out. Moisy the last, carrying the dog. Had it been worth it?

Chris Andersen smiled in the backyard of his home. He stood with his family staring up into the sky with them. Staring at the first star of the night.

Had it been worth it?

'How's that?' said Brian down the phone line.

'Brian...' he laughed. 'You're a good man.'

# Acknowledgments

I would like to thank the following, in no particular order of importance. Sarah Watt, Clem McInnes, Stella McInnes, William West, Phillip Greenwood, Vanessa Radnidge, Rick MaCosker, Bernadette 'Batman' Foley, Amy Hurrell and all at Hachette Livre Australia.

Thank you.